A Horse Named Sorrow

Terrace Books, a trade imprint of the University of Wisconsin Press, takes its name from the Memorial Union Terrace, located at the University of Wisconsin–Madison. Since its inception in 1907, the Wisconsin Union has provided a venue for students, faculty, staff, and alumni to debate art, music, politics, and the issues of the day. It is a place where theater, music, drama, literature, dance, outdoor activities, and major speakers are made available to the campus and the community. To learn more about the Union, visit www.union.wisc.edu.

A Horse
Named Sorrow

Trebor Healey

Terrace Books
A trade imprint of the University of Wisconsin Press

The author wishes to thank the **Morris Graves Foundation** for their generous support in providing a writing residency where much of this story first emerged.

Terrace Books
A trade imprint of the University of Wisconsin Press
1930 Monroe Street, 3rd Floor
Madison, Wisconsin 53711-2059
uwpress.wisc.edu

3 Henrietta Street
London WC2E 8LU, England
eurospanbookstore.com

Printed in the United States of America

Library of Congress Cataloging-in-Publication Data

Healey, Trebor, 1962–
A horse named Sorrow / Trebor Healey.
    p.   cm.
ISBN 978-0-299-28970-6 (cloth: alk. paper)
ISBN 978-0-299-28973-7 (e-book)
  1. Gay men—Fiction. I. Title.
PS3608.E24H67   2012
        813'.6—dc23
        2012009961

Parts of this book have been published in earlier versions. An initial short draft first appeared online as "The Mercy Seat" in *Blithe House Quarterly* 8, no. 2 (Spring 2004). Chapters 28 and 30 first appeared as "Boy Who Don't Talk" in *Blithe House Quarterly* 3, no. 3 (Summer 1999). Chapter 3 first appeared as "Jimmy in the Bath" in *Quickies 3*, edited by James C. Johnstone (Vancouver: Arsenal Pulp Press, 2003). Chapter 43 first appeared as "St. Andy" in *Big Trips*, edited by Raphael Kadushin (Madison: University of Wisconsin Press, 2008).

For

Alex Nowik

Daniel Kopyc

Ezequiel Yedro

And the carny had a horse, all skin and bone ...
that he named Sorrow

Nick Cave, "The Carny Song"

A Horse Named Sorrow

"Yellowdog, where does sorrow go?"

He held his heart. "Lives here, in each of us."

"So why was it running around in that horse?"

"Sometimes it does that. I've seen fear do that, and once I saw hate do that in a pack of stray dogs. When there's too much of something in one place, it runs around." He motioned with his hand. "Once I saw a whole buffalo herd named Sorrow. It happens. Now, put your story in the fire."

Prologue: Rusty

I'm a clown. And I don't mean that in the sense of being a fool either—although I've been that too. I mean, I'm an *actual* clown—as in I wear face paint (an exaggerated frown, of course), a big red nose, balloon pants, and giant orange shoes. I juggle; I fall; I'm a fool for hire now instead of just doing it pro bono. I'm not so different from any other clown except for my prosthetic leg, which I use to great effect. I've got my clown pants put together in such a way that I can knock it out from under me. Then I'm able to use it as a prop: putting it back on upside down, or carrying it around under my arm while I hop about; I shake it at children; toss it sometimes into the audience if the kids are old enough to catch. They either howl with laughter or are reduced to utter silence. The two most important things in the world right there in the same place.

Imagine that.

They call me Rusty.

And I don't speak. Ever.

So I guess you could say I'm a mime too. That's on account of Jimmy, who always told me I talked too much, and Eugene, who showed me how not to.

The hardest part is not singing, of course.

But I do hum and laugh and groan and make all the animal noises.

I became a clown for the usual reasons—because things didn't work out. On a grand scale. That's the cliché of clown stories, I know. Yet I

3

didn't go bankrupt or lose my family in a tornado or anything like that. I just lost Jimmy, which amounted to the same thing, and then some.

Because it *was* like a tornado, the way it came, leaving nothing behind but dust and ruination—and Jimmy's voice as he grabbed hard ahold of my wrist with what strength he had left, his big hollow dark eyes looking at me: "Don't forget to take me back the way I came, Seamus . . . road's the place for lost souls."

The question that was my face.

"Promise?"

I nodded. Then I kissed him on the forehead and sat holding his hand, listening to the rhythm of his breathing—and humming along with it—as he made his way toward sleep.

Jimmy was a song, see? And the song's over. Let me tell you the story. You read and I'll hum.

1

Jimmy came from Buffalo, New York, and he had the acronym with him on the train platform the day I met him. Along with everything else: the bicycle he'd named *Chief Joseph*, the pannier bags, the tattoo of the Chinese character for "good" etched where his right sideburn should have been and the little bull's-eye tattoo smack dab between his eyes (he'd later tell me it was his third), the four thousand dollars in cash tucked inside that book, *Bury My Heart at Wounded Knee*, and his made-up mind. Made me close shut what I'd been reading: *Useless Facts & Other Fauna.*

He looked cute and interesting, and I stared at him and studied him, waiting to see if he'd look back my way for too long or not. His hair was a grown-out dye-blond, black as engine grease underneath, and he was wearing old green army fatigue cutoffs that hung loose around his insubstantial waist. He had a waif's long bony chest and knobby shoulders under his black long-sleeved T-shirt with the big red asterisk/mandala symbol of the Red Hot Chili Peppers on it.

I'd been wallowing for hours in one of my dark moods, meandering around Oakland so as to avoid seeing anyone I knew, taking a break from San Francisco, making my rounds of the sacred places of my own lesser mythology—the museum, the lake, coffee shops under the forlorn, all-is-vanity flashing of the big neon sign at the Grand Lake movie theater—and wondering and pleading with each for a sign, a finger pointing to where I should go with my stalled-out little life, as if these landmarks were great cromlechs or Easter Island stone heads imbued with wisdom.

And then Jimmy: a handsome stranger from faraway, and with a mystical steed too because there were strings tied all over his bike—so many, you couldn't even tell what color it was underneath.

And, sure enough, when I raised my eyes, his were looking back at me. And for the briefest of moments we stared. His perfect chin and scruff, his wide mouth, his cheekbones. Then he looked away, and there followed the nonchalant slow return—and me doing the same—and round in circles it goes: the timeless dance of the sugar plum faeries.

A lit match.

And I was tow. Because despondency always made me feel epically horny. Maybe it was just my low-intensity suicidal thoughts—the last stand of my gonads? One last statement before oblivion? Or perhaps my body just knew it was the only way to get me to stick around and thus roused me from my stupor with that old standby lust, promising connection and reminding me there were things here otherworldly and transcendent already—that "little death" that beat all swan dives off the Golden Gate.

Consequently, any boy who appeared at such a time was bound to carry a certain weight, a sort of saving grace, a fateful kind of gravity. Which perked me up like no monthly five-minute appointment with yawning, obese Dr. Pinski at County Mental Health ever could. Pinski, who couldn't have spotted a suicide if the malcontent's errant bullet ricocheted off his desk and grazed him with a flesh wound. And chances are it would be a flesh wound, because he was packing. Flesh. Lots of it, too. Pinski, who, just last week, after cursorily poking around my psyche, quickly wrote me a prescription for the latest antidepressant, in the middle of which he pulled back his sleeve to check his watch, tearing the scrip from his little pad, proffering it, and impatiently blurting out: "Call me if there are side effects. See you next time."

"What kind of side effects?" I furrowed my brow, looking at the latest ominous drug name with its characteristic z's and x's.

"Ask the pharmacist; nothing major—vertigo, dry mouth, seizures," he'd snapped, as he'd hefted his substantial girth onto its feet and reached across the desk one more time to shake my hand, grinning like a car salesman.

Therapy, the lemon.

But the drugs were all free: Prozac, Paxil, Zoloft—like some sick pantheon of old gods who sounded anything but cheerful.

Happy as a clam.

I gobbled up Pinski's SSRIs—but sure as the stranger standing on the train platform fifteen feet in front of me, I knew in my bones only a boy could heal me.

The sweet junk of him filled my veins. Endorphin, Andy Orphan, Orphan Andy. Because San Francisco was a refugee camp of orphans, and he looked far from home and unkempt. Fate, sure thing.

And I was feeling grateful for it just then, full of a familiar greed to hear his voice. A crowded train arrived. People poured on and off. And he just kept on looking about and then right back at me. For too long. And it wasn't just the look in his case. Everything about him was long: his long torso and the long knobby legs and arms; his long journey and his long nose; his long face, and later his long dick and his long, long story. A horseboy, that's what he was.

Pawing the pavement.

"I think you gotta wait," I said loudly across the now deserted platform so he'd hear me. He looked up at the dusty, grimed clock to see it was 5:03. "Rush hour; no bikes till six," I sighed.

"And who are you—the station master?" he flirted.

"Me? I'm just a whelp—I got no authority."

"A whelp?"

"A baby tiger." And I strolled over and showed him my book of useless facts with its long lists that were suddenly useful.

"You look full-grown to me."

"Trust me, I'm half-baked."

"Why a tiger?"

"A whelp."

"Well, why a whelp then?"

"I just like the word. I could as well be a pullet. That's a baby hen. Shoat's a baby pig. Elver's a baby eel." (And I began to read compulsively, masking my nerves—or not.) But I soon grew afraid of being a bore, so I shifted to questioning him. "Where'd you come from?" I queried, looking at the bike and its strings—me, a nervous pullet of chatter.

"Buffalo."

"Buffalo. Let's see—" (consulting my book) "that'd be a calf." I looked at him regretfully. "Sorry."

"Don't apologize, I hate the place. Besides, I'm all grown up." And he grinned again.

I smiled back. "Did you ride this bike all the way from Buffalo?"

He nodded, arching his brows.

The passion: a dye-blond crown of thorns.

My emotions were like a crowd. Give 'em what they want. Barabbas or the J-man. There's gonna be a crucifixion. Well, more or less. Because if you ask me, purveyor of useless facts, the promise of sex with someone you're starting to like puts you smack dab in the center of time, history, and the universe itself. Right there in West Oakland no less. The birth of a new religion, and all the madness that ensues.

I smiled and held out my hand. "I'm Seamus."

He paused and looked at my hand before taking it, reminding me what a distancing a handshake always was. A safe distance. Gay people don't generally shake hands, not when they've already traversed the distance of acknowledging who and what they are. But it was too early for a hug or a kiss. Instead, he surprised me, grabbing my outstretched hand by the wrist, bending forward and pulling it to his lips, kissing it with a smack like some fairy-tale prince. "Seamus, the whelp," he said triumphantly.

"The pullet," I blushed, disarmed.

"I'm Jimmy."

"You're no calf."

8

"No? What am I?"

I could have said a lost puppy, on account of those big brown eyes, or a bantam rooster, with that spiked crest of bleached hair, but I opened the book instead, flipping madly, thinking: *I better pick the right one.* But I already knew he was a colt. I just didn't want to give myself away.

"You've traveled a great distance; you must be a smolt."

"What's a smolt?"

"Baby salmon."

"That doesn't follow, Seamus."

"Why not?"

"The baby hasn't been anywhere. I'm an old salmon; the trip's over."

He looked away momentarily, a hint of sadness in his voice, and being that it was 1990 and he was a young gay man, I knew what he meant straightaway.

"This book doesn't have the old ones," I offered, at a loss.

He shook his head back and forth, as if he knew that.

"Ex-smolt?" I offered, arching my brows, chancing a smile. He grinned. "Wanna go somewhere 'til six?" He raised his brows. "Like food, beer, something like that?" I persisted.

He hesitated. Then: "Sure."

And off we went, bike in tow. Bike like a horse. Jimmy too. With his long face and big-lashed dark brown eyes; the long slender nose. Strong and free and just a tad startled. Worn-out by miles too. Half salmon and half Pony Express. Some kind of mythic animal that hadn't even been thought up yet.

But he looked nothing like a fish, of course. The fish was inside, in the river of him.

And, truth be told, I didn't look anything like a whelp either. That was lost somewhere way inside of me too. I was no tiger—if I could have mustered a feline at all, it'd just be a little stray kitten. Unselfconfident and somewhat befuddled by life, I had a wide-open, disarming face that made me look like I was always in the middle of asking a question, or perhaps just waiting for an answer, question posed or no. My hair was just brown then, its normal color; kind of long, curly, always messy—a right when you have curls. My eyes were gray like slate, but they turned blue when I was unsure. They were blue almost all the time then.

"What do I look like, Jimmy?" I asked him after he'd negotiated the exit gate. He gave me that one arched brow of his. "I mean—like which animal?"

"I don't know, Seamus. A dog, I guess. A lost dog. A mutt." I frowned. "Friendly," he said with a smile.

"Loyal, a good companion," I added.

And then we were on the sidewalk, in the afternoon sun.

"So what's with the strings?" I inquired, looking more closely at the bike and its adornment in every color of thread and twine.

"Each one's a poem. I hope." He laughed. "I just collect 'em as I go, and when I have the time, I'll tell their story."

"Looks like a long friggin' story."

He sighed. And we stood there and smiled, gazing at his threads.

I didn't actually know a place to go around there. It was a rough neighborhood, West Oakland: an old-style ghetto, houses always burning down. Beautiful old burnt-down houses from high above, out the windows of the BART train. Lots of liquor stores and wide empty avenues, crowded street corners with all number of children and teenagers swatting each other. A place most people only passed through—or over, actually—admiring the public sculpture of incinerated domiciles.

We ended up sharing a forty-ouncer. On the curb, in a brown paper bag, a block from the station.

"Where you goin' now, Jimmy?"

"This is it, man. This is my destination."

"This street corner?"

He grinned. "San Francisco."

"That's not very original, Jimmy. And you're not quite there yet."

He grinned again. "Not till six, at least. So what brings you here, Mr. . . . ?"

"Blake."

"Like *tiger, tiger burning bright*?"

Oxidation, I wanted to say, but I was always careful not to betray my cynicism to potential quarry. "Yeah, sure, but you'd have to substitute a whelp."

"Whelp, whelp burning bright. Doesn't work, Seamus."

"Try pullet."

"Pullet, pullet burning bright. Nah, sounds like a rotisserie."

"Elver?" He just looked at me. "Electric eel?" My eyes matched my face, a big wide question.

"You didn't answer my question," he said.

"That makes two of us."

He rolled his eyes. "So you're as unoriginal as I am."

"No, even more so. I was born here!" And I said it with great enthusiasm, proud of my inconsequence. "Oakland, that is."

He laughed. "You *are* a whelp." And he patted my thigh affectionately, which sent my heart racing. Then he got himself up. "Must be six by now."

I didn't stand up with him, just looked up at him, his body making shade all over me in the lengthening rays of the setting sun that were turning the sky heartbreakingly orange-pink-purple right then and making of Jimmy an angel among the litter and the empty lots and burnt-out houses, loitering children, and liquor stores of West Oakland.

"Where you goin', Jimmy?"

"Goin' to California."

I threw out my arms and looked around, a big car-salesman smile on my face.

"You're a weirdo, Seamus," he said with a grin, but I was suddenly ecstatic, as he added: "—and that's a good thing."

"Stay here in California with me, Jimmy," I said, patting the concrete sidewalk next to me where he'd been sitting just moments before.

He sat down heavily again and looked at me, as if he were thinking. Then, gravely, he ventured: "You know, I need a place to crash."

"Coming right up!" I shouted. "You can stay with me."

11

He squinted his eyes at me, considering it.

I hopped up, tore a page out of my useless book, and dug a pen out of my pocket. "Can I get you something to drink, sir?"

"Forty-ouncer." He chuckled bashfully.

"Coming right up." And back I went down the block to the liquor store, the old black proprietor, his glasses and steel-wool gray hair; his curious way of looking at me, an odd pullet in the neighborhood. The news was going on the TV behind him, and there was the smell of wet boxes and spilled soda, old and sticky; and there was dust, dust everywhere; and cigarettes, liquor, lottery tickets, blistered old plastic Pepsi and Miller signs, crooked and burnt by years of bad fluorescence.

"Don't drink it all in one place," he chuckled wryly.

But that was just what we did. And then I took Jimmy home.

2

I ended up right back on that same platform a year later. Alone. And
going in the opposite direction. But the bike was the same, and the
panniers—even the clothes on my back were the same, since they were
Jimmy's: the baggy army cutoffs, the Red Hot Chili Peppers T-shirt.
Even a new tattoo: on my left ankle, the Chinese symbol for "dog,"
inspired by Jimmy—or his goodness, or both.

And second thoughts, of course. Eyes a vivid blue.

The bike was still covered in those strings—he'd only gotten to a
few dozen, and there were hundreds: every sort of string imaginable—
from all colors of cotton thread to skeins of silk, and even braided hair
and plastic fishing line. There was a short section of some of that yellow
police tape, and a twisted length of shimmering tinsel from some old
Christmas tree; a thong of leather, some Mardi Gras beads, and even
plastic ties from food bags in yellow, blue, and white. And there was yarn
and hemp and tangles of packaging twine. There were the shimmering
brown remains of cassette tapes—I wondered what songs? There were
twisted pieces of ribbon—cherry red, navy, kelly green—and even a
frayed knot of rope. And the name, painted over where it used to say
Schwinn on the front handlebar post of the bike—scrawled in Jimmy
dime-store model paint: *Chief Joseph*.

And Jimmy, of course, in an old purple velvet bag with gold draw-
strings, all ten pounds of him, tied tight around the center of the handlebars. *Taking him back the way he came*, just like he'd asked.

3

I'd yanked a coarse blue thread off the seat cushion on the BART train that day we'd met as we sped along under the bay toward San Francisco, lights flashing by that I always liked to believe were those deep-sea fish with organic lightbulbs on their heads. But they weren't; the tube was concrete and not a window in it anywhere.

"Here, Jimmy, your final string."

He gave me that quick smile of his, leaned forward, and tied it onto the frame, right under the handlebars, which brought me face to face with *Chief Joseph*.

"What's with the name?"

He looked at me, like I'd already asked too many questions, and then he looked at it, and contemplated it for a minute. "There's a long answer and a short one to that," he offered somewhat reluctantly, enigmatically.

"You don't gotta tell me at all, if you don't want to; I was just curious."

Whoosh, whoosh, went the BART train, people yammering above the din.

"Chief Joseph said, 'I will fight no more forever.' That's why." But he wasn't looking at me when he said it. The short answer. I let it drop as the train beeped and we emerged under downtown, the platform a scurrying anthill of suits and hairdos. Jimmy perked up and looked slightly alarmed, but I shook my head no: "Four more stops, Jimmy."

Beep, beep, like the roadrunner, and the windows exploded with light and faces for the fifth time.

We came up the escalator from underneath, the BART tube under the Bay having now delivered us from Oakland like a birth canal to the garden of earthly delights at 16th and Mission, ground zero for the lost youth of America come to San Francisco. They were all there in their skinny checkered pants and knit caps, with their tattoos and their piercings, among the vendors of *elotes* and pork skins and tacos, a portly Mexican in a white shirt and tie bellowing out Spanish Jesus-talk from a bullhorn. And there were the homeless too, heaped in coats and plastic bags, and the ubiquitous Central American women, kids in tow, wearing their T-shirts and skirts and grim brown shoes—and on the uncomfortable-looking benches: indigent youths and hustlers, speed freaks and men with canes dealing crack cocaine and heroin. On the chained-to-a-pole newspaper vending machine, a plethora of Queer Nation stickers barked out their messages in primary colors: *Rugmuncher, Buttfucker*, and *What Causes Heterosexuality?*

"You made it, Jimmy." His sideways grin, rattling the bike off the escalator and across the dinful plaza. He played it cool, but I could see he was taking it all in. I should have put him back up on the bike and led him by the halter so he could better look around as I guided him along toward my own private manger in Bethlehem on Shotwell Street, just a few blocks beyond.

I had a slew of roommates, a sort of musical chairs of roommates, in the big flat where I'd lived the past year. They'd come and go with circumstances, or fall in love and get driven out by the others who didn't want a fifth or sixth to share the bathroom with and to clean up after. I was the only one who hadn't pulled that, but now here I was—and he had a bike with him too, and stuffed-to-bursting panniers that hung on either side of the back wheel. They wouldn't read *him* as a one-night stand, no sirree.

"I don't know how long you can stay, Jimmy, but at least a few nights before they turn on you," I sheepishly told him, rounding the

15

corner, anticipating furrowed brows and general passive aggressiveness that wouldn't go full-blown until midweek at the earliest. It was a tolerant city after all. Tolerant until it wasn't, and then you were cooked good. Such was our fair PC city.

Jimmy just smiled at my warnings, seemingly unconcerned.

The crowds dwindled, but never entirely—not in San Francisco—as we got further from Mission Street. And then there were some big scraggly dusty-green acacia trees, and we turned left, and there it was—the dilapidated brown and white as-yet-to-be-refurbished Victorian, sitting on its grand wooden haunches, lost in the leafy shade of a big unpollarded sycamore tree.

I held the door, and Jimmy rolled in. And I grabbed the back wheel while he held the front handlebars, as up the stairs we guided his steed.

The shower was broken in our apartment, so everyone had to take a bath—which was ridiculous because baths take time and four or five people with one bathroom don't have time. Myself, I rarely bathed there, swimming most days at the nearby YMCA and taking a shower in the locker room.

But I couldn't think of a better thing just then than bathing Jimmy. I'd never bathed anything but a dog, but suddenly it seemed like just the thing to do.

I needed to bathe Jimmy.

Jesus Jimmy.

I needed to oil his feet.

4

Riding the elevator down, with its buttons for *1*, *2*, *Fire*, I looked at the purple velvet bag full of his ashes under that fluorescent hospital-like light inside those stainless steel walls, standing on that filthy gray rubber floor, with its stuck gum, scraps of paper, and greasy who-knows-what, and I felt shock. Shock that receding foot by foot above me through space and time—not yet a year—was the boy on the platform, with the body he'd lived in, and its wasted, trashed half-bleached over-dyed hair, its intelligent furrowed brow, its long nose and knobby knees, its pronounced shoulders and delicate clavicles—its lungs that breathed, its kidneys that purified and its intestines that digested, its liver that kept working even as it got overtaxed by medicines; its heart that I loved and that loved me, the lips that first touched my hand, the eyes that looked too long, the say-nothing smile—gone and not coming back.

And the elevator opened to the busy crisscrossing of suits and dresses and a newspaper vendor, and a young woman who just dropped her cup of coffee, transfixed over it momentarily. Will she walk on, curse, or look for a janitor? She walked on, the coffee abandoned, running in rivulets among the greasy, shoe-scuffed tiles that made the whole station look like an enormous public restroom.

I rolled up to the booth so the lady could let me through the gate since the bike wouldn't fit through the turnstile. She waved, went out and around, and, fumbling with her huge key ring, let me out with a smile. Then she ran my ticket through the machine and it buzzed.

"You're short," she informed me.

"Really?"

"Ten cents."

I dug in my pocket and handed her a dime. What she'd said had reminded me of my father, since that word always did. Which was complicated, as I'd never met him. But he'd been *short* too. Until I was eight, I thought he was a dwarf. "If he was short, how'd he end up getting shot?" I'd asked my mother one rainy Saturday while we played dominoes.

She'd given me the quizzical look over the edge of her glass as she sipped her old-fashioned. "Short doesn't protect you."

"Sure it does; he's closer to the ground," I'd responded, as if she were stupid.

She'd sighed then, and, taking my little hand in hers, she explained what "short" was for the first time. He was scheduled to be heading home in ten days when it happened, and in Vietnam "short" was jargon for almost done with your tour.

Like Jimmy, my father died in a hail of acronyms: ARVN and NVA, and VC, and NCO, and PFC, and LZ, and KIA, USA—and all the rest of them in that pile of papers my mother bequeathed to me on my eighteenth birthday. I counted and found that all twenty-six letters were involved; not a one guiltless. An orgy of acronyms; a PTA of them.

Can I have the cherry?"

She delicately pulled the maraschino out of her glass and handed it to me. Then she got up and headed toward the kitchen and her next old-fashioned while I went to put on the records because that's what had to be done when I brought up my father. Otherwise, she'd watch TV and drink far into the night and not do the dishes and act curt the next day.

My mother had a whole record collection of *him*. That's where he lived, in *their* songs, and those that followed in the wake of his disappearance. Which meant we lived in the summer of love and then some, on up into the early '70s, riding the wave of her once-upon-a-time as we played dominoes, mahjong, Yahtzee, and Scrabble. I'd memorize lyrics I liked and that I knew pleased her, which gave her no end of amusement: *Feeling good was good enough for me,* and *Let me sleep all night in your soul kitchen,* and *Do you know the way to San Jose?* I did, and pointed.

5

We parked the bike in the hall and tossed his gear in my cluttered, messy little windowless room, and I marched him grinning into the bathroom, which was miraculously empty. And I turned the lock behind us and ignored what came to six knocks during the course of our bath.

Jimmy let me pull his shirt off and unbutton his trousers. It was no lusty come-on kind of thing either. Not at first anyway. It was just me preparing to bathe Jimmy. But I got all bunched up and heartbeat-giddy when I had him down to his shorts, and with sighing smiles we looked straight at each other and kissed long and crazy. I don't remember how the rest of our clothes came off, but they did and fast, and the water making a racket filling the tub behind us, and his skin so silky and his scent so horse-sweat sweet—and someone knocking on the door.

And then Jimmy had me balanced up on the sink, all naked, with my lanky limbs clinging to him like a spider, and he grabbed my face in both his hands as our cocks swung around like antennae, and he said, "Hey Seamus, whelp, I got something I gotta tell ya." He stared for another second. "I got *it*."

Any faggot worth his salt knew what *it* was too. My heart skipped a beat all the same, not because it was news—I'd figured it on the platform when he'd called himself a salmon—but because words from the source make it more real, and because I didn't want to say the wrong thing.

"I know, Jimmy. I'm not afraid."

20

Lie. But a white lie.

He looked down at his feet momentarily, and then we both opened our mouths and kissed deep and crazy, and I wrapped my legs around his back and squeezed.

And off we went, galloping until with a shuddering groan and clenched brow, every mile of America was flying out of him and onto me, and without a lot of choice in the matter—in bodily enthusiastic courtesy—I gave him back my own paltry travels, which ran off his pale waifish chest and belly like lost—no, not lost at all anymore—tears.

Then Jimmy in the bath, and the wet dark roots under his platinum hair, and the muted green of his pale skin, and how dark he was under his arms and at his waist. I went to work with a big loofah sponge, and I scrubbed Jimmy's back, and his bony shoulders, all around his little dark nipples, each with a single hair, and up under his hairy armpits, where he captured my hands and then leaned forward and kissed me long and deep. Then I made him stand up as I scrubbed his dark-haired shins and his long chicken-thin thighs. I soaped all around his cock and held the heft of his balls as I soaped up his sweet perineum. And every part of his body I washed, I sealed with a kiss.

And then I pulled him down to rinse him off.

And Jimmy said, "I don't want your pity."

My stomach sank and I just looked back at him. At a loss. I handed him the sponge: "Here."

But Jimmy surprised me with a quick little upturn of his mouth, and then he sponged the whole of me from behind while he hugged me close and nibbled my neck.

He dried me off and I dried him off as he shivered, arms tucked close against his chest. I got a little carried away drying his cock and balls and hairy ass crack, and before I could mutter my awe or cry my sweet sadness, Jimmy was down on the floor with me and 69 trombones in the big parade, and then he was asking me for a condom, which put me up against the door, my hands pressing into it as someone on the other side knocked rhythmically in perfect harmony with Jimmy.

21

6

I hadn't packed up and left right away, thinking it a fool's errand—which everyone agreed it was. And yet I *was* a fool, so what kind of argument did that make? Besides, he'd asked and I'd promised, and all the naysayers with their chorus of "dementia, Seamus" couldn't put Humpty Dumpty back together again. Fact was, I couldn't bear our place on Guerrero Street once he was gone anyway, even though I never left it for more than beer, coffee, and ramen.

Something there watching me all the same, telling me to pull. Pull myself together. I'd look at that bike in front of the fireplace, and the two Best Foods mayonnaise jars on the mantel that were Jimmy. They'd tried to talk me into urns and wooden boxes and other bourgeois accoutrements at the crematorium. No sir, as in life, so in death—Jimmy goes in a jar. Best food I ever had. *Let Them Eat Mayonnaise* mocked one of my horrible Marie Antoinette paintings staring down at me from the wall.

I'm the first to admit I had little if any talent, but it was San Francisco, so of course I had to be an artist. Besides, I was an emotional wreck and being an artist gave that some dignity, nobility, cachet. Consolation, if nothing else. So I painted, mostly therapeutic black-and-green abstracts, with flashes of orange when I was feeling particularly anxious or had had too much coffee. I liked doing it, and there was a scene of folks who even thought my paintings were good. I'd hang them in cafés, have openings, the whole charade. People even bought them. I was too guilty to sell them for more than a hundred bucks, so I got a name as a real cool artist: "The real thing—he's not in it for the money." And what *was* I in it for? I never painted anything that was worth more than the canvas it was spilled on, so who can explain the added value of ninety dollars? It was just a guilty Catholic's version of greed (highly discounted, but still profitable). Or maybe it was more about the greed of just being somebody, because I had a vague sense that deep down I wasn't anybody at all.

"Let them buy shitty paintings!" Marie Antoinette would say if she were me, which is a ridiculous hypothetical notion. But I painted her all the time after that, since it seemed appropriate.

Let Them Buy Timeshares, Let Them Get 2 for 1, Let Them Shop 24 Hours a Day, Let Them Gobble Prozac.

Jaded. I never understood the term. Jade is pretty and worth something, yes? I was rusted if I was anything. Too long in the rain. Going out in an orange blaze of muted, anonymous, common-as-dirt oxidation. Nothing pretty or valuable about it.

And then Jimmy . . . in the nick of time.

7

After the bath, Jimmy had pulled out his maps and showed me how he'd traveled. One long red squiggly line, from Buffalo to Eugene, Oregon—with circles where he'd stayed the night—and then down the coast to San Francisco.

"Why'd you go all the way up to Eugene, Jimmy?" My brows arched.

"I knew some people there," he said with a shrug. Short answer.

I looked at the bike. "And you picked up all those strings right along that red line."

"Every one of 'em." And he let the map fall to the floor. "I'm so tired." And he kissed me on the forehead, lay back, and just like that, closed his eyes. And then after a while, Jimmy curled in on himself, like a cat.

I awoke early and petted his wrecked hair and his knobby shoulder, and then I got up, threw on some clothes from one of the piles on the floor, and snuck out of the room, spying my new bottle of Zoloft on the bookshelf near the door, which I grabbed and—once in the hall—pitched out the window before leaping, three steps at a time, down the stairs and through the door, to go fetch coffee and food.

I was on Jimmy! Like a PhD or MFCC was his saving pedigree—Jimmy Keane, SSRI.

Past the madding crowd of 16th and Mission I hurried, and up two blocks to the coffee shops, where I ordered two triple lattes and bagels and ran into my ex-boyfriend Lawrence.

"Hey Shame, what's up?"

"Oh hi, Lawrence," I said distractedly, paying my tab while he beamed next to me as my mood rapidly deflated. I was hoping I could make a quick getaway. Lawrence was annoying, unresolved, hot, charming, lethal, desired and undesired in ways I couldn't get a handle on.

"I got a show coming up." He smiled seductively.

Of course he had a show coming up. Handsome Lawrence with his big handsome nose and glittering green eyes, his sultry smile. Chemistry. We'd met at an art show as we both painted, though that had little to do with it since we were alterna-boys and attended all the ACT UP and Queer Nation benefits and art happenings and would have met anyway. He was a "serious" artist, he'd reminded me on several occasions, as he attended the Art Institute and I didn't. Be that as it may, we'd urgently needed to fuck each other the minute we met, and within a few hours were doing just that.

"Cool. Where?"

He handed me the little orange postcard from his stack. I saw he was still doing big bold-colored phallic flowers with titles like *Bob*, *Mike*, *Jim* (his sacred/profane shtick).

"OK, I'll try to make it," I lied.

"What are you working on?"

"Oh, haven't been doing much lately," I fudged. Actually I'd been painting like a fiend, but saw no point in bringing it up as he didn't really care anyway. I knew what Lawrence wanted; what he always wanted.

"Check it out." And Lawrence, shifting his gaze to his waist and leading mine with his, pulled the front of his pants down a bit so I could see his underwear's elastic band, revealing what he'd written there in black magic marker: *This is the Body of Christ*. It was all an inside joke with us, this underwear business, a natural progression from the endless variations of Queer Nation stickers. We'd worked it to death, so that even then I still had loads of jockey shorts and boxers left over from our

25

affair, stenciled with *Om Mani Padme Hum, What Me Worry, Joe Boner, To Buttfuck Just Lift Handle*, etc. We'd even put our phone number on there one day, in search of a third.

I smiled, inadvertently admiring his happy trail, but also remembering that the actual body of Christ was back in my bed asleep on Shotwell Street. Which made Lawrence what?—the Prince of Darkness himself? Or just another false prophet? What boyfriend wasn't in the end?

"See you later, Lawrence," I dodged, and out the door I fled.

It was simply the pinball machine that was San Francisco—it couldn't be helped. You ran into everyone, and nothing could be done about it. It worked wonders for activism and art happenings as the place functioned like a village, rumors and plans blowing about and around like a thorough little wind, reaching every nook and cranny of the city. But it wreaked havoc on any hope for privacy or sexual discipline.

Well, Lawrence wasn't so bad. We'd had our fun, I had to admit nostalgically. We'd gone to Queer Nation kiss-ins at department stores downtown, walked around shirtless on San Francisco's rare sunny days, drawing all over each other with Sharpies. Once we'd gotten royally stoned on sensimilla and wandered the streets in the rain for hours, laughing at absurdities: a Baptist church marquee that read "Come Worship"; a new Korean restaurant named Young Dong; streets named after bad presidents: Pierce, Fillmore, Buchanan. "Where was Nixon Street? Where was Harding?" Bush Street loomed around the next corner.

Back through the squirming crowd I hurried, feeling guilty as I rushed by the homeless men with their cups out, wondering always if they were veterans and if they'd known my dad. I got to Shotwell, where I turned left and then left again up our chipped, rotting front steps, hurrying through the door and back up the stairs, balancing the coffee and the bag, imagining the handsome boy asleep or smiling, dressed or naked, my tiger's quarry hung from the limb of a tree—Jimmy.

But when I opened my bedroom door, I found an empty bed. Something sank in me and something indifferently cruel followed it,

26

ran its fingernails down the inside of my spine and vanished into the floor as I swung my head around to double-check that I had in fact just run past the bike. Yes. I calmly put down the food and coffee on the bookshelf, felt my heart banging around with the dread of *jilted*, and went to look for him in the bathroom. No Jimmy, in the bath or otherwise indisposed. I went out to the common room and the kitchen. No Jimmy on the couch or making me tea. Just Tanya, in her school-marm black-framed glasses, sitting calmly on her stool, reading the newspaper, drinking her coffee.

She didn't even look up when she said it. "He can't stay here."

"I know, Tanya," I said irritably. I was shaky, like I'd just had eight cups of coffee already, when I'd in fact had only a few sips.

She looked directly at me. "I'm not waiting an hour for the bathroom in my own house, ever again, no way."

"Sorry, uh . . ." But I was already heading back down the hall, in no way able to deal with her harangue.

"What were you doing in there—I knocked!"

"Have you seen him?" I yelled back to her.

"Just briefly."

I turned and headed back to the kitchen. "What do you mean?"

"I told him what I'm telling you."

"Shit, Tanya, that's fucking rude. Where's your hospitality?"

"My hospitality? You never told any of us you had a guest coming."

"I just met him!" She rolled her eyes. "Where'd he go?" I demanded. "Did you ask him to leave?"

"No," she said glibly, which made me suspicious. "He asked to use the phone for a local call, grabbed his bags and went downstairs, and someone came and picked him up." She shrugged and returned to her newspaper.

"Did he say where he was going?"

"No." I marched away frustrated, and she barked after me. "You can't leave that bike in the hall either." I grabbed it by the handlebars in a fury and rolled it into my room, slamming it into my easel and knocking my latest to the floor: *Let Them Read My Lips.*

She appeared at the door as I struggled to get the painting upright.

"Happy?" I snapped sarcastically.

"No; it's not about that. Accountability, Seamus. Being responsible."

"You're a bureaucrat, Tanya."

"We've talked about this before." (I'd royally screwed up last month's utility bill as it was my turn to pay, and the power had gone off right as the sun went down and Tanya was firing up her juicer.)

"Okay, okay," I muttered, but she'd proceeded to the bathroom and out of earshot. She was Queen Bee. Only because she'd been there the longest and was older than the rest of us. Like all bureaucracies, it was all about seniority. But her name wasn't even on the lease. The name on the lease, we'd learned, was someone none of us knew. Such was San Francisco. Rooms were passed on like sex partners, the common cold, or currency.

We'd only found out who was in fact on the lease when Darren was dating Cynthia and she'd shown up with an enormous duffle bag. This after Darren had already proved himself a jerk on several counts in the paltry three months he'd lived there: dirty dishes, late-night TV, loud music.

After Cynthia had disappeared into the bathroom, Tanya cornered Darren in the common area, which consisted of two couches, a TV, a dining-room table, and a fireplace, with surrounding built-in bookshelves—like the walls, all paneled in mahogany, or something that looked like it anyway.

"She's not moving in here," Tanya stated calmly.

"Says who?" Darren responded defensively.

"Says me."

"And you're the landlord?" he said mockingly.

"I've been here the longest." She raised her voice.

"So what?" he'd snapped back, "your name's not on the lease."

She just stared back. An admission.

"Whose name *is* on the lease?" I'd ventured from the corner dining table, where I was flipping through a pile of photographs from my latest "art project," a study of shoes (and a rich vein it had proven to be: the endless color variations of Converse hightops, often mismatched on the same biped; prescription shoes for clubfeet; stickered Doc Martens; dozens of paratroopers' boots, and not once on a paratrooper).

"I don't know," Tanya answered matter-of-factly.

"Well, let's find out," Darren demanded self-righteously (he of three-month tenancy). He was one of those swing music guys, a sax player, though he'd kept that to himself when he'd interviewed for a room, mentioning only his day job—word processing downtown (read: safe bet). He wore thin ties and played the morose, put-upon genius, and kept to himself generally until he had a gig. Then he'd don his trim black suit and pork-pie hat, snort some speed, and get all chummy before jerking jauntily down the front steps, off to play with his band, 22 Fillmore, which was named for a local bus line.

Tanya dug self-righteously and intently through a box in the kitchen, and when she'd found what she was looking for, she stopped, put on her glasses, and sauntered back out, Darren impatiently snapping, "Well?"

"Someone named John Galt," she said dryly.

Proving nothing but the absurdity of them both as well as the whole concept of private property, tenancy—even Tanya's precious "accountability."

"John Galt's gonna hear about this!" I snapped.

Tanya glared at me, but I looked at Darren, wanting to ask, but balking: *So what'll it be, Darren: Cynthia or the sax?* I could take Tanya's stares—I even sort of liked her for some odd reason I had yet to understand—but Darren's arrogance riled me. I smiled. He sneered.

"Darren?" Tanya said, folding her arms across her chest.

He didn't even look at her as he shouted: "Cynthia!"

"Just a minute," we heard her reply from behind the bathroom door far down the hall as he stormed off to his room and loudly began to pack up, calling out as he did:

"I'm outta here and I'm not giving thirty days."

Tanya didn't protest.

29

I got Darren's old room after that, which beat the back room where I'd been before—it listed toward the alley, abutted the forever-utilized bathroom, and smelled of mold and Pine Sol.

I sat down on the bed and slowly drank both coffees, nibbled a bagel, worried, and waited. *He'll be back*, I thought. But why'd he take the bags? I sat and ruminated about those moments of emotional distance that always held the clues to a boy's disappearance—in Jimmy's case, the comment about pity, the short answer regarding *Chief Joseph*, and the loss of eye contact after he told me he had *it*.

Finally I sighed, took a deep breath, and began to clean up my room. And it was only then, when my eyes passed over the bike, that I looked again at the strings all over it. No one would abandon a bike like that— would they?

8

I reached down and grabbed my water bottle, quaffed a gulp, and returned it to its holder on the bike frame. Then I hopped on the bike and rode down the very same street Jimmy and I had wandered a year ago, only now it was misted with morning fog. There was the empty sidewalk and the curb and the open lot, and the fennel-choked cyclone fence where we sat and drank King Cobra and discussed the virtues of infant critters, the life cycle of salmon, the dream of California—the colors of that not very long-ago sunset unimaginable in the morning gray.

I went by the corner liquor store next, and out front with a broom I saw the steel-wool proprietor. I hoped he wouldn't recognize me, as I hadn't taken his advice, about the forty-ouncer or Jimmy. But he didn't even look up.

And neither did I much, after that. Which means I ran red lights and stop signs and angered drivers, who angered me in return. But I did what my mother always taught me to do: *When you get angry, sing a song*, she'd said. And it worked too. Humming Leonard Cohen's "Suzanne," I couldn't stay mad *among the garbage and the flowers*, which I soon learned is what the shoulder of every road is made of.

Pinski'd once warned me about such music: "No '70s folk music," he'd barked. "Do you know how many people have gone over the edge listening to that stuff?"

I hate rhetorical questions. What do I get if I guess right? A trip to Mexico? What are we—the sad legions—jelly beans? "3,456," I answered him.

He'd looked at me, vexed, but ever distracted and short on time, he dismissed it, not having expected an answer anyway. "And why are you wearing those gloves?"

I had scabs on my knuckles from my habit of dragging them along brick walls, but I wasn't going to share that with him, although just then some of the scabs on my knuckles were sticking to the cotton, making me wince. "It's the cold, Doc; it's just the cold."

Because I didn't tell Pinski much of anything. Not only because there wasn't time, but because I didn't want to talk to him. He was a drug dealer. I wanted the pills. Even though they never worked.

Well, fine then, I'd tried and I could rust in peace.

. . . *all men will be sailors then until the sea shall free them.*

I watched the fog down those intermittent street crossings as it pulled back out of the bay and over the Golden Gate Bridge like a slow tongue, serpentine and torporous—the whole Bay Area a sleeping dragon just like how the Chinese immigrants of gold rush days described it, with each peak—Tamalpais to the north, Mt. Diablo to the east, Mt. Hamilton to the south—the spikes of its back. And right in the center, encircled, was its treasure: Gold Mountain, San Francisco. Or maybe it wasn't a treasure at all—such a trickster of a city. Maybe it was a little anthill and the fog wasn't a dragon's tongue but an anteater's snout, its long tongue reaching in and pulling out tasty morsels like Jimmy, one by one.

9

A week went by after that blissful truncated honeymoon and not a word from Jimmy. So, after a dubious digging around in the alley looking for my discarded Zoloft with no success—to think I'd thought I could escape the warlock Pinski so easily—I attempted to go about my business, slinging coffee at Java Baklava, all the while playing the B-52s to steady my nerves (something askew in their rhythms comforted me), but still assailed by anxiety, tempted to blame Tanya, but guessing it was probably something in me that had driven him away.

I drank too much coffee, drew no hearts in the foam of the lattes I made (part of my job description), and when I went to the YMCA, where I tutored kids twice a week in the after-school program, I was curt and impatient.

And as luck would have it I got stuck helping Ivan with his spelling. "Ivan, there is a letter missing from this word."

He'd peer at it with great concentration. "It says 'mountan.'"

"Correct—but a letter is missing." He then proceeded to place a *w* after the *u*.

"No, I think it's a vowel." Various efforts at placing *a*'s and *e*'s around in the word were met with frowns on my end until he gave up with a growl, at which point I told him, raising my voice in frustration, that the missing vowel was in fact an *i*. "Now, where does it go?"

"Nowhere."

"I'm telling you that's the missing letter," I explained irritably. "So it doesn't go *nowhere*. It goes in that word." And I hammered the word with my index finger.

"No, it doesn't."

I jerked my head backward, quickly reviewed the arguments for and against swatting a child (just a mental exercise), took a deep breath, and looked at him. Then I showed him where the letter went, raising my brows, "Okay?" He raised his brows in response. Smartass. Then I turned the paper over and asked him to re-spell the word, which he spelled without the "i" once again.

"Ivan, where is the *i*?"

"Next to the nose."

"Wise guy, eh? Where's the *i*?"

"It's outside having a cigarette."

"Ivan—"

"It called in sick."

"Ivan—"

"It died."

"Ivan," I exhaled impatiently, "how could *you* be here if the letter *i* died? There's an *i* in your name!"

He considered my remark, shrugged.

I looked around the room and crossed the line of sight of Miguel, unattended and frisky (he with the choicest cowlick I've ever seen).

"Why can't I vote?" he demanded, brash as ever. He'd get no straight answer from me. I always answered questions with more questions.

"Why do you think?"

"I don't know—you're the teacher."

"Nah, I'm just a tutor. Come on, Miguel. Why do you think kids can't vote? See if you can figure it out yourself."

"They're stupid?" He hunched his shoulders.

"Are kids stupid?"

"Some are."

"Try again."

"Uh . . ." And then he began thinking in earnest. His eyes rolled back into his head. Then he abruptly dropped his gaze back toward mine. "We're too short," he announced with astounding confidence. Case closed as far as he was concerned.

"What does that have to do with it? Short people can vote," I retorted.

"No . . . see . . . if they ask everybody to raise their hands, they won't see the kids' hands, so . . ." And he looked at me triumphantly, not even bothering to finish the sentence, as I shook my head no.

"I like your reasoning, Miguel. But you're wrong."

"Well, why then?" he challenged me.

"I'll never tell."

He sighed with his whole body. Then the bell went off like a Jeopardy *too-late*.

"Think it over and tell me next time." I raised my voice, hoarse above the din of the now-departing kids, gleeful and screeching as they gathered their backpacks and cleaned up their work tables.

Normally, after class, I'd consider heading downstairs to the gym part of the YMCA to take a shower and scope out cute boys, for though it was the Young Men's Christian Association, Paul of Tarsus had little to do with it. The showers were cruisy, and the sauna even more so, while the steamroom was like a primordial swamp, with slithering creatures, their copious juices of saliva and semen flung about carelessly as they emerged and then retreated back into the mists. But I had a reputation to uphold—I was a tutor—so I laid low or, when I just couldn't resist, dragged my prey into the nearby toilet stalls.

Upstairs, we kept our pants on.

Some days I'd read them stories about insects and monsters. I'd half a mind to take them on a tour downstairs to see some in the flesh. They hollered and screamed when I told them there were zombies and trolls right here at the Y.

"Where, where?!"

"Downstairs, in the bowels of the building." (Pun intended, which flew sailing over their heads.) "You know how trolls live under bridges? They live under classrooms too." And I bugged out my eyes at them. Of course, it wasn't *all* fun. Some children are worse than adults, and more rigid and moralistic too. An annoying little girl named Alice was a case in point. She berated me whenever I wore my pearl necklace: "Pearls are for girls. You can't wear them. Are you a girl? It's wrong!"

But there were others of endless delight. For instance, a little Chinese girl named, of all things, Eustacia. (The grandiosity of some of these kids' names was staggering. There was Mohammed, Jesus, and a girl named Shiva. All we needed was a Buddha and Quetzalcoatl, perhaps a Kali—there had to be a little black girl named Isis somewhere in this town—to turn the whole program into an ecumenical acid trip.)

Eustacia liked the oddest animals (possums, wombats, Tasmanian devils, javelinas and ocelots, newts and mudpuppies) and treated me like an encyclopedia/library, massaging my adult ego endlessly with questions about habitat and behavior, while smiling charmingly, and continually thanking and flattering me for my substantial knowledge and assistance (much of it faked). Eustacia was, in fact, responsible for my finding *Useless Facts & Other Fauna*, rummaging as I'd been forced to do, because of her insatiable mental appetite, at various thrift shops and used bookstores.

"What's the 'Eus'!" I'd call to her in greeting, which made her giggle and scrunch up in her seat.

They ultimately got around to asking about where babies came from, of course. I was hardly the right person to ask, but I certainly would never throw them off the scent with a stork.

"Well, what do you think?" The second half of the question accompanied by the voices of Eustacia and Mo (short for the prophet of Allah) and a few others, since they were used to this ruse of mine.

They discussed it among themselves.

Win said they came from kissing. This was followed by snickers and Miguel's announcement that his mother kissed him all the time and he'd never had a baby. The kids laughed, and the collective adrenaline amped up Mo's ADD.

"Quit banging your pencil, Mo."

"I can't stop."

"I'm asking you to stop."

"It does it by itself," he pleaded.

"Babies just come by themselves!" Ivan roared.

"Like a disease!" Carlos chimed in. The others howled.

"Okay, lesson in neurology," I digressed, having lost control, holding Mo's hand up as if he were the victor of something. "You have a brain and your brain has these nerves. They're like wires, electric. You can tell your hand to stop."

"No, I can't," Mo offered, looking completely sincere.

"Explain to me why you can't."

"Well, see, I think there is a brain in my hand that is different than the one in my head." Clever, sure, but it sounded like a serial killer's court defense. The class groaned.

"I don't believe it, and the judge won't either."

"What judge?"

"In time, Mo, in time. Put the pencil down."

"But what about the sweet little babies?" Eustacia now whimpered, clearly mocking the subject. If anybody knows, it's her.

"Well?"

Total silence, all eyes on her.

"Win is right, but it's a certain kind of kiss," she said matter-of-factly. Hoots again, and ring went the bell.

Class dismissed, I lolled home down the busy Central American streets of the Mission, past the popsicle vendors and the short Guatemalan mothers with their strollered babies, their little daughters in Mary Janes, shiny as beetles, their little boys with filthy hands and faces, ecstatic with the action of the world, the circus of it, the promise of adventure and mischief. A thousand windows beckoned to them to step right up and covet Gameboys, soldiers and Transformers, airplanes and cars. How many of these children would one day be queer? How many felled by the acronym? How many by something else? How many would forget the circus? How many would never see it at all? How many would join?

Rounding Shotwell, and clumping up the stairs, my stomach clenching at the sound of Tanya's juicer, dreading all of a sudden what I may have forgotten to do, I stopped and turned around, deciding instead to walk, which was really the only way I knew to calm the roiling, boiling soup that was my mind.

A superstitious ex-Catholic, I soon began bargaining with the God I no longer believed in via signal lights (three greens in a row means Jimmy will appear—father, the son, and the holy ghost), songs heard in shops as omens (happy love songs or sad, laying down their prophecies: *love will keep us together . . .* and *everybody's got a hungry heart . . .*), clouds passing in front of the sun (he loves me, he loves me not), spiraling into superstitions about whether to go left or right around a telephone pole or tree, this street or that (the horrifying responsibility of free will and choice)—each decision a fateful algebra determining whether Jimmy would reappear or not.

But after a week and a half of No-Jimmy, way too much coffee, annoying children who couldn't spell, who badgered me with beautiful questions that unnerved me (why does red mean stop and green go? How come there are wars? Why do people die? Why is there cold anyway?), I was tired and anxious to bursting.

Little Miguel at the Y, who previous to then I'd thought was utterly devoid of compassion, put his arm on my arm, reminding me why I tutored these kids and that they trumped SSRIs even on their worst day. He said, "Seamus, what's the matter? You sad?"

"Well, a little bit, Miguel. But I'll be okay." I was an adult, I told myself (at least relative to them), and I had to make it look like sadness was not a big deal, though come to think of it, kids appear less afraid of it than the rest of us.

"What's the matter?" he persisted. I didn't want him prying, and besides, I was a homo—what could I say?

"A friend of mine went away, Miguel, and I don't know if I'll ever see him again."

"You think he's dead?"

I laughed. "No, I don't think he's dead. It's just like he moved away or something."

"Maybe he'll send you a postcard."

I nodded, and we got back to work on Miguel's math. If only love could be as simple as addition and subtraction, division, sets and multiplication. I thought math beautiful just then. Beautiful like a lie of simplicity. White lie. Love was actually more like calculus or physics. What was the half-life of love? Did it have cosigns and slopes, or quarks that morphed from wave to particle faster than you could say, *please don't leave?* Love was unpredictable, unquantifiable, or so multidimensional it was like string theory, and not even geniuses could form an equation that worked. People avoided those they loved; hated them; killed them; renounced them; ran away from them; called out their names; embraced them; kissed them; made sweet love to them; fucked them like dogs; telephoned them; comforted them and offered consolation; did just the opposite.

Perhaps Miguel had been right—Jimmy had been murdered, or run down in a crosswalk by a MUNI bus.

I groaned audibly, marching down one street after another, tempted to drag my knuckles along the brick walls, but stopping myself on account of hope—because bloodied knuckles were no good for safe sex with Jimmy. And then I felt the dread of not knowing. How long *had* he been positive? I just assumed not long because he was young. But he was twenty-eight. That wasn't young considering—but it used to be. Maybe he was really sick. Maybe he'd already checked in to one of the city's many hospices that had sprung up like mushrooms to handle the huge numbers of ill and dying men in those days.

No way.

Healthy as a horse.

I grabbed my camera and started photographing hospices, ACT UP posters, billboards about safe sex, all the little '50s-style boys and girls with arms akimbo that had sprung up wheat-pasted on walls and trashcans, newspaper racks and mailboxes.

Maybe he'd figured I was negative and he just wasn't up for the hassle of dealing with the mix. Maybe he was just horny. Maybe this, maybe that, and a long line of conjecture, honking and maneuvering for position in the traffic of my wracked mind.

But the bath. The bath. That wasn't casual sex—*was it?*

Maybe I no longer knew the difference. Since Lawrence, and even most of the time *during* Lawrence (him and me both—we had an "open" relationship), I'd been a true fisher of men. Catch and release. I slept with hundreds of boys. I drank them up like water, bolted them like food. Because in San Francisco, when you're twenty and aimless and willing, you can literally fuck your way up and down whole streets—paint the town white, and then go back and start over and put on another coat. The world is your oyster, they say, so fill it with pearls of semen. Pearls before, on the chest of, up the alimentary canal of, and down the gullet of—*swine*. Downright biblical. And though San Francisco's a small city, and you might think it likely that one would run out of new men—not to worry: thousands of new ones arrived each day, pouring out of Greyhounds down on 6th Street like well-hung locusts. San Francisco was like Ellis Island back in the day when you didn't even need papers or so much as a name. Desire alone was the ticket.

I did come up for air now and again. Usually when I got VD or crabs. Then I'd reconsider what the hell I was doing, how close to the acronym I was getting, not to mention what effect my constant fucking around might be having on my mind. Even Pinski had said: "Don't focus on outward means of satisfaction if you want to be happy." I suspected he was right, so I dabbled in yoga and Buddhism, but in the end I returned to seeing my brains as soup. Soup with too much salt. My mom had come up with that: "There's nothing wrong with you, Seamus. It's just your soup. A little too much salt." And she'd smile. I'm not sure I totally got it, but soup, soup was a comfort.

And boys—boys were like sailors from a sea of it. Merchants from the Maldives. San Francisco wasn't a candy store; it was a spice rack. How about a little of this, or a little of that to flavor your soup? Imagine a world of boys named Tarragon, Sage, and Thyme. And wouldn't you know it, in San Francisco there were actually dozens of boys who went by such monikers. I actually met two Sages, blew a Catnip, fucked a Fennel, and jacked-off with a Willow.

Tasty boys.

Their rose hips.

Whatever ideas I'd had about true love, or convictions about inward means of satisfaction, had paled next to the endless outward thrills. Beige vs. brilliant white? True love's like a job. Who needs it when you got food stamps? True love can wait.

But fate wouldn't. And suddenly I didn't want anybody but Jimmy.

10

And pretty soon I'm in Berkeley—and rising above the campus in front of the steep dark green hills, I can see the Campanile Tower, like some phallic monument to my dashed college career. I'd lasted but a semester—not so much due to the difficulty of my studies as by my decision one afternoon—while defecating in the basement bathroom of Wheeler Hall no less—to finally act on my long-dormant sexual desires.

I may have been a bit neurotic, but that bathroom was madness incarnate.

Once I'd succumbed, courtesy of a track star named Kevin at the urinal next to mine, I returned almost daily to all number of sexual acrobatics: from sticking my dick through glory holes to lustful embraces with anonymous fratboys, our T-shirts yanked back behind our necks, constraining our shoulders, while our pants dropped in heaps to the floor, semen sloppily catapulted this way and that, busy with some agenda of its own we hardly had a say in. Within a few weeks, I had joined the cast of regulars, and having done nearly all of them, soon became bored, and felt the need to expand my sexual orbit to the local bars, and finally to San Francisco, from which no faggot can ever return. Needless to say, my grades plummeted and my class attendance suffered, with irreversible consequences.

My mother admonished me. The university threatened expulsion. But it was just too late to salvage my academic career, for though I may have been the answer to x in the quadratic equations of some of those wild sexcapades, I didn't like math—in fact, there was no major for what I wanted to study.

I didn't even return for the spring term, for it was during the holidays that I came out to my mother and assorted others, and somehow something shifted and Berkeley was like some place I'd graduated from, in a sense, already.

"What will you do now?" my mother asked me, exasperated and still stunned I'd ever gotten into Cal in the first place.

"Move to San Francisco, of course," was my too-fast answer.

"To do what?"

"To explore my sexuality."

"But I thought you knew what it was."

"Well, you know what I mean." I could have illustrated my point with one of "our songs" (Karen Carpenter belting out "We've Only Just Begun"), but we never listened to music together anymore.

"Solace for my soup" would have been an honest answer. Either way, it was to be a grand adventure, and I was a ship cutting through the waves, full sail, intent on Eldorado, with its towering palm trees swaying in the breeze and loaded with coconuts. A new world and I was greedy as a Spaniard.

Until I met Jimmy, of course. Jimmy, who educated me better than any university ever could.

U.C. Jimmy.

11

I found a postcard of the old chief in a card shop and pinned it on the wall over my bed, hoping to conjure the boy I'd lost.

I turned and saw Tanya, leaning on the doorjamb, and I gave her a sheepish glance.

"Don't pine, Shame. Do something constructive."

What was she, my big sister? Well, sort of.

And then she was rushing around, gathering her things, shoving folders, flyers, cards into her backpack with its ACT UP buttons and Queer Nation stickers plastered all over it. There was an ACT UP meeting that night and she was heading there. She went all the time, was on a committee even. I'd been before, but my attendance was spotty, predicated more on a vague sense of guilt, on righteous anger, and because it was the scene for cute boys with the sex appeal of radical politics. I'd gone to street protests and taken pictures, but I didn't like to think about the acronym too much except for how not to get it, and when I spent too much time thinking about it, I got depressed and paranoid. And I was afraid of depression and paranoia almost as much as the acronym. I preferred Queer Nation kiss-ins at downtown department stores. Tanya turned and looked at me as I sat and stared at her collecting her things. "Come on."

At the ACT UP meeting, I just sat there and listened, slouched next to Tanya with her set jaw, surrounded by the earnest multitude, who ranged from the leather-jacketed pierced intellectuals who ran the show to assorted hot young artfags and desiccated '70s-era guys—men who'd seen so many deaths, I feared they were death itself. There were bouncy, rotund baby dykes and menacing butches, smiling holy men, reassuring Venus of Willendorf sex workers, and several male couples with their hands gripped so tightly their knuckles were white. There were guys who looked like they'd never have been at such a meeting if it hadn't been for the great equalizer of the acronym, and there were the wackjobs who existed among all scenes in San Francisco and could be found wherever subversives gathered.

Tanya got up and spoke and said something about Burroughs Wellcome and AZT, and then they spilled out of her—acronym after acronym: CDC and NIH, FDA and PWA, PCP, ddI and ddC, Compound Q.

She was the real thing and I admired that and knew then that's why I sorta liked her despite how we clashed over things around the house. But I still hated those acronyms more than I liked her and wanted to swat them away like mosquitoes.

"I think I'm gonna go, Tanya," I whispered to her after she'd sat down post-speech. She put her hand on my thigh to keep me there, but I squirmed free, inconsolable despite the playful antics of the moderator, who had a lampshade on his head and strings of Mardi Gras beads across his chest.

He looked at me, grinning, when I got up: "Bye," he minced.

I waved sheepishly, mortified at the public flirtation that put me on the spot.

Off I went to walk and ruminate, hurrying up 18th Street from the meeting at the Women's Building, and through Dolores Park, which was living up to its name just then, misty and shadowed in the growing darkness. And in spilled the fog, huge banks of it over Twin Peaks, silent, crashing and breaking like a slow wave, then creeping and foaming around corners, slipping down alleyways and loitering among the buildings, moving heavy and steady like a giant slug ghost down hill-sides and streets, or surreptitiously whispering through the cypress trees, insinuating itself.

The city was full of smoke. And where there's smoke, there's fire, each infection like a red-hot coal, waiting to catch enough wind to blow into flame.

Halfway up Portola, the lone walker on the sidewalk, a terrible feeling of loneliness overcame me. Icarus, but in the darkness and mist this time, falling not because of the melting wax of my wings, but because there was no updraft to keep me aloft. I turned and went back down the hill, snaking down among the empty streets and Victorian corner markets into Noe Valley, intent on the Mission, where I just *had to* find him.

First I went to Kaos on Valencia Street, where all the cute ACT UP boys went after meetings, all of whom would arrive soon—and who knows, maybe Jimmy had already joined up and just hadn't been at tonight's meeting or had arrived after I'd left. In which case, he'd appear here? But no Jimmy among the tacky neon décor and smiling boy-crowd, all sweating and shirtless on the cramped dance floor, or crowded around the little tables, hip to bursting, young and full of promise and hormones. I drank too much, ran into Lawrence and assorted others, even made out with some lanky dark Italian boy named Limbo, who wasn't even nice. But my loneliness needed a tit to suckle and he was it on the Naugahyde couch. I tore myself away when he commented on how weirdly blue my eyes were. Off I went, home to masturbate, thinking of my horseboy and how gray he could make my eyes.

12

Berkeley became Albany became El Cerrito became Richmond—like biblical begetting, the miles passed me and that bike from one on to the other, like the word of God (or in this case, the words of Jimmy—In the beginning was the word, and his were: *take me back the way I came*). And into the hills past Richmond, past housing tracts and industry, determined and pumping away, the bay still out there, the big pill-shaped oil storage tanks on the golden summer-desiccated hillsides. I'd catch a glimpse now and again of the Amtrak train, rushing down the tracks to who knows where. Or I'd look out to the water to see a ferry bouncing along over the waves, heading for the dream city that stood out there like a promise, beckoning. And always the whoosh, whoosh of cars passing me. And Richmond became Hercules became Crockett, and pretty soon I was crossing over the Carquinez Strait itself, looking down into the slow-moving end of rivers. I tried to remember their names and how many: the Sacramento, the San Joaquin, the Napa, and the Mokelumne—and before them, having merged with the growing flood miles inland: the Tuolumne, the Stanislaus, the American, the Cosumnes, the Merced. All come to San Francisco, just like Jimmy had.

I looked at Jimmy's strings then—rivers all—going back now to wherever they came from. Was I supposed to return each one of them? How would I ever find their source? What garments, what bags or awnings, what rags and carpets? What tasks were completed with the frayed remnants of rope? What packages were held secure with that twine? And who were the sheep? Where were the cotton fields? What bleak West Texas plain had the synthetics been once spit up out of? Who'd worked to transform them in refineries and factories and sweatshops? How many people and how many things were involved to discard a string on the side of the road for a young man dying to find and tie to his bike, resolved to tell its story, but running out of time and never quite getting the chance?

I remembered then his long beautiful fingers laying the strings out on a café table, the wrinkles on his knuckles, the scar on his thumb, how it felt to hold his warm alive hand.

13

The next day I went to Crystal Pistol, figuring Jimmy just had to eventually appear at one of these sideshows of choice for the lost young punky boys who came to San Francisco, who did things like collect strings, and—like Jimmy—ravaged their scalps with color. Which reminded me to be thorough in my search. His scalp might have morphed to hot pink by now—or green or blue. I had to be vigilant and keep an eye out.

But no dice at the Crystal Pistol.

On Saturday, to Klubstitute I scurried, swirling through the retro circus of young multi-gendered boys, some with rhinestones ensconced between their eyes, tiaras on their shaved heads, dresses and combat boots highlighting their skinned, hairy knees; there was lots of slopped-on eyeliner, garish crabapple red lipstick, darling chin stubble. I saw some friends and even wanted to stay, but without knowing where Jimmy was, I found it hard to socialize with anyone, my face a question, obsessively worrying that somewhere my *answer* was laughing and drinking, dancing and jawing on and on about infant critters to a steady stream of cute available boys. I downed proffered kamikazes foolishly and careened toward a pathetic drunkenness.

A boy got ahold of my left buttcheek and held it like a potter would clay. I smiled politely into his lascivious eyes, but I was through with suckling—my thirst would only be slaked by Jimmy. I walked, all through and up and down the streets of the Castro, where I doubted I'd

49

find him. Sometimes I'd stand on a corner and just watch the parade. The screeching and slap-happy weekend queens, the bow-legged diesels and swaggering butches, the golden-age-of-Hollywood lipsticks, the snooty sweater guys, the quiet watchful artists, the jabbering mainstream social crowd, the gaggles of serious ACT UP boys in small black leather jackets and paratrooper boots, the playful babydykes, the drunks, the broken, the loners, the addicts, and the mad. To some I said "hi"; to others whom I didn't know, I just smiled, investing perhaps in future liaisons as we'd thus now noted each other on the scene. But really, I just wanted to ask all and any of them if they'd seen Jimmy. *And how would I describe him?...* "Horseboy,... sloppy bleach job,... gangly,... doorknobs for shoulders, knees, and elbows, ... pants baggy—there's not a belt that could hold anything around that waist, ... eyes, eyes that ... that ... *Here, look into mine*—they match these like an electric cord matches a wall socket."

A few nights later, I went to the End Up for Club Uranus. My last chance. And that's where I saw him. Out on the patio, smoking a cigarette, alone.

I swallowed what felt like a whole hard-boiled egg.

It was crowded and I was on the other side of the patio, so he didn't see me as I scooted myself up onto the bench that ran along a sad little hedge of neurasthenic bushes. And I just stared across at him. No way was I going to walk up to him. Someone else did though and tried to chat him up. He didn't even smile, just took a hard drag off the cigarette, nodded his head, and looked away. Which made the point. Then he was alone again.

I leaned forward, wanting to be the next someone, but hesitated. I was dying to give him a hug is the honest truth, grab him like he'd survived a natural disaster and squeeze him until my teeth unclenched and I could breathe easy again. But I couldn't let him see I wanted him that badly. That'd finish it. He might even push me away, repulsed by my presumption. I breathed deep to calm my beating heart. He was like the deer in my sights and I couldn't shoot.

I stared at my shoes, scuffed black clownish-looking things I'd found at Community Thrift, and I must have been looking down at them when he spotted me. I'd stopped my head halfway up when I saw he'd discovered me, and I eyed him from under my brows, with my chin still almost touching my chest. That was probably what made him laugh, which momentarily made me blush, and then made my face erupt into a smile that almost hurt, it stretched my face so.

He walked over, pushing through the drinking crowd.

"Well, if it ain't Mr. Blake, the station master," he beamed.

"Hey Jimmy," I answered back, my heart bouncing off my sternum like a rubber ball, the dog in me wanting to jump up barking and lick his face. I knew better.

"How you been?" And his hand went to my shoulder and shook it lightly.

"Uh, okay, I guess. How about you?"

I was still sitting down, and he bent his knees to crouch down in front of me, grabbing my hand as he did and kissing it, like he had on the platform.

My lashes fluttered, my heart and stomach leapt, my legs and arms tingled, my throat caught. *Don't do this, you dog.* He kissed me on the lips next, and I leaned into the kiss.

"I'm glad I found ya," he said.

Found me? I wanted to say, . . . *but you knew where I was all along, Jimmy.* I didn't dare. And I was never going to admit I'd been looking for *him.* "Here I am." I raised my eyebrows. In the background the music throbbed—Soft Cell: "Tainted Love."

"Aren't you gonna ask me where I've been?" Jimmy said then.

I gave him a long, hard look, my eyes bluer than ever, no doubt. "California?" He guffawed and cuffed me on the shoulder. "Okay," I said demurely, "Where you been, Jimmy?"

"Building a foundation," he said obliquely. Short answer. And then the long. How he'd finally reached Sam and Julie—friends of friends he'd been calling for weeks—that very morning I'd run out for coffee and bagels. And then there'd just been so much to do.

"But why didn't you leave a note, Jimmy?"

"I'm a poet." And he stood back up.

"Uh, what does that mean?" And I stood up then too.

"I left the bike, didn't I?"

I screwed up my brows.

He put his arm on my shoulder then. A lit match. "You didn't think I'd come back for it?"

My shoulders and brows went up.

"I thought you knew it was like the most important thing. I figured I could trust it with you, and that you knew of course I'd come back for it." His big smile, his fangs a little bit too pronounced.

Gulp. I smiled shyly. Then I hugged him full force and he hugged me back the same way.

"Come see my new place," he invited.

My brows went up again.

But before I could inquire, he'd grabbed my hand and, pulling me to my feet, we weaved through the smokers, squirmed through the patio door, parted the drinkers and the dancers as the music enveloped us, jostling our way toward the exit, past the haystack bouncers and the big knot of folks at the entrance, before stumbling onto the sidewalk, out among the smoking modern primitives and garish clubsters in skinny ties and kelly green slacks. The fog was everywhere, sifting down like a floury mist—so heavy that you could barely see a block ahead of you.

He yanked me by the arm and he ran me like a dog all the way down Harrison Street, and then along under the overhead freeway, sometimes grinning, or laughing when cabs blasted their horns because we never stopped at corners until we hit the Mission District and had to on account of serious traffic. By then we were sweating, the hot sweat of the dance, our cheeks rosy in the cold, the mistiness of the air making us damp and clammy, both of us breathing steam like horses. We were so alive right then, re-found, come to life, that that moment sticks forever in my mind—the wetness of his skin, droplets all beaded up on his chin scruff like dew, the wide-eyed look in the bracing cold, his pronounced Adam's apple and slightly turned-up nose, what it felt like to stand there next to him—the lucky prizewinner—my calloused toe rubbed raw in my stiff black leather clown shoes, the way my boxer shorts' sweaty elastic band was sticking to my belly, my toothache and hangnail, my cock coming to life in anticipation, the blinking neon of the Zeitgeist Bar that made rainbows on the damp sidewalk at our feet, and the intermittent voices as the bar's door opened and closed, the bass thump coming through the walls, the dandelion pod headlights coming toward us on Valencia Street and the fuzzy red balls that slowly receded away from us once they'd passed—his half-cold, half-warm hand in mine, squeezing.

He kissed me hungrily, his mouth warm and gooey in the cold—like that warm, soft Szechuan tofu I liked so much at Much Luck Express on 17th Street. Then he eyed the hill before us, laughed at it, and ran me south to 15th where we could cut up to Guerrero without ascending 14th Street. That took us past the projects, which I usually avoided since fags had been bashed there a lot—and, well, like any city, it was full of poor young men, emasculated and angry. I guess it helped to be running because we encountered no trouble and arrived at Guerrero without incident, walking the rest of the way until we reached his gate, at which point he smiled—"here we are"—and dragged me, clumping up the stairs, the two of us half-stumbling in the light of a single bare bulb hanging precipitously from what was once probably a legitimate fixture. The walls were a faded glossy cobalt, decorated with wild-colored paisleys and mandalas, an obvious holdover from some San Francisco psychedelic dream of twenty years previous.

At the door, Jimmy pulled out his single key and turned the deadbolt, then the lock, and, pulling me in, shut the door on what smelled like ginger and bok choy and steamed rice, which permeated his landing like a perfume. It ceased once inside his room and so I figured it was from across the hall.

"Time for another bath, Shame." And he went into the bathroom, leaving me standing in the single empty room of the studio, staring at the empty fireplace, the mantle where he'd already left change, his wallet, the lease, and matches. In one corner was a kitchen counter built against the wall, with a sink, an oven overhead, and a stove and cupboards. In the corner opposite, his sleeping bag and the two panniers. There was a big bay window that dominated the front of the room, and naturally, like a kid, I was drawn to it. I walked over to look out just as I heard the plumbing roused to life somewhere behind me, and there below was a corner liquor store under a fuzzy befogged streetlight, all of it shrouded by a big acacia tree that was buckling the sidewalk in front, where a young man leaned into a pay phone attached to the wall.

That's when I felt him bear-hug me from behind.

We were a cold, wet mess, and in no time at all, we were naked too, our cocks bobbing in front of us as we slurped at each other's mouths—and then he pulled me into the bathroom, and into the gray steam rising out of the tub—a whole different kinda fog—and all I could say between kisses was "Jimmy, Jimmy," keeping to myself the end of that sentence, which rolled on and on into *thank God I found you; tell me everything; hold me forever; don't ever leave again.*

Didn't dare enunciate that.

Otherwise, there was just the sound of the choppy back-and-forth waves of the bath, the slurps and grunts and giggles, the sexy smell of Jimmy's sweat, the taste of cigarettes in his mouth, the sweet thought of living out good luck, and all the different textures of him: scruffy chin, slippery lips, the soft leather of his cock skin, the cold slippery yellow-rain-jacket feel of his back, the soft tender skin stretched tight on his belly, the thick, hard rubbery stiffness of his nipples, the endless cartographic texture of his balls and his rough hairy shins and bony feet, his shoulders like bald tennis balls—and I was a dog for them.

We bobbed for apples.

Jimmy pulled me up onto my feet after we'd slaked our thirst. "Come on, Shame, my turn." And he handed me a condom and up inside him I went: the rollercoaster, and no one driving. Just two boys along for the ride—and then like the sun from behind a cloud, a flashing burst of warmth and light, and ooh-ahh, and a great vista appeared with a meadow laid out before us, which was him and me and the night we would spend together—and the dreams there, the moon and stars.

14

The wine country was beautiful and all that, and the redwoods too, but everything I saw wasn't really itself, but just something that in some way reminded me of Jimmy. I suppose I looked for him—or couldn't stop looking for him—and so I'd find him in things: the melancholy sound of a breeze, or the way a door slammed in a house a hundred yards back from the road that had just a hint of a Buffalo twang. And there were oak trees, of course, that gestured with their branches just like he did; granite stones in the golden oak-studded hills that shared cheekbones with him; rounded grassy slopes that looked like him sleeping under blankets; rivers dimpled and smiling and full of his words; clouds that were his thoughts, wind his breath. Once, courtesy of a creek, I even heard the sweet sound of him peeing in the filthy little bathroom on Guerrero Street. And sun-dappled that pissy creek was too, from the overhanging buckeyes—trees that were just like Jimmy because they lost all their leaves too soon and died mid-summer.

And at night, the mummy sleeping bag, which held me like he had.

15

Lucky we were both so skinny because Jimmy and I had to sleep that first night together on Guerrero Street in his sleeping bag, which left no room for anything but an embrace. When his eyes opened, I told him he needed a bed, and that we should go out today and get one for him.

"Yeah, you're right," he said groggily, "how 'bout we go get yours."

Eyebrows high, the question that was my face. "Sure," I agreed, "let's go." But I was careful not to act too enthused. Horses scared easy, like deer, birds, and stray dogs.

Moving by cab was not uncommon in San Francisco, and that's just what we did. It was a transient city, after all, so no one had much stuff and they were constantly relocating, either due to the complicated evictions of scheming landlords dodging the strict tenants'-rights laws, or due to new lovers, irreconcilable differences with roommates, wanderlust propelling them to the far ends of the earth, or perhaps new jobs that necessitated more convenient commutes, which in San Francisco meant not more than ten blocks or so—or if further, then at least accessible via a direct bus or rail line.

Not that it was ever simple.

"You gotta give thirty days, Shame."

I just looked at her.

"Isn't there someone?"

"You know anyone?—reliable?"

Tanya was right, and while I was flaky and irresponsible, I wasn't a jerk and wasn't going to stick it to her. Besides, after the recent ACT UP meeting, I had a newfound respect and admiration for Tanya, as well as a sudden ability to forgive her for sending Jimmy packing, since I'd tracked him down and was now about to be living with him. I didn't always like her style, but she was just and at least deserved justice in return.

"I'll find someone, don't you worry." But my only friends were six-year-olds at the YMCA. Or boys I'd hooked up with. And contacting them—which likely would entail bodily contact—was no longer an option now that Jimmy was in the picture.

I certainly couldn't afford paying rent in two places, even though Jimmy said I didn't have to pay rent the first month. But, as it turned out, Tanya found someone through ACT UP and I was off the hook. I was glad she'd found someone because then she wouldn't blame me if my choice turned out to be a fuck-up, which was about 75 percent likely.

Where'd you get the money for this place, and how'd you get it without a job?" I asked Jimmy, hefting a box up the long stairwell from the sidewalk where my pile of boxes sat post-cab ride. The cabbie had even agreed to take the bike, though we'd had to hang it out the back of the trunk. Just then, Jimmy carried it up the stairs before me on his shoulder.

"I gave him six months, up front."

I did a quick calculation. That had to be three thousand dollars, give or take. A lot of money. And Jimmy didn't look to me like the kind of guy who would have that kind of money.

"Where'd you get the money?" I looked at him, incredulous, as we reached the landing.

"I found it." He gave me a quick smile over his shoulder, but by the time I registered the oddity of that response, he'd vanished through the door and into the apartment, where he placed the bike carefully in front of the fireplace.

"Where?"

"In Eugene," he answered, without turning around.

"How do you find that kind of money?" I asked suspiciously.

He turned and laughed and said: "By reading books."

"What?" I felt like I was talking to Ivan.

"Uh-huh," he said and changed the subject before I could ask where. "Let's go get that mattress."

Of course we had to carry the mattress and box springs ourselves, on top of our heads, as no cab could accommodate their dimensions. But it wasn't more than twelve blocks anyway, so like ants with our prized sugar we set off—for what lovemaking would soon sprout like flowers upon our holy platform, and feed us all the short days of our betrothal. We were a psalm. And it was right to hold the bed high like a king and carry it above our heads across town, intermittently laughing as we pumped it up and down to prevent our muscles from stiffening.

Arriving at Jimmy's door, we met the twins. They'd peeked out previously when we'd unloaded all the boxes from the cab, a wind of ginger, garlic, and sesame oil at their backs. But they'd quickly slammed the door when we got within five steps of the landing. When we'd showed up with the mattress, however, they'd gotten up the nerve to come out— perhaps emboldened by the fact that our limbs were all occupied with the mattress and we were clearly compromised as predators. Dressed in identical Taiwanese sweat suits, with the small-billed caps to match, they couldn't have been more than six or seven years old.

As we maneuvered this way and that, they not only came out and watched us get it stuck in the downstairs doorway but went so far as to direct us the minute we got through and up the first few steps.

"Oh, oh, no this way. . . . No, it's hitting the wall!"

"The light!"

"No, up this way—wait!" And like little mice they ran up and down the stairs, under the mattress and in between us, laughing, shouting, and throttling each other.

"Hey, you guys aren't helping," Jimmy gruffly announced. "Besides, it's a mattress; it doesn't matter if it hits the walls!"

"Let's drop it on them, Jimmy," I threatened playfully.

They howled then, and went careening out the door and into the street.

When we finally achieved the threshold and got the mattress in the door, we went back down to get the box spring that we'd left leaning on the wall outside.

And there they were bouncing themselves off it.

"Hey!" Jimmy barked and down the street they ran, yipping and clipping at each other.

"Antidepressants," I commented in a deadpan to Jimmy.

He rolled his eyes. "You like kids?"

I nodded enthusiastically. "I even tutor them, down at the Y."

"Tutor them in what?"

"Whatever. It's like study hall." I didn't go on to explain that I went to be tutored by them more than the other way around. They were far better therapy than Pinski, serotonin reuptake-*inhibitoraderos* all. Or maybe they just made me try a little harder, since having nervous breakdowns around small children was just not kosher.

Jimmy stood and looked at me for a few frozen minutes.

"I don't know. I don't like kids, but I like people who do."

"Well, then you like me," I said triumphantly.

He grabbed me. "You ever read Burroughs?"

"Sure."

"*Wild Boys?*" His face was full of mischief. "Wanna go make a spirit baby, Shame?"

I nodded emphatically.

Up the stairs with the box springs. We threw the bed together like a giant sandwich, and then I guess you could say we ate it. Or made the mayonnaise to moisten it up. Same difference. Garnished each other with kisses.

Lying there spent and naked, up on his elbows, with his cock rakishly splayed across his left thigh, Jimmy winked at me. And then he jumped up and went and gathered strings like berries off his bike, untying several.

Then Jimmy sat down Indian-style in the middle of the bed, saying, "Let me show you something"—and he tied a yellow string around my wrist and told me: "That one came from a rag that was blowing in the wind, caught on a barbed-wire fence near Gillette, Wyoming. It's for you." I nodded a respectful thanks, though I couldn't imagine why he gave me that one. But I kept listening because there was a whole load of such stories tied all up and down that bike and I wanted to hear them. He stretched out a blue string that he could only remember was somehow about time—"from either Dayville, Oregon, or Ten Sleep, Wyoming, I can't remember which." There was a red thread he said belonged to a gay priest in Preston, Iowa, who'd asked but hadn't received on account of Jimmy wasn't interested in anything but a place to lay his sleeping bag in the rectory.

"This one"—and he held up a dingy dark blue-green thread—"I yanked off the blood pressure Velcro thingy the day I found out."

16

Up in Sonoma County someone had painted that Katmandu Buddha on a barn and it made me think of Jimmy's third-eye tattoo. "It was very cool once," he'd said as we lolled on the bed, "but so were a lot of things. I wanna get rid of it." I agreed with him, it was sort of ridiculous, especially compared with the beautiful Chinese one etched on his sideburn that reminded me of his goodness. Yet after a while the third-eye tattoo seemed so sweet. Jimmy's mistake. Jimmy'd get shy when I'd run my finger around it. It was a black circle with a red dot in the center, more a bull's-eye than a human eye.

"The third eye *is* the bull's-eye, silly," he'd razzed me when I'd mentioned it looked more like a dartboard than an ophthalmological specimen.

"How 'bout adding a tear?" I said animatedly.

"I never killed anybody. Shut up," he said, furrowing his brow.

"So, the real third eye—is it open, Jimmy?"

"I found you, didn't I? Must be." He winked.

"Ah, Jimmy, I'm not third-eye stuff. Hell, I wouldn't even wanna know what I looked like through a third eye. Probably like one of my friggin' paintings."

He looked offended and furrowed his brow again. "Hey, I like your paintings."

"Do you really?"

"Yeah, I do."

"Why?"

"I don't know, it's like you turn your anger into something funny. I don't know how to do that. I mean, my poetry isn't funny."

"Your tattoo is funny."

"Fuck you," he said with a smile. The timbre of his voice.

"Your anger is actually kinda sexy, Jimmy."

"Nice to know it makes someone happy."

"See? You're sarcastic. That's a kind of funny."

He nodded and sighed.

"If we were clowns, Jimmy, you'd be like the hobo clown with the frown . . . and I'd be like the white facepaint psycho kind."

He guffawed. "You're not as crazy as you think you are."

"And you're not as serious, Jimmy. You always laugh after you cum."

"Maybe that's because sex is sort of ridiculous once you've gotten it out of your system."

"Or maybe we need to have more sex so things are funnier?" Brows high, the question that was my face.

He guffawed again. "You are crazy." And he kissed me. And not long after that we were naked and pretty soon we were laughing too.

And then Jimmy was up on his feet and ready to go out for coffee.

And like we did a million times (I wish, but it was more like a few dozen, Jimmy not being here that long—it felt like a million all the same), off we'd go to sit in cafés like two kids with our projects. He'd lay out his strings, a handful he'd tied to his wrist that morning after removing them from the bike. Me, I'd sit and sketch up new Marie Antoinette ideas: as Ronald Reagan (*let them eat ketchup*); as a Palestinian teenager (*let them live in refugee camps for three generations*); as two guys having sex (*let them laugh like clowns*).

"You're more of a performer than a painter, I think," Jimmy said.

"I'm no artist, am I, Jimmy? These things are crap."

He laughed, and then he stopped when he saw I wasn't saying it humorously.

"Maybe you should take an acting class or something."

"Yeah, then we could become porn stars and laugh at each other," I sighed.

He rolled his eyes. "I just mean it's good to try something different for a change."

"Like fight no more forever?"

He nodded with gravity, as if he weren't sure whether I meant it like he'd mean it or if I was just being smart-aleck ironic and/or defensive.

"I'm sorry, Jimmy . . . I just meant . . ."

Funny till I wasn't. Then I'd get all apologetic and it would annoy him. "Sorry, Jimmy. Good Mr. Jimmy. Sorry to bring you down."

He knew where that was going. He reached over and shook me hard by the shoulder. "Hey. Pull yourself together. What's the matter?"

"I talk too much. I say the wrong shit all the time." And I shook my head.

"Just stop." He shrugged. Easy for him to say.

I looked at him. "It's just the soup, Jimmy."

"Pull."

"I don't know how to love you," I said, but in my mind I was singing *Jesus Christ Superstar*.

He put his finger to his mouth, then leaned across the table and kissed me on the forehead. "That's how."

He went back to his strings, and I pulled.

And *pull* meant all sorts of things: shut up and pull yourself together; pull the rope of your life—because I'd let it all run out all over the floor with my endless chatter. Or it was like skeet-shooting even: pull, concentrate, aim, and fire.

Jimmy in a white T-shirt with his ratty green sweater over it, the dark scruff of his chin running all the way down to his Adam's apple, which was a red delicious, so pronounced it was. He'd stop on the sidewalk and I wouldn't notice until I was ten feet past him, so lost I'd been in my musings about Ivan or Tanya or my mother's preference for Jim Croce over Joni Mitchell.

Pull.

He'd catch up then and grab ahold of my hand, maybe bite my ear. And sometimes he'd run me like a dog down the block. Because I really was like a dog to Jimmy. A good companion. And he knew how to calm my barking.

Sometimes he just grabbed me. The steadying embrace of James Damon Keane. Pulling me. Squeezing me. Making a bowl for my soup.

Jimmy loved to dance, while I'd go on and on about how I didn't like to dance and didn't know why, and maybe it was the places, or the people, or the music, or maybe there was just something wrong with me. He'd just look at me and say: "Seamus . . . pull." Then he'd give me a big hug, and I'd go and just find a nice place to sit more often than not, with my sketchpad, or put back beers and smoke cigarettes or pot and watch Jimmy like some mom at a soccer game. How he danced all alone in his own little trance, his head rolled back past his shoulders, the Chinese sideburn tattoo on his pale skin like a beacon to spot him by. He danced sort of like Pig Pen, and dressed like him too, all grungy.

And I sat and watched him a lot, whether it was dancing or when he was reading his poems.

Because Jimmy had quickly become a little sensation in the SF poetry scene—and not just because he was cute and edgy, with that tattooed face, but because he was different in that he wrote no poems about Jimmy or gimmicky hipster drama. He was never arch. He wrote poems about nothing places and the nobody people whom he described in vivid colors—little knots in his long, long string:

> Men who look like frogs
> And gather bullet casings from highway ditches
> With their tongues
> Men like flies who smell the shit of consumption
> And gather
> Men like big wandering hairy children
> Who've turned in their stingray bikes for F-150s

They know the earth in the way that children do
By its trash and its puddles
Men
Like frogs
Tadpoles of a promising four-legged, croaking death

Hot damn Jimmy and the silences he wrought. The timbre of his
voice.

17

Jimmy had gotten a job through Sam and Julie, those same friends who snatched him away from me after the bath. Good thing too because he'd get insurance eventually, but not for six months, at which point we'd also learn it didn't cover pre-existing conditions. So much for that.

Well, he got paid at least. He worked at the blood bank, as a warehouse man. Funny Jimmy. Dark Jimmy. A vampire at the blood bank. He was the warehouse man, shipped the blood all around.

"You ever drop it, Jimmy?"

"Yeah, and it bounces." His little grin.

"Never breaks?"

"Nah, the bags are thick and rubbery."

"Do you get to drink for free like I do at the coffee shop?"

"No, but I smear it all over my face when I'm angry—what do you think?" Jimmy would get tired of my caffeine-blitzed chatter after work, especially if he wasn't feeling well. And I talked on and on while I opened mail, folded clothes, listened to phone messages, throwing out my doubts and anxieties and talking my endless nonsense. Sometimes he'd grab me—and squeeze, and squeeze, until it was like all the caffeine went right out of me, and then we were kissing, and our clothes were being pulled by the other, and we were naked, our eager cocks poking at each other, the dark hair around his cock as black as his chin's, and me muttering, "Jimmy, Jimmy, oh fuck, Jimmy."

"Shame," and he'd look me in the eye. And then he held his finger to his mouth, "shhhh."

It's like he fucked the madness right out of me.

"I fuckin' love you, Jimmy."

"Oh yeah?" Deadpan Jimmy.

And I'd squeeze him back, hoping to squeeze out of him what ran through *his* blood. And sometimes I convinced myself that I was doing just that. Sex magic—and I thought of my semen as a healing balm when it jetted out of my cock and onto his chest. And I rubbed it around all over his lovely long pale chest and pronounced clavicles like it was Vicks VapoRub, lying with him, kissing him, telling him he was my new favorite thing.

"What's the old one?"

"Well, they come and go, you know?"

"So you don't remember?"

"Well, probably this little girl, Eustacia."

He looked at me, brows furrowed.

"She's one of the kids I tutor."

He nodded. "So, what? Am I like her?"

I had to think about that. "Come to think of it, yeah. Sorta."

"Hmm, this should be interesting. She's what?—eight?"

"Yeah. She's cute and she likes me. Maybe it's as simple as that."

"Ah, give me a little more than that, Shame."

"Uh, she's Chinese, has this really cool, long silky black hair that shines."

"Well, I'm not Chinese and my hair is blond."

"You dye it," I corrected him. "Same roots? I don't know, Jimmy— shit, you make me want to smile and cry all at the same time. How's that?"

"Hmm. Better. What's her sad part? I know mine."

He didn't want my pity, so I checked it. "I don't know her that well. She's a kid. I mean, it's sad to be a kid. It's not easy, or carefree and fun like people think and choose to remember it. Kids are . . ." But I didn't

67

say it. I was thinking "powerless." He didn't want my pity. "It's nothing specific, Jimmy. I think when you love somebody that's just how it feels. A little sad. I mean, we're all fucked ultimately."

"Vulnerable, right?"

"Yeah, sure, that's a good word for it."

"I'm not a kid, Shame. You don't have to take care of me."

"Jimmy," and I ran my hand through his chaff-like golden scalp. He sat up then.

"You're gonna probably leave when things get fucked up, Shame."

"I don't think so." And I sat up then too, hands around my legs, head between my knees.

"I think so, Shame. And maybe we need to take a little break, see some other people or something."

I said nothing to that; felt offended in fact and thought of a new Marie: *Let Them Go Find Some Other Boy Even Though They Found the One They Love Already.*

"What do you mean, Jimmy? You want me to go away?"

"Shame, I came here with a lot of intention, you know?"

"Yeah, I know," and I looked down.

"I came here to die, okay? Fight no more forever." And he reached over and lifted my chin with those long fingers of his. "Shame . . . I'm not pushing you away; I'm just not pulling you down with me." And his eyes were all glassy after he said it. Jimmy, who didn't cry.

"You aren't pulling me down, Jimmy . . . you pick me up."

I got a pained look on my face then and he got up and walked to the window and the fire escape, and looked out at the acacia tree, and the corner liquor store and the pay phone and the buckled sidewalk, and he said without turning around:

"You ever been there for it? Someone dying slow and ugly? Huh, Shame?"

"Stop, Jimmy."

"Huh, Shame?" And he turned around. "It's not pretty; it's very fucked up. I didn't expect I'd meet somebody the day I got here, you know?"

He kicked a shoe, "Dammit."

I didn't wanna be Jimmy's problem.

"I can leave then, Jimmy." And I got up and started grabbing stuff. Dramatic, yes, but I was twenty-one and I wanted him to show me he wanted me to stay.

"Shame," he barked, and he took my arm and made me drop the handful of T-shirts I'd started gathering from the floor. Tight, tight, tight he held my arm. "Just let me figure this out. I'm trying to do right by you. I came here and figured if I met somebody . . . If I met somebody . . . it wouldn't be like all the other times . . ." And he looked away. And then he looked back at me intently: "If I met somebody to . . . if I met somebody to love (his eyes all glassy), . . . I was gonna love and take nothing back . . ."

I wanted to grab and hold him so bad right then, but I checked myself. He didn't want pity. I kept reminding myself of that, though he kept teasing me to express it. Instead, I argued: "Jimmy, you don't take nothing . . . you're like . . . like the lottery or something . . . I'm . . ."

"Shame . . . I'm gonna take everything you got, man." And he dropped my arm and looked at the floor. "My numbers are bad, Shame." And he raised his face again, his long eyelashes and creamy pale-skinned healthy young handsome face. "This disease, it fucking wrecks people."

I could put out my hand. And I did. And he took it. Two young naked men. Too young. "It's not gonna wreck you, Jimmy. Besides, you're young and strong . . . and now there's like AZT and like . . . ddI . . ." But I stopped. I'd been to ACT UP meetings; I knew how dubious those drugs were.

He took my other hand then, and we came slowly together into a tender embrace. And I started dancing with him then, holding his naked body close. And soon enough, we were waltzing around that little apartment, dodging combat boots and paperbacks, humming songs from *2001: A Space Odyssey* because Strauss's were the only waltzes I knew. I hated to dance but knew how to make him laugh. And soon enough, his drawn face, with its black-as-iron-filings chin scruff, the slightly turned-up nose, the doe eyes, and the Blakean angelic crown of spiked blond hair, smiled, listening to me hum *The Blue Danube* as we danced faster and faster.

"Crazy motherfucker," he said.

I just nodded in the affirmative.

We showered and got dressed and I made Jimmy tea, and we sat on the fire escape and Jimmy told me all sorts of long stories while the cars passed back and forth below us and the wind rippled the acacia tree. Man of few words, Jimmy . . . man of short answers, let out the line and didn't pull until the very end.

"I always went out with older guys, Shame." And he told me about Franco the dancer and Thomas the poet. "But I couldn't really deal with it when they got sick."

Jimmy went inside and dug around in the piles up on the mantel. He came back out with an old coffee-stained envelope. And he opened it, and there was Franco, a handsome Italian-looking Argentine with a big smile holding Jimmy close against his shoulder, and Thomas, a serious priestly looking man, standing next to Jimmy. Jimmy had dark hair in all those pics and he looked eager and boyish and enthusiastic. Not so tentative and horse-like. He told me how he met them and what they were like and where they lived and what they liked to do—Thomas had been his English professor at Empire State College one semester, and with Franco he'd lived in Alphabet City after college. And then he started in with the acronyms. I, who didn't want to hear it, listened, but I preferred having Jimmy to myself, with no past—just my William Blake angel appearing on the train platform coming for to carry me home.

But he continued: "I always found some way to pull away, and then I'd end up in some whole other city." By then he was looking out into the street, talking to himself really. "It was easy to come up with reasons to leave upstate. New York City too, I guess, 'cause it wears people down. People disappear from there all the time."

I nodded, and we just sat in silence, watching cars and the corner liquor store and the people going in and out. Then I started suggesting

70

places we could go, talking about museums I wanted to show him, the statue of Georgia O'Keeffe in Sydney Walton Square where the cherry blossoms always accidentally bloomed in February and got torn away by the rains; the Bufano sculptures scattered about the city; the churches and bloody Jesuses I'd found. "Let's go to the Cliff House, Jimmy."

Jimmy put the envelope back and off we went to Land's End.

He must have had a sense. Two weeks later he was sniffling and coughing, moaning with a cold. A cold that turned to pneumonia. I made chicken soup, I did laundry and everything I could so he wouldn't ask me to go away again. I smiled, kept quiet, and didn't mope once. I pulled. On account of Jimmy, I pulled.

He came home from the doctor's one day feeling much better—and with a doll, the first. "Here, a spirit baby—it's for you," he'd said. "Give him a name."

"Little Joseph," I said spontaneously. A fat little plastic-headed boy, with plastic arms and legs and a cloth body full of sand. Hourglass boy. "He's got your nose, Jimmy."

Later he'd bring home Elmer and Genevieve, Sebastian and Victoria, who all nestled together on the mantle, leaning on Our Lady of Guadalupe candles and plastic tubs of lube. Our family. World without end.

I'll light the fire . . . and you place the flowers in the vase . . . that you bought today . . .

18

I slept in campgrounds—all up California, all the way to Eugene—among redwoods, on rivers, sometimes near motorhomes or young hikers with tents. I always camped a ways off though, on my own in just my sleeping bag on a foam pad, with Jimmy, a pile of dust in a velvet bag, held close against my belly in the pocket of me, under a huge vault of stars and a traveling moon.

And I wondered if I'd ever tell anyone about Jimmy. And what would I say? "Grungy, scruffy . . . horseboy . . . sloppy bleach job . . . gangly . . . doorknobs for shoulders, knees, and elbows . . . pants baggy—there's not a belt that could hold anything around that waist . . . eyes, eyes that . . . that . . . *Here, look into mine*—they matched these like an electric cord matches a wall socket."

Sometimes cars would come into the campgrounds late, and there'd be that searchlight swing of the headlamps that would pass over me, reminding me of when I was a little boy after Mom had tucked me into my bed in the apartment in San Leandro, and I would watch all the lights flashing across my ceiling, which Mom told me were angels and shooting stars. But, in fact, they were the headlights of cars from the freeway, named for animals and Indians: Pintos and Cherokees, Dodge Dakotas and Falcons, Winnebagos—and even some with names from deep space: Vegas, Coronas, Novas, and Corollas. All going who knows where.

In the woods, there were shooting stars for real, and they got me remembering the plastic glowing ones Jimmy and I pasted on the ceiling in Guerrero Street—and the string of Christmas lights we wrapped around his bike for the holidays that blinked at five different speeds in five different colors.

Looking up at those Day-Glo stars, I'd ask him, "Who are the Three Wisemen, Jimmy?"

"Jimmy, Seamus, and Priapus," he'd snicker, right on cue, his biceps flexing as he pulled a reversal and pinned me with a kiss. And the gifts we gave? Cock, and ass, mouth and nipple and belly and flank, leg and arm and foot and hand—and things from way inside: our saliva, our cum, our hearts. Little drummer boys. And we drummed each other good too.

I had half a mind to make love to Jimmy when I'd get to thinking like that. To drive my slimed member into the dust of him. Jimmy, who I held close to me like a warm chunk of coal that I'd heard the Japanese Zen monks use at night in the monasteries high up in the mountains where it's cold and they have no furnace. Just a lump of coal they hold to their heart.

Because it was cold among the redwoods at night. San Francisco cold, but no Jimmy and the silk warmth of him.

What does love feel like to the touch? The silk of skin. What does it look like? Tall, brown-eyed, horsey, with knobby knees and shoulders. How does it taste? Like cold water on a hot day, or jasmine tea when it's raining outside. And what does it sound like? Buffalo twang. And how does it smell? Like Clorox.

Yeah, and bleach kills everything.

All I am is clean. Clean out. Clean outta Jimmy.

19

Jimmy made really good miso soup and we ate it all winter long, with different vegetables we'd scrounge up at Rainbow Market, the big co-op on Valencia Street. One night it would be purple potatoes, beets, and burdock root with tempeh; and the next green cabbage, carrots, and acorn squash with tofu. The night following would be sweet potatoes, zucchini, mushrooms, and asparagus, with sweet mochi on the side. Jimmy'd direct me like a master chef: cut these, sauté those, run down to the corner liquor and get us some salt. And off I'd go. I'd love going out on errands because it meant I could come back, and I always liked coming back to Jimmy, seeing him from behind working the stove, the spikey hair and the way the steam floated through it. One time, he turned and his eyes were puffy with tears from cutting onions. Jimmy who never cried.

On weekend mornings we'd go for coffee and sit for hours riding the caffeine high, discussing all manner of topics, from the alienating horrors of Republican politics to literature, movies, and art.

Jimmy would look at something and he'd say, "How would you make art out of that?" He'd do this randomly, regarding a plant, a shoe, a street sign, some argument between two people on a sidewalk. He was pointing at a gaudily painted Edwardian across the street. I hated all the quaint Victorians because they suggested too much, had way too many stories coming out of them. In fact, to me, they looked like stages—like if they didn't have a story they'd insist upon telling one regardless. They were self-consciously of another time and too much had happened in them, much of it dissonant to their appearance; too many different things. So I told Jimmy I'd gather together all the people in one room who had lived in that house since it was built: top-hatted and corseted Victorians, labor movement dock workers, giant Irish families, hippies, People's Temple and Krsna devotees, Rajneeshis, Chinese people who painted it green and red for luck, Mexicans who packed each room with five young men—finally gay guys fucking each other with tubs of Crisco.

"What is this, Shame?—a painting, a play?"

"Uh, yeah, a play." Overwhelmed, I could only express myself in collage or absurdity. He sat back and listened. "Or I could speed it all up, do it like a video, compress it so that people get lost and disoriented—I could call it 'Time and Space Are Bunk'—and some dude in a top hat would be blowing Jim Jones to a Grateful Dead soundtrack, with everything falling around them in an earthquake, Sir Francis Drake riding the edifice down like a bucking bronco. And Dan White just blasting away at the windows from out on the sidewalk, killing Harvey Milk first, then Moscone, then Feinstein, then Warren Harding, Gerald Ford, Jack Kerouac, and Jim Jones, Joe Montana and Dwight Clark in bed together, Billie Holiday, Allen Ginsberg—everyone of any consequence who ever stepped foot in this city, Dan gets them. Twinkies like snow falling. Or maybe something sexier, more vulgar . . ."

"More vulgar?" He smiled.

"How about porn pictures, like with little Victorians instead of penises going up guys' butts or into girls' pussies? Or I could have like a dollhouse-scale Victorian and have guys fucking all the windows, the cum dripping down a big funnel inside that directs it out and onto the front steps where it would run like blood down an Aztec pyramid. I'd call it 'Aztlan, Ass-tlan,' 'The Sword and the Cross,' 'Montezuma's Rear End' . . . your turn, Jimmy."

He'd begged off, laughing, saying, "You are sorta insane . . . in a good way, of course . . . I was just curious what was on your mind."

75

What could I do but smile? A backassward compliment. My soup for brains.

"So, Jimmy, I'm waiting . . ."

"I'm a poet, I'd just look at it until something happened and then I'd report back with everything associated with that moment."

"That's boring, Jimmy."

"Is not." He smiled.

"Is so."

"Funny isn't everything."

"Is so." He rolled his eyes.

"Why don't you paint me, Shame?"

"If you write a poem about me, I will."

"He
can't see
the forest
for
the trees.
There."

"Smartass."

But I wouldn't paint him because the image that kept coming up was him nailed to a cross, and he would have seen that as pity.

Let Them Die for Your Sins.

But they did crucify him. Or *IT* did. The mother of all acronyms, like the artist formerly known as . . . I don't dignify it with a name. KIA, AZT, INRI: Here's the King of the Jews.

I thought I could wander around with him forever like some disciple, fishing, sitting under palm trees, visiting wells, watching him walk on water . . . Jimmy did enjoy balancing tightrope-like on curbs and cement walls when he'd find them. And there was always a timeless miraculousness when we got naked and he climbed on top of me and kissed me—*I was blind and now I can see.* But it was me who liked St. John of the Cross poems and Rumi. Jimmy, he liked Lorca and Ingeborg Bachmann.

In the storm of roses, thorns illuminate the night . . .

The nails went in, one by one just as soon as the weather turned, not two months into our love. Illness after illness. Endless colds that turned to pneumocystis: left hand to crossbeam; two blows with the hammer will do. In December, thrush: right hand to crossbeam. February was shingles: let's just pile one foot atop the other and blow through 'em both with one big nail . . .

He wasn't what you'd call a good patient. In fact, he wasn't patient at all.

Jimmy got angry.

"I'm sorry, Jimmy."

"Not your fault, Shame." And "I don't want your pity."

I didn't give it to him. I held my breath and made him soup, fed him his meds and helped him bathe. I held my breath and told myself he'd get better because he always did. For a while.

I touched his forehead when he slept and saw how long his roots were getting. His brows would furrow during dreams.

How could I not tear up?

But Jimmy admonished me if I showed a long face. "Don't go there, Shame, come on, please." Jimmy, who didn't cry, which just made me want to cry all the time.

So I had to go somewhere else to cry. To blubber really. *Pull yourself to-fucking-gether,* I'd shout at myself on the street. *Pull.*

Growling and barking helped. Sometimes I dragged my knuckles down brick walls until they bled, like old times, pre-Jimmy. That made me smile. That worked. Yes, out on the street, I could fall apart. In the name of Jimmy. And I'd murmur prayers to the Virgin, even, like Mom and I used to do, stop and light candles. I'd look up at the sky and plead and feel foolish. *Who was I talking to?* Because if God lives at all in this sorry rusted world, he's the flow of tears, the breath in and the breath out. Oxidation. And it's just a world of iron faces in the rain. And God— God ain't nothing but chemistry. And this motherfuckin' acronym that took Jimmy away? *This here's the King of the Jews.*

So I never painted Jimmy. In fact, I gave up painting when the fumes started to bother him. I dusted off my Canon that Mom had given me for high school graduation and went back to photography, since I was taking more and more walks anyway. I always saw things worth recording: faces, trees, buildings, a street called Easy Street that looked anything but. Tattoos of course: copulating elves, a well-hung Porky Pig in a fedora; and nails embedded in foreheads too; earlobes with holes big enough to hang iron skillets from (one boy I found had a mouse who liked to hang by its tail from such a hole). Tanya's old girlfriend Chloe had a forearm tattooed between her tits that ran down to her belly. I thought it looked like a big cock, the fist at the bottom being the cock-head, with her tits as its balls. Found art. I found lots of it. Like Dr. Pinski, and the rest of the numerous hungry ghosts who lurked around that city, I got into quantity.

But I never photographed Jimmy.

20

Out on the road, I made a habit of stopping at Catholic churches whenever I'd see them on account of an old superstition of my mother's that I always thought was swell. It goes like this: if you are a baptized Catholic, you get three wishes every time you enter a Catholic church that you've never been in before. I doubt she expected I'd still be practicing this after I'd left the church and childhood behind, but then again she probably hadn't expected I'd drop out of college and end up with soup for brains either—or widowed at twenty-one.

And since I'd never been to church in Napa, Geyserville, Ukiah, Willits, Laytonville, Garberville, or anywhere north of Vallejo for that matter, my trip was turning into a real jackpot, with lots more where that came from. But being of little faith, I always wished for the same thing, counting on a squeaky-wheel-gets-the-grease metaphysics. Or maybe I *only truly had* just three wishes.

In a little clapboard chapel in a place called Middletown, with nice, tall, stained-glass windows, and a cheesy '70s-era Stations of the Cross (all abstract and Braque-esque)—an obviously well-intentioned enhancement via Vatican II that aesthetically missed the mark—as well as some tired-looking velvet banners hanging from the ceiling, I plopped down in a pew and hummed my tune. Because that's what a prayer is, was, and will ever be—a song. All through my youth I'd sung pop songs to the Mother of God: *Hold me in your arms, just like a bunch of flowers, sing to me your sweetest song.*

Pull and wish. And I'd wish that Mom stopped drinking, that my dad was at peace wherever he was, and that Jimmy was okay in the bardo. Because according to the *Tibetan Book of the Dead*, which we read in bed once together—and which Jimmy suspected was close to the truth—Jimmy wasn't anywhere yet. He was still in the bardo—the in-between state, the space between lives, as in reincarnation—and according to the high lamas of Tibet it lasted forty-nine days. He was wandering—hopefully on his game—going toward the right lights and all. There were so many in that book and of every color and brightness— and you had to pick the right ones. Which is which? Like a cosmic SAT it was. Bad scores don't get you into college. You'll end up back here, or worse. Just forty-nine days, like a sale. And when the time expires, the jig is up and you're reborn wherever: womb, Buddhafield, celestial or hell realm; as a hungry ghost with a huge appetite and stomach and a mouth like a pinhole; or as an animal even. Well, as I understood it, anyway. And I was one sorry-ass Buddhist.

Still I counted each and every day for Jimmy. He'd been gone for about five weeks—thirty-three days to be exact—so he had two more weeks to go. They say if you're on your game early awareness-wise, you're out of the whole program by the first few days—sort of like passing out of freshman English. But that was only for Gandhi-type people or saints. The rest of us take the full forty-nine and are reborn.

"Hang in there, Jimmy."

Pull.

And then I remembered, thirty-three days too late, that someone was supposed to read that book over you when you died. Something else to feel guilty about. Well, it's never too late. I could still chatter at him with what of it I remembered: *"Listen, o nobly born, to what I tell you now . . .* none of it's real, Jimmy. It's all a big show and a circus. Only love, Jimmy."

But, in fact, it was *his* voice I heard—backasswards—reading to *me*: *Listen, o nobly born . . . listen.* Okay then.

There were, of course, precious few, if any, Buddhist temples on the American road, so I just kept visiting those churches. Genie in a bottle

80

called a chapel. A wishing well is God. And I always prayed and made my wishes before the Virgin statues. I wanted nothing to do with the dudes, Jesus and the Father. The Father was mean and withholding, and Jesus looked already put upon up there on the cross. I didn't want to bother him. And I certainly didn't trust priests.

Not after Father Cavanaugh anyway. But it wasn't the usual story you hear. In fact, I'd pursued *him*, and my crush played out one day right under the big Easter banner after rehearsal for the passion play. I was playing Christ. No kidding. Stuff about how big I was getting, what it must feel like to be growing up. I was thirteen and he'd seen that twinkle in my eye, my too-long looks his way, noted my insistence on playing Jesus straight up, in a loincloth. Having to explain to me it wasn't appropriate in our community.

"But what about the truth, Father Cavanaugh?" I'd pleaded.

I remember exactly what he said: "Well, Seamus, the truth is not always appropriate. Some truths need to stay hidden. You know what I mean?" And he'd smiled.

I sure did. I was a bastard. And a little homo too. I got it.

Even then, just trying to find my way to my father. Just wanted the truth. Sort of. I think.

Then Father made his move. "One of those truths is, some boys like boys instead of girls."

"I know," I'd answered.

Silence.

Can I show you my loincloth? crossed my mind, but I wasn't that precocious.

Maybe I wasn't interested in the truth at all. Maybe I was just crazy hot for Father Cavanaugh. He was what you'd called Black Irish. All the church ladies were crushed out on him.

But I got him.

I was blown away.

I remember wanting to wear a mink coat after that, which confused me considerably. Something about being his pet, all furry, self-contained, like a little nest.

I gave the church ladies odd looks during mass that unnerved them.

I got a new down jacket and pretended.

It was like twice a week for a month, and then the maid walked in.

I never saw him again. The worst part. They sent him away. He wasn't the bad guy. They were. But somehow I ended up taking the fall.

My mother, a mess of tears when I came home and began denying it all when she asked. I'd never seen her do anything but the weeping kind of crying, but she was really putting it out that afternoon. I was scared. I was nailed. And I was the last to know.

Inappropriate.

I ran. She screamed after me, heartbroken.

I couldn't help it—tears just erupted.

I ran harder.

Maybe I should have stopped.

I didn't dare.

I ran all the way to the BART station, no small distance. I figured I'd take BART to San Francisco and look for a homeless Vietnam vet to take me in. All about my father, the whole mess.

As it turned out, I didn't have enough money for BART.

So I went to Ricky's, but he wasn't home. Ricky was one of my only friends. Another kid who didn't have many. He was also a goth and had all sorts of pagan ideas about the power of nature. We had a special place we'd go to—a little ravine up in the hills, full of oaks and rocks, a creek bed that was usually dry. I remember always getting burrs in my socks coming and going. The price of satori. What Ricky really needed was a disciple, but I actually was more interested in him because he was cute and all serious. He had the palest skin and the darkest hair, with eyes as blue as a husky dog's. He'd make circles with rocks under the oak trees, and tell me about druids and serpent power and that we needed to find some human bones.

But I didn't need bones just then. I needed to calm my nerves. I climbed in his window and found his pot, scrounged for what money he had and stole it. Eight dollars and twenty-three cents.

Then I ran up to our secret place in the hills.

I got myself royally stoned on his pot and calmed down some. I needed a plan. I had eight dollars, which would cover BART, the cost of some dog biscuits for the vet's dog, and a few bucks left over for a bottle of Thunderbird.

But what I really wanted to do was find out where Cavanaugh was. I'd rather live with him. Mink coats, my own chalice, and all the communion wafers I could stomach. Dipped in guacamole, with sacramental wine for a chaser.

I knew I was talking crazy, thinking crazy. The dread was creeping up on me. I'd done a terrible thing. Untenable. What was I thinking? My mother. I'd wounded my mother. My poor wounded mother. Bleeding already, and I'd gone and shot her again. I was just like my father.

I cried.

I knew I couldn't escape.

Well, the game was indeed up.

No ability back then to pull.

Nobody to squeeze it out of me.

It hit me then that I'd killed my dad (his memory so holy and intimate that anything that hurt my mother killed him all over again, not to mention my birth coming right after his death, which forever implicated me) and now quite possibly my mom—who knows who else would follow like some sick chain reaction? Maybe people will figure Ricky's a fag since he's my friend and they'll kill him too. And it will be my fault. I realized, in my thirteen-ness, that I was a serial killer without ever having done anything but take off my clothes. Betrayed everyone who loved me. Didn't even get a bag of silver out of it. What a rip-off. Well, Cavanaugh was my bag of silver. Same size when I cupped them in my hand.

Well, he was gone. So be it, I concluded high-mindedly. It was my duty to put a stop to the whole mess. I'd started it, I'd finish it.

Eight dollars was plenty.

What I had to do was get to Rexall Drugs.

I went to Rexall, and tried to buy all three bottles of Robitussin at once. But the clerk, a high school kid, clean-cut and no stranger to robotards, said "limit one per customer" in a snooty smirk. It wasn't like he cared; he just wanted to bully a little kid and make it hard for him to get high. What had the world come to?

"I have twelve brothers and sisters; they're all sick."

"You don't look Mexican," he snapped racistly.

I assured him: "My name's Jesús."

He sold me one bottle, and so I had to go over to Longs and then Payless. All they had was cherry-flavored in each place, which I didn't like. "Beggars can't be choosers," Mom would have said. Thanks, Mom. Always lending a helping hand, even on suicide watch.

I returned with my booty to the hills, which got me thinking about Ricky, who was going to be mad at me for stealing his money and pot. He might even be there waiting for me, conjuring up something worse than death by Robitussin. I didn't want to suffer. Ricky was into black magic. Lately, he'd been attempting to curse several teachers with hairballs and such—and he'd started talking about girls and how we could use certain candles to get them to like us.

And right then, as I crested the hill to find he was not there, gazing out across our ritual circle of stones—sorry to have stolen from him and devastated that he was trying to conjure up girls—some other part of my screeching, bird-fallen-out-of-its-nest heart cracked like a little robin's egg. I was in love with him.

Life was so sad.

Yes, like a bad cough. I downed one bottle straight up, laid back, and whimpered. Then I started on the second, which made me feel profoundly nauseous.

Down the hatch it went.

Ten minutes later, I barfed, which probably saved my life. The first bottle took though, as I started hearing voices: my mother calling my name, ghostly: "Seamus." Oh shit. Then my own voice, out loud and with gravity, saying, "I think this was a bad idea."

Too late now.

I put on my Walkman and played my Beach Boys: *Wouldn't it be nice if we could wake up . . .*

It made me cry because I was a homo and it wasn't gonna be nice for me either. Not with Cavanaugh, not with Ricky, not with anybody ever. And what's more, it was a song my mom wouldn't allow in the house. Even though I'd hunt down these golden oldies just to sing with her, I'd sometimes get it wrong. There were certain songs that were okay: "Hurdy Gurdy Man," "Quinn the Eskimo," "Bobby McGee" — songs about someone who was still out there somewhere. "Eleanor Rigby," for instance, had been another mistake. Because my mom kind of was Eleanor Rigby: a more modern, prettier Eleanor to be sure, but a Rigby all the same. She didn't keep her face in a jar by the door, but she kept her past there. Actually, she had a box for it, under her vanity in the bathroom.

I found it one afternoon, during the latchkey period of my matriculation when I was about ten. I'd been snooping about, looking for my father. I found him in the oddest places: pictures secreted away in spice jars in the kitchen; a shaving kit behind books on a shelf; a pair of his aviator sunglasses in the glove compartment of the Vega. Mom's box was under her dressing table, and it was a major jackpot. Not only was there a Jimi Hendrix sticker on the top of it, but it was chock full of cool '60s stuff she never used anymore. There was white nail polish and blue eyeliner, pictures of her and my dad from those little photo booths — man, he had a smile! And his hair was curly like mine but cut so short you could barely tell. There was one of his old worn-out wallets, with a California ID inside — so Wally Cleaver in his checkered short-sleeve shirt: James Owen Blake. There was a shiny stainless steel cigarette lighter too, and gaudy, colorful beads, and big gold hoop earrings.

I couldn't resist.

She walked in on me dancing in a polka-dot sundress I'd unearthed from the far back of the closet, my eyelids blazing turquoise and my nails all painted white—both feet and hands; her big hoop earrings dangled from my earlobes, catching the waning sunlight from the window, and her multicolored beads jangled on my flat little chest like a tambourine, while I sang along to the Archies:

Sugar . . . oh, honey, honey . . .

She dropped her groceries and her jaw. Her eyes blazed vengeance. I stopped and looked at her. I think I smiled contritely, but I may have frowned, as I recall thinking how drab she looked. How drab she'd always looked. It was hard to imagine she'd once worn colorful flowery or polka-dot dresses, and this wild jewelry. As I knew her, she usually wore things like camel skirts and ivory blouses. Her earrings were always little studs, her hair groomed professionally for her office job.

She was turning red. "Seamus, how dare you!" She gave chase, while the song went on at top volume:

. . . Put a little sugar on it baby!

I didn't quite understand at the time whether it was me dressing like a girl, or the particular choice of my drag—or maybe it was even the song. I only knew she was miffed.

The needle skidded across the record; she spanked and dragged me by the bicep. I never did put up much resistance after my initial flights. She pulled the dress off me, yanked off the earrings—which hurt; almost strangled me pulling the necklaces over my head. She pulled me by the forearm into the bathroom and went to work, scrubbing my eyelids and painting all my nails with remover. She did it quickly and ruthlessly, ending with a "Never, ever do that again."

I looked her in the eye with fear and conviction and nodded my head. The box vanished and she never mentioned it again.

And Ricky found me. Probably came looking for his stolen money and pot. I was staggering around. I had a sense that there were gophers

86

everywhere under me and they were all about to come out like Viet Cong from their tunnels. I heard helicopters scouring the hills. And then here comes Ricky, and I swear to God he looked like a clown. He often used some white makeup with his goth getup, so maybe I just hallucinated the rest. But I distinctly recall a big red nose and a frown painted in green around his mouth.

I probably tried to run, but wasn't able to, and apparently when I tried, I tripped and collapsed into unconsciousness.

The temptation must have been there for Ricky to pour lye on me and make use of the jackpot of bones I could provide for his rituals, but in a pinch Ricky came through as a good middle-class kid. He carried me home and called 911. He was no stranger to robo-tripping. Maybe he was only saving his own skin, figuring he'd be implicated as he was the one who first turned me onto it three months before—and had unintentionally financed this trip besides.

Maybe he just loved me.

Fat chance. And not how I wanted.

But enough of Ricky. It was the look on my mother's face later at the hospital that changed everything. It was I who had done something wrong. How could I? She called Cavanaugh a weak soul and me a little devil. Thanks to my sorry little suicide attempt, I'd found a way to corner the market on guilt in the whole mess, while Cavanaugh was in clover in Mission Viejo I think it was, down among the lotus-eaters of Orange County. I'd saved him.

My mother loved me but she'd be damned if I took the church or myself from her. As for them taking me from her, she didn't see it that way now that I'd just tried to take my life. The only danger to me was myself.

"Think of your father," she'd admonished.

"I do. I think about him all the time."

And she burst into tears and hurried out of the room.

If I hadn't been such a wackjob and she hadn't been such a victim, I could have at least demanded a chunk of change out of the church and made Cavanaugh sweat some. I didn't begrudge him the sex—I liked it. But in time, as he never came back or wrote or anything, I grew angry and felt he'd abandoned me, run off—and for that I hated the coward.

Men and abandonment.

Oh well. After all, I'd gotten my little bag of silver; I really had.

Though it ended up in a piggy bank. Compounding interest. My cock in trust until I went off to college and it got loose again. Like a credit card.

Maybe I'd found my father after all. Hanging between my legs.

And I'd gotten the message from my mother, in no uncertain terms, that my little briefs were the frame on the TV where he needed to stay.

Well then, every church is my father's gravestone, I suppose. He's up there on the cross. And now it's Jimmy's too, but he was no Jesus. He wasn't really St. Sebastian like all the other homos either. Maybe he and I were the two thieves. Butt pirates after all.

So how long do I have to hang here alone?

21

Jimmy gave me a fighting chance, that's what he did. Jimmy liked keeping things in line. He'd had a string of disobedient pets as a child, and he'd learned he had a gift for an odd kind of discipline: pull, Seamus; sit, roll over.

The dog biscuit of his love.

Because Jimmy was someone you just wanted to please after a while. Or I did anyway. Maybe it's that Jimmy had a whole lot of trouble, but didn't complain. Not much anyway. Or maybe it was just that he was the cutest guy I'd ever set eyes on, with his big brown eyes under the pronounced and serious brows, those cheekbones and that perfect mouth, the Adam's apple, the chest—and all the way down to his cute long bony feet. A marvel. But beauty was never enough—I'd had the billion one-night stands to know that much. It was his kindness that got my tail wagging. Not big stuff either. It was that he helped people in small, seemingly insignificant ways. And it was always the most troubled people he helped: a homeless woman who needed toilet paper; a disoriented old man on the bus who suddenly panicked when he forgot where he lived. Jimmy asked him for his license, and together we walked Stan home and ate Fig Newtons with him. Jimmy made him coffee and called his niece.

Jimmy also volunteered with the needle exchange program and handed out hypodermics to junkies on 15th Street at the Armory. That's how he got to know Tanya. And pretty soon they were friends. "I see why you pined, Shame. He's a keeper," Tanya told me.

I admired Jimmy, that's what kept me hooked. He was strange, and a bit moody, but in a good way. Different. I'd go about my day, quaffing coffee at Muddy Waters, having panic attacks, arguing spelling with young tykes at the Y, handing out quarters to the legions of the wacked that patrolled the streets of the Mission District, all the while wondering what Jimmy was up to, slinging blood and doing small favors, being more effective than I could ever be. *How'd he do it?*

"How do you do it, Jimmy?"

"There's no trick, Seamus. Seeing what needs to be done and doing it."

All I ever needed to know. All that falls with the rain and rises each morning with the sun.

But I was someone who needed tricks to get out of bed, to eat, to work, to go to a movie. I needed tricks for everything. Without tricks, I'd likely never get out of bed at all. Bargains and promises and obsessive worries: *The world might end today—you don't want to be in bed for that.* Or, *someone might set this building on fire, so you better get up and go somewhere else.* How about: *If you go to tutoring today, a parent might see how well you treat their child and hand you a check for ten grand so you'll never have to get out of bed again—at least not for a good long while.* These tricks weren't even believable (like, I only worked with low-income single-parent kids). They were my soup-for-brain's way of expressing superstition, I suppose. And what the hell is superstition anyway but the desperate rationality of the panicked, who've come face to face with the fact that it's all chaos, and goddamn they need a story—and fast!

Tricks.

Wishes.

Seeing's what it was. No tricks with Jimmy. You could trust Jimmy, marvel at his sanity. Jimmy and Jimmy's ideas were strange to me because they looked like the God's honest truth. He was different and he was certainly different than me. And so he remained a sort of holy intimate stranger. I'm not so sure what I was to him. I don't think he thought me particularly unique or admirable. But Jimmy didn't seem to want anything in particular from me.

"What is it, Jimmy—what do you see in me?"

"You got a good heart, Shame. That's enough." And he'd smile and turn out the light.

On another occasion when I asked, he said: "Who says I see anything in you? You're like a window, Shame. I see right through you." And he'd chuckled.

"How's the view, Jimmy?"

"I like it, Shame. I've always liked ruins." Winking Jimmy.

"Yeah, well maybe I oughta charge admission. I'll put a turnstile right on my back belt loop. One dollar a ride, just like the MUNI bus, Jimmy. Pay or get out."

"I'd jump the turnstile."

"You'd be arrested and fined."

"Gladly. I'd charm the judge and jury. Exhibit A: your cock. B: your sweet little ass. C: your beautiful face. Crime of passion." And he'd grin like a winner. Charming son-of-a-bitch, Jimmy was.

"Jimmy, you make me frisky. All I did was ask a question."

"That'll learn ya," he liked to say as he took to wrestling with me.

And it's those little phrases lifted from Nina Simone records and who knows where else that catch in my throat. And then he'd be pulling at my clothes. "I like the view, Shame; let me see the view." And through the turnstile we'd go.

And black is the color of my true love's hair—even if he always dyed it blond.

I know why I loved him. He lacked the profit motive. And of all the supermarkets in all the broken-down strip malls of the world, he walked into mine. Across the linoleum he trundled his shopping cart all tied with strings, peering up at the little signs over each aisle: coffee, canned fruit, beverages, boys. Would they hang us like at the butcher's? Or just stand us up like cans or cereal boxes? And there I was, having fallen off the shelf, a sort of dented box of love, but still with a good bit of shelf-life.

22

Each morning out on the road I'd rise not long after the sun, moving about quickly in the cold, climbing into my sweat-dried, stiffening shorts and salt-stained Red Hot Chili Peppers T-shirt. Then I'd get Jimmy up and tie him on the handlebars, quickly pack the sleeping bag, mount my humble vehicle, and move out from whatever campground I'd found in search of a diner, where I always ordered the same thing: pancakes. They always came in stacks of three, just like wishes in a church. Everything a trinity. I clung to the magic I knew. Which pancake's the father? Which the son? And which the holy ghost? The kingdom of carbohydrates; their power; and the glory of how far they could take me each day—one hundred miles.

All of which led to me to saying grace and a prayer for the souls of Jimmy Keane, James Owen Blake, and my wounded mother. Take this cup of coffee, I'd mutter, hoisting it to my chapped lips. And then I'd douse the offering in syrup—three supersized eucharists, amen. I crossed myself, and bolted them down.

23

Jimmy grew impatient with illness and suggested we start going to ACT UP weekly.

"What about *fight no more forever*, Jimmy?"

"It won't be forever, trust me."

It was somewhere to vent, but also: seeing what needs to be done and doing it.

Jimmy joined the media committee and wrote press releases and called news outlets.

It became our social life. ACT UP gave me a sort of team feeling, a kind of power I'd never been familiar with, loner that I was. Although it often felt hopeless too, reminding me of what a vale of tears life was. Of course, it helped that ACT UP was loaded with cute guys. And angry cute guys at that, which gave them sex appeal—and made me feel guilty.

Mostly I took pictures, so I made it art and history too, which was something—and I needed something. Because Jimmy was going to die and then I'd have nothing.

So, in the end, as always, the guys and girls at ACT UP, like the kids at the Y, gave me more than I ever gave them. I showed up, did my little part, and I appreciated that they never asked any more from anyone than what they wanted to give. They were mostly young guys in their twenties, many of whom, like Jimmy, had *it*, disabusing me once and for all that *it* was a '70s-guy disease. These were young punky guys in leather jackets and Mohawks, babydykes with nails through their noses, radicalized middle-aged men who'd lost their safe place in the gay bourgeoisie. And Tanya of course, and even Lawrence sometimes too.

I'd first gone a year before I'd met Jimmy, because, like I said, it was the cool in-crowd to hang out with, and because Lawrence went all the time, mostly to meet guys—but also for contacts, networking, to promote himself and his art career. And I suppose because Lawrence cared too. In his way. Just as I did, and Tanya did of course. Tanya, who always encouraged me to do the right thing.

Later, it became a constructive distraction in the struggle to stay sane dealing with Jimmy that brought me back each week. I didn't believe we'd ever kill the dragon—the dragons, I should say, because there were so many: the disease itself, Republicans, the pharmaceutical industry, the city, the county, the state, the church, the feds, the NIH, the CDC, the older queens who hated us postering their precious Victorian neighborhood with leaflets and flyers and art—and the biggest dragon of all: that it was probably far too late for Jimmy to benefit from anything we did.

But it was fun, too, in a carnivalesque way, with different facilitators each week who dressed for the occasion in drag, crazy hats, and jewelry. One week a lipsticked boy with a beehive, the next a girl with a penciled-in mustache in a three-piece suit.

Each week, we talked and argued, got crushes, and planned actions.

A black-clad procession, marching.

I dreamed at night that we walked with huge tigers and lions on big chain leashes. And I woke up scared.

Mostly I remember whistles, deafening and shrill.

They were blown to signal the beginnings of marches, or whenever we stopped, or when the cops blocked our way, or if there was any bashing danger present. In the middle of California Street, while policemen on motorcycles called us "fags," dozens of boys lay down and we quickly drew chalk lines around them. One time I lingered too long outlining Jimmy, and boy did I get a truncheon bruise.

Jimmy got arrested a lot before he started to worry about being stuck sick in jail. Then he just showed up at the end of marches, holding a sage stick, which burned slow and smoky. He was wearing an old green army coat by then and his hair, having grown out, was mostly black, with just the tips still golden. Sometimes he wore a brown and white Andean wool cap with the extended ties that dangled around his lovely scruffy neck. So I always knew where Jimmy was . . . the one green coat, the one Peruvian head, the one smoke-surrounded character with the sage stick.

Jimmy and all the others got arrested or sick or both, and all I did was run around with chalk and a camera.

And I think we were more afraid, the negative boys. The positive guys had gotten it over with, even though they hadn't. Not the hard part. What I mean is they didn't have to worry about getting *it* anymore. Some of them actually seemed relieved and liberated in their strange fashion. They were kind of like guys who'd made the varsity team or been drafted, or joined the Marines. You didn't really want what they had going, but you looked up to them as manlier in the twisted way men do. Jimmy had it: that hot positive-guy air to him that negative guys fetishized and felt guilty about. Motherfucking star.

So I had the secret pride of having a cute poz boyfriend. Some consolation. I tried not to gloat. Which ended up doubling the guilt.

Jimmy said: "Hey Shame, gloat while you can."

Winked at me.

Well, I didn't gloat much, being that I was scared stiff. I'd even sneak off now and again and go to the forty-eight-hour clinic on Haight Straight, where for forty bucks you could get test results back in two days, unlike the health department's testing center, which took two weeks. I didn't have the nerves for two weeks. No sir.

I never told Jimmy I went there, but I'd go now and again when I noticed a cut in my mouth and started tripping on which blowjob when.

Once these two yuppie guys came running out of the place as I approached. They were all smiles, hopping into their Jeep and

French-kissing. I knew what that was. Getting negative results made you wanna fuck like crazy. Saved for another day.

I'd feel it too, but only a little bit, and it had nowhere to go. Because if one of you wasn't negative, it just wasn't that exciting.

I went home to Jimmy and to being careful.

After a while, he wouldn't even let me blow him anymore.

"Ah come on, Jimmy," I drooled despairingly like a dog.

"Fuck no," he snapped, annoyed.

"You like it, don't ya?"

"Not about me, Shame. Get a clue." And he'd get up and go to the bathroom.

"What you wanna do then, Jimmy? What *can* I do?" I continued once he'd returned.

"Quit asking questions." And out went the light.

"I hate this."

"Well, you can leave."

"Jimmy, fuck, don't say that. I don't mean you."

"This is me, Seamus. Take it or leave it."

I wouldn't pity him. He'd asked me not to, and I wouldn't. So I'd lie there quietly and I'd wait for him to reach out and hold *me*.

24

When I couldn't find a campground or state park near Jimmy's red hoops, I'd stay in whatever small town was nearby. Like me, Jimmy obviously liked back roads and empty places as that's where his red line took me. I'd sit in diners, or coffee shops, wondering what it was like to live there, especially for queers. And I'd look at the chairs and booths and people's clothes and wonder if any of their threads had made it onto Jimmy's bike. I'd see possibilities and make up stories about how Jimmy had done them some small kindness and secretly yanked a string from their sleeve.

In Hayfork, out on Highway 3, I came upon a sock lying on the sidewalk as I exited St. Brigid's, three wishes the richer. And I picked it up, and that's when I started collecting strings too. Not for poems—I think they were prayers or wishes, but even I wasn't totally sure. They gave me an idea for a new kind of Marie Antoinette painting: *Let Them Be Lost Souls* and *Let Them Ride Bicycles Cross-Country Taking Their Lovers' Ashes Back the Way They Came*, and *Let Them Pull*. This time, though, Marie Antoinette would merge with Our Lady of Guadalupe, whom I'd just seen in all her glory and wished before in the church. I liked how she was clothed in the sun, mandala-like, and she'd been my favorite Virgin Mary for years besides as I'd always known she was actually Tonanztin, an Aztec goddess who'd been co-opted by the Spaniards. Queer that way (that's why me and Jimmy had her in jar candles all over the house). I suddenly wanted to paint her a thousand times and garland her in strings and mayonnaise jars, bicycle parts, bandages, AZT pills, third eyes, and Chinese characters for good, holy, and better. But never any image of Jimmy. No sir. Jimmy was the light behind her.

When Jimmy had started to lose interest in the scene of San Francisco, we went to the ocean or the woods, or both. Handy Jimmy sewed straps on his panniers, so we could each carry one to use as a backpack. Of course I needed a sleeping bag and found an old Boy Scout bag at Community Thrift.

"Maybe I should get a bike too, eh Jimmy?"

But he just looked at me.

"Nah, biking's over." Never once did he ride *Chief Joseph* in San Francisco. Jimmy had a way of letting you know some questions he didn't want to answer—a look away and down—so I didn't ask, or just let them fall aside, ignored.

Once, we took a bus out to Mt. Tamalpais and walked the rest of the way into the hills to a campground he'd read about that looked out through the oak trees to the Pacific beyond. We watched the sunset there and made a fire and baked zucchini and potatoes all wrapped up in foil, with tofu dogs we cooked on sticks. We smoked pot and drank whiskey from a pint flask, and then we talked about Tom Spanbauer's *The Man Who Fell in Love with the Moon*, a magical story about a bisexual Indian boy and a cowboy and the higher form of homosexual love that they found together alone in the wilderness. I can still see Jimmy's face in the firelight, the shadows that his pronounced brows and chin and Adam's apple made, flitting about him while he went on and on about how important a book he felt it was. Then we made love the same way they did in the book. No, there was nobody like Jimmy—my cowboy, my Indian.

Another time we hiked the whole Dipsea Trail, from Mill Valley all the way out to Stinson Beach, through redwoods and over creeks, across wind-waving fields of green yellow-flowered grass, through groves of squat little oaks so dense we had to bushwhack through their branches and made a racket trudging through their heaped-up fallen leaves. Then I picked more of those leaves out of his spikey rapidly blackening mane above his say-nothing smile.

We went south too to the reservoirs on the peninsula, and east to the redwoods above Oakland and the forested canyon behind U.C. Berkeley.

I followed after Jimmy, his cute horsey behind in his faded jeans, his ratty green sweater, his head like a star thistle gone to seed, dry and fading, going who knows where up the trail before me.

And then one day we never left town again.

25

Back in San Francisco, we'd go up to Dolores Park to amble, sit somewhere, amble some more under the big date palms, amid the shiny-eyed Guatemalan boys dealing weed and grinning—because long before the cannabis club, we had to buy Jimmy pot for his appetite on the street or in the parks.

There were children there, evident from the unattended multicolored balls that would bounce by, and off into the street. A small brown kid would inevitably appear and give chase right to the curb, at which point he'd stop as if having reached a river. Sometimes I'd go after the ball then, reminding the kid to never go into the street, as his mother came hobbling along thirty yards behind, two other tykes in tow. I'd have left Jimmy back at the corner, and there he waited for me in his army coat, all bundled up now even though it was summer, and looking very alone.

We walked on to where the tanning queens staked out the upper reaches of the park, near where the J Church trolley stopped after coming out of the trees where the green parrots lived—legend had it that they'd begun as one or two escapees and had now burgeoned into a squawking colony. They weren't the talking kind, but we imagined if they were: cruisy come-ons and drug marketing would erupt from their screeching beaks: "suck my cock, yeah boy; weed, weed; fuck me, fuck me; dime bag?"

"San Francisco, Jimmy."

"Yeah." His deadpan.

With Jimmy I tried mightily to be agreeable, even when he wasn't. Usually, I'd go out for walks when Jimmy was sleeping or in difficult moods. I felt guilty leaving him of course, but I was also freaked out considerably, and besides I felt justified in that he was taking out all his frustrations on me of late. But I tried to keep my head up. He was dying after all.

Still I got pissed off at him, lost my patience. "Fuck off, Jimmy," I barked when he chastised me about forgetting to go to the food bank. His harangue had begun with my unemployment (I'd started giving deep discounts at Java Baklava one day because it felt good to do so, but soon was caught in the act and dismissed), moved on to my forgetfulness, my general unreliability, and my utter lack of focus. All true, sure, but still deserving of a "fuck off" for one as stretched thin as myself during those times.

"Didn't you mean to add *and die* to that, Seamus?"

I glared.

"'Cause you're killing me." His little smile.

"Bitch," I said with disdain.

"Pull, Shame."

I walked out and slammed the door, running into Michael (one of the twins) in the stairwell. The part of me that wanted to kick his seven-year-old good cheer and innocence down the stairs was quickly subsumed by his look of concern. "Is diarrhea boy sick?"

It was a harsh nickname, but Jimmy'd had a bad afternoon in the stairwell two months before that the twins and their mother, Mrs. Hsieh, had witnessed. We'd all tried to joke through it as I got him upstairs—to save face, retain human dignity, all that. Nothing could wipe a smile off Mrs. Hsieh's face of course. She'd have smiled as an earthquake brought the building down, all in the service of not freaking out the twins.

"Diarrhea Boy is okay," I answered, offering him a cursory smile as I stepped past him and proceeded down the stairs. I'd have liked to sit down and explain it all as a responsible adult, but being a responsible adult was even harder than explaining it.

101

"Where you going?" he called after me.

"Goin' to California!" That's what I always said to him, and it got him to smile and wave sadly as I turned and saluted him from the landing.

Then I'd roar down the streets, hands in pockets, knit cap pulled low on my eyes to indicate my unavailability for human interaction, carrying on long conversations with Jimmy, trying to find new ways to dodge his anger, new methods of rationalization, new five-year plans (more like five-day) to make things work. I'd rehearse dramatic breakup scenes, holier-than-thou tirades, fantasies of him throwing me out so I wouldn't have to bear the agony of *leaving him* to die alone, resolving always in the end to become positive so he'd quit treating me like the lucky, clueless one and take care of me instead.

Checkmate.

That's what the acronym was and will always be. A better chess player than the rest of us. Bobby Fischer.

From that hopeless place, I'd spin off into my imagination, where I'd get a medical degree, cure *it*, assassinate Jesse Helms, William Dannemeyer, and George Bush, burn down all the Baptist churches, and legalize love. By that point, I'd be in the Excelsior, having traversed all of the Mission on my forced march. I'd turn and head into Noe Valley, then up over the hill and through the Castro, where I'd get offers to buy drugs and sexual come-ons via fixed stares and smiles (the finest escape of all, but I'd balk), before climbing up into Buena Vista Park for the view and more furtive looks and temptations. Finally, I'd shamble down into the Haight Ashbury and cut back through the Lower Haight. On really bad days, before returning home, I'd end up stumbling tired into a South of Market gay dive where I'd drop my pants for a blowjob, rationalizing my infidelity around Jimmy's cruelty, and, as I zipped up, reviewing the whole scene to make sure I'd played safe (avoiding the disease that was destroying my domestic life by playing right up against it as well as worrying about any other disease I might thus bring home to my immuno-compromised boyfriend. Oh the guilt). Then I'd realize, as I hoofed those final blocks home, that my resolve to get infected could only involve the agent being Jimmy. Then, and only then, I'd finally cry. On a random doorstep, or as time progressed and I got used to it, just while I walked. Who cares what they think? I certainly couldn't risk such an outburst at home.

I'd be clumping up the stairs by the time it occurred to me that I'd still failed to go by the food bank, and then I'd have to turn around and go all the way back up toward City Hall to get our allotted food. By then I was plain punchdrunk. For Jimmy! *Ain't no mountain high enough, ain't no valley low enough!* I'd bellow sarcastically into the incoming fog. That's usually when I'd run into someone I knew—an old friend, or some trick from a past encounter.

"Can't talk." On a mission for Jimmy.

"Okay man, catch you later."

Toward the end, only ACT UP people were immune from my avoidance. Black riders, they too were all wrapped up in the ring. "Fuck!" I'd exclaim and fall into their arms. Then I'd unload. "He's driving me fucking crazy, he's this, he's that . . ." The looming question of dementia, writ subtly on the brow of my confessor.

But not Jimmy. "No, Jimmy's just . . . moody." (I'd wanted to say "an asshole.") "He's not demented." I'd battle with saying things I might regret, comments I'd never be able to live down, like: *I only wish he were demented.*

To the food bank we'd go together. And all the way home too. Freelance social workers those ACT UP boys and girls were. Most of them were older than me, and I leaned on them. My father was long dead, my mother was useless to me in this, and my country didn't care. So the boys and girls of ACT UP were all I really had.

Back home, they'd accompany me up the stairs for hellos to Jimmy because he knew them all too from the meetings, even though Jimmy didn't go anymore.

"Fight no more forever!" he'd shout at me when I'd invite him along now.

"How, Kemo Sabe," and I'd throw my *Star Trek* hand up for goodbye.

Very bad joke. And cruel.

Sorry.

So we fought, and I fought back. No pity. He didn't want pity.

He'd lie there in bed, reading and asking me questions I didn't want to answer.

"Have you looked into some jobs?"

"No," I answered impatiently, busying myself with the dinner I was making.

"Why not?"

"'Cause I'm busy."

"With what?"

I glared.

"This isn't a job, Seamus, no one is paying you for this."

"Damn straight."

"Aren't you enjoying it?"

"Short answer or long answer?"

He sighed. "You need to get a job, Seamus—if not for yourself, for me. We're running out of money."

"Maybe you need to start going to used bookstores to find some more."

I felt his paperback hit me square in the back. I exploded, turning around and picking it up and throwing it back at him, along with a shoe, an orange, one of the dolls that was on the kitchen counter for some reason—Genevieve I think it was. Then I dumped the whole meal into the sink and started breaking dishes, and he struggled out of bed and came over and grabbed me, and for the first time ever, I struggled to get away from him. He gripped me tighter and tighter, until I gave up and cried.

But after I'd composed myself a tad, Jimmy went right on with it: "You gotta pull, Shame."

He hobbled back to bed then, and once under the covers, he added: "You gotta clean this place up."

I didn't say a word to Jimmy for two days.

Maybe we need couples counseling?" I threw out cynically when I finally re-emerged from my self-imposed exile.

And he laughed and laughed. And I started to laugh with him. And Jimmy was suddenly vital, gesturing and mincing. Jimmy, sitting in his sentinel chair where he often sat now at the window, giggling, imitating a therapist. ". . . Maybe your illness is a metaphor for your lover's mind . . . or maybe you're just tired of diarrhea . . . honey, think of all the poor constipated souls . . . in India . . . Not."

"Norway!" I shouted. And I laughed from the belly, long and hard, and dropped onto the floor, and I hugged his lovely ankles. And I laid there like that for a long time. "I'm sorry, Jimmy."

"I'm a bastard, Shame—it's okay."

"You are a bastard, and a motherfucker too."

"True, true . . . you and me both."

"And I love you, Jimmy—too, too much. And I'm a fuckup . . . and I'm trying."

"Better luck next time." And he ran his bony foot through my hair.

I got up on my knees and looked him in the eye. "You're hard on me, Jimmy."

He looked at me earnestly then. "I'm sick, Shame."

His dear face that I reached out to touch with my hand. Pity.

"Don't." And he pulled his face away.

So I climbed up and sat myself in his lap: "Is this okay?"

His hollow-eyed smile indicated it wasn't really, but he nodded in the affirmative.

Our own kind of pieta, Jimmy and me. Backasswards.

26

It rained on and off over the pass out of California, Mt. Shasta obscured and looming among the clouds, intermittently appearing and disappearing, but ever-present all the same. Hunched over in Jimmy's blue nylon poncho, I couldn't turn my back on it. Had to have just one more look. Lot's wife or Jimmy's. One could do worse than become a pillar of salt. Mt. Shasta was just a heap of ash, the spent side of an hourglass: Jimmy grown huge in death.

I was a long way from Guerrero Street. But no matter how bad it got, the road would always conjure some reminder of Jimmy, and then I'd be inside and warm with him . . . drinking tea, watching him unspool strings from *Chief Joseph*, watching his big brown eyes grow larger as his lovely cheekbones and chin and Adam's apple grew more pronounced, his hair more black.

I tooled along a frontage road that paralleled Interstate 5 for several miles, but eventually I had to merge onto it as it was the only road through; I had to crawl like a little ant along its shoulder, buffeted by truck wind and thoughts of bloody mayhem — recalling stories of highway workers and civilians changing tires who'd lost their lives quick into pulp. I conjured up visions of my bicycle flung into the ditch, Jimmy like a chemical spill spread out all across Highway 5. What would they think he was? Would they stop all the traffic to investigate, to make sure he wasn't toxic, flammable, or poisonous? Radio communications echoed through my head: "Roger, roger, flaming homosexual. Correction:

highly flame-able at one time, but now rendered unto dust. Give 'em the all clear."

And into Oregon I went, where it began to rain in earnest. I had to stay in a Motel 6 in Ashland—miles short of Grants Pass and Jimmy's red hoop—home to a giant Shakespeare festival, which meant all night I thought of my Romeo and how Falstaff I'd been and how much a Tempest was the world.

And to think I'd once stood on the corner, on the buckled sidewalk under the acacia tree, and I'd shouted up to him on the fire escape as if he were my queerboy Juliet, shirtless in his cutoffs, his long thin chest and scruffy chin, his messy spiked straw-colored hair with his hand running through it: "What kind of milk you want, Jimmy—whole or 2 percent?"

One fairer than my love?

When I reached Medford the next morning, only two hours down the road, my bike and poncho and Hefty-bagged panniers were soaked again. Fuck it, I'm not riding in the rain no more.

I hobbled into the Happy Rogue diner. Everything was "rogue" around there on account of the local river's name, or so they told me. Rogue motels (roach?) and Rogue Inn (hair transplants for rogues?)—a Rogue Federal even, which begged the question: who would trust their money to a rogue? A few days ago, I'd passed through a town named Mad River, where everything was mad—Mad Videos and Mad Markets, mad people too—and even a Mad High, which sounded like a slasher film featuring manic depressive kids. They'd even dammed the river with a Mad Dam, which seemed like a bad idea to me. Madness needs to move. Madness is a rogue.

There was a pay phone in the waiting area, reminding me that I owed my mother a phone call, but I wasn't in the mood, so I plunked down in the nearest sticky red Naugahyde booth and opened the laminated menu to pictures of prettied-up carcasses—and, of course, pancakes. And I sat there at the window, watching the rain increase, apprehensive and stubborn in my resolve not to go back out into it as I unenthusiastically ordered and then wolfed down another stack of pancakes. *For thine is the kingdom, the power, and the glory*—Dispense with the storm then, dude!

I suppose I could have stopped.

I didn't dare.

And all the time, the question that is my face inviting people.

A big strapping blond guy in a blue sweatshirt was at the counter and looked my way. "That your bike?" he asked.

"Yup," I said despondently.

"Where you goin' on it?"

"All the way across." And I motioned my arm perfunctorily toward the far window.

"Across where?"

I'd have said the acronym, but why be off-putting? I liked strangers. "America," I answered, which always embarrassed me somewhat. America sounds so Pollyanna, with its Kate Smith–rendered purple-mountain majesty, amber fields, and shiny sea B.S. But I can't love an acronym, so America it is.

"Hmm, north-south?"

"Uh, no, west-east," I corrected him, hiding my annoyance. How backasswards a question is that? Whatever traveling north-south is called, it's not *across*.

"What are you on the 5 North for?"

A good question, I suppose, come to think of it. I wanted to reply: I'm a whelp, sir. "Uh, I'm going to Eugene; then I head east."

"Well, it's a nasty day for riding."

I agreed with a nod and a sigh.

"I can give you a lift as far as Roseburg if you'd like. I'm heading to Coos Bay—in a rig." And he motioned with his head out into the parking lot to a big shiny yellow Mack truck (yellowjacket?) towing a trailer full of—what? Venom or honey—same difference.

I imagined some kind of hairy blowjob scene, which made me hesitate, so I stalled. "Oh yeah?"

"Well, I'm heading out of here in five minutes. Take it or leave it."
He turned and ordered a coffee to go, cream and sugar both.

"I'll take it," I said, forcing a smile. I pulled myself up out of the booth with a ripping sound, as I was stuck to it, and hobbling over to the counter—God how the stiff muscles in my thighs burned today—I paid my bill and ordered a coffee to go. And I stood there in Jimmy's soaked, wrecked hightops, his army cutoffs, cradling his ashes and wrestling with folding up the poncho like some pathetic grief-ridden idiot—better luck next time—while the trucker headed off to the bathroom. I considered slipping away out the door. I hadn't even asked for this ride. He'd offered. He must be queer. Was I really willing to go through with it to stay dry and make it to the next red hoop? God knows, the world's full of homos with trucker fantasies, but I wasn't one of them.

What you hauling? How long you done this? Where you from? And what were you before?

To Ralph I talked a blue streak. Because I didn't feel I had a choice. A hitchhiker owes his ride wisdom or entertainment, as I see it. There's no better way to stretch a ride this side of sex. And if sex is what you're afraid of, there's no better way to take it down a few notches from someone's projected fantasy of you than to talk, and thus become "somebody" and all the annoying unsexy things that accompany such a condition.

Ralph wanted to talk about young people. Uh-oh. At twenty-two, there was always the chance I was too old, of course. He also wanted to talk about drugs and alcohol and divorce and all number of social ills, each and every one of which he bemoaned. Well, at least it was a buffet.

I opted for divorce, something I knew nothing about, to keep him off the scent of my drug-addled sodomite matriculation. And I talked and talked because, like I said, a hitchhiker is a prostitute and if there's to be no sex, then he's gotta give the client what the client truly, underneath it all, wants: someone to talk to.

Ralph wanted to fix the world. He talked about how it was and how it should be. Well, it beat a serial killer or a lech. I just let Jimmy talk through me, as I didn't have much to say. I sat back and listened to them both: Jimmy's Buffalo childhood and his parents' divorce versus Ralph's Ohio alcoholic father—gone by his fifth birthday—and the delightful drunken stepfather who replaced him. It was a tennis match of misery.

"Kids need guidance and discipline," he announced. "They need a father in the home. They need structure and a purpose. When you have children . . ."

Aye, hell'll freeze over. Then again, as he seemed so keen on fatherhood, perhaps I could sell him on the idea of two fathers being better than one—or maybe even spirit babies. But I didn't want to fix the world or Ralph. Unfixable. All I wanted was a little peace.

"You got a family of your own, Ralph?" I ventured.

And so it commenced. "And she this, and she that, and her . . ." Suffice it to say, there was acrimony involved, and then some. "It got me sober, I'll tell you that," Ralph continued.

"So you don't drink anymore?" And here I'd been about to suggest a couple forty-ouncers for the ride.

"No." And he shook his head.

"Were you doing drugs too?"

"Was I!?" he chortled, pulling on the horn strap that hung from the ceiling of the cab, letting out a comic blast. "Why do you think I'm telling you all this?"

I wanted to say I hated cautionary tales, but he was the ride, so I let him run. Before he found sobriety and Jesus—*take this cup* before I fill it up again—Ralph found cocaine and speed.

He talked on and on, the miles peeling away in the rain. I felt suddenly very old, like I'd heard it all so many times before. I turned to look out the rain-streaked window at a dilapidated barn as his words faded into another song: . . . *everybody's talking at me* . . .

Ralph had been through it. And come out of it alive. Why'd he make it after all that, and not Jimmy, who'd never even had drug issues? I felt almost mad at Ralph then and wanted to shout out that I knew a dozen men not even twenty-five who never got a second chance. But that wasn't Ralph's fault; he'd done me a kindness besides, so I held my tongue.

Ralph was all good cheer as he let me off at the truck stop (the rain was still coming down and I was calling it a day, even if it was still early afternoon and Jimmy's hoop was another fifty miles north. He never said take me back at the same speed, just *take me back "the way"*).

"Jesus loves you," he shouted.

"Right on." I jutted my thumb in the air because I did sort of like Ralph, Jesus or no.

Oh—he was hauling palm oil, for cookies, crackers, and other snack foods: hydrogenated, lethal to the heart. Poor Ralph, spreading love and death, spreading it like margarine. And how the heart aches.

America, this is the house that Ralph built. Made of fat, cocaine, and Jesus.

I waited until he was out of sight to make a beeline for the liquor store, where I procured a foul-looking packaged burrito (gotta support Ralph's hydrogenated economy) and a forty-ouncer—just in case Jimmy manifested, thirsty and randy.

Then I mounted my steed and pedaled quickly to the nearby Red Rose Motel. Things had gone mad and roguish, and now everything was rosy in Roseburg.

In the amber light of the little office, a woman who looked like a giant bullfrog gave me a room. "With a view" I requested roguishly, but she didn't get the joke, or care, and I felt all alone in the mad rain, my bike up on my shoulder, climbing the stairs to room 206, with the view of an empty trash-filled lot, the big double bed, and the freeway beyond. No place like home—and home was there in the bag, gone, a pile of ashes. They burned our house down.

I put my Converses on the radiator to dry and I can't say whether it was the rain and Jimmy, or the fact that I was avoiding calling my mother, or just Ralph's tale of woe, but I felt so sad that I climbed into bed and watched out that window as I, a bit too quickly, upended the consolation that was Crazy Horse malt liquor and ended up making love to Jimmy phantoms with my blistered, calloused hand, not wanting to admit to myself that I wished Ralph and Jesus were both there with us.

What a fourway: the hairy stocky jewboy with the big Mediterranean dick, my sweet horseboy Jimmy, and the beefy uncut cokehead who likely fucks like a jackrabbit. My first trucker fantasy.

27

Jimmy got philosophical, which made me worry about dementia. An El Greco-looking saint muttering mysticisms. He talked about Indians—Chief Joseph and Crazy Horse and Sitting Bull—while we waited in clinics with water bottles and little Playmates to keep food and medicine cool.

"Crazy Horse said two things it's hard to forget. *Hoka hey*—it's a good day to die—and when they tried to photograph him: 'Why would I let you take from me my shadow?'"

"Do you think he said *Hoka hey* the day he died, Jimmy?"

He looked at me. "They shot him in the back, Shame. He used to say *Hoka hey* when he went into battle, but yeah, I guess he probably said it every day when he woke up. You gotta understand Zen to understand Crazy Horse, I think. *Hoka hey* is like a koan."

"One cannot understand Zen," I responded in my best Japanese Buddhist monk mimic.

He popped me lightly on the head.

He's not demented, I thought, relieved. His wan smile.

I didn't just lose Jimmy. He was torn from me, slowly, like how they took the land from the Indians. Sometimes I'd have much rather he'd gone off and died in Vietnam like my father. There's a mercy in sudden death. But the slow reduction of life, like starvation—he grew too thin to even have a shadow to take.

I remember a sick man at one clinic, his lover like a Birkenau survivor, shriveled to a skeleton. "When they prove the government created this disease, we'll have our Israel," he'd said defiantly. He was angry, and my throat caught to hear his defiance framed in the idea of a place of respite; a sanctuary. It was the kind of anger that made me want to cry.

I didn't dare.

Because I felt guilty. That I'd been spared. But I felt even guiltier that I found the dying beautiful. And I don't mean in some poetic way. I thought they were hot is what I mean. I tried to shake it out of my head. These tiny, shriveled gray men, with big eyes (is it as simple as that? Hello Kitty?). They all looked like boys at the end. And all of them seemingly abandoned—if not by family, then by nation, by history, by the fact that all their friends had already died.

I don't know, but I fell in love or lust a thousand times in those clinics. And Jimmy, I got hotter for him as he withered, and I couldn't tell if it was love for his sweet, plump heart, or for the appearance of those ribs that surrounded it.

I felt bad for being attracted to him then.

"I'm sorry."

"Why are you sorry? It makes me happy. We're lucky."

Sweet Jimmy, who could no longer do a thing but lean against me as I'd spill all over him. "You'll never not be hot to me, Jimmy. Never. You're beautiful and the best luck ever."

His sighing smile.

One fairer than my love?

Nah, not gonna happen. Ever.

28

In Eugene, Oregon, next stop north of Roseburg, I got a fateful, hankering hunger for one of Jimmy's favorite foods: tempeh. And in a place like Eugene, all you have to do is look. And I saw. The characteristic plants and benches out front, the sun and cornucopia painted on its wooden sign, and the '70s peace-and-love people-of-color mural on the old cement wall of the parking lot. Bingo, tempehland.

I marched into that market in Jimmy's tattered army shorts and Converse hightops; Jimmy's stinking Red Hot Chili Peppers T-shirt; Jimmy in my arms and Jimmy's food on my mind. Right back through the hippie wooden décor of the place to the rattling refrigerator where I didn't see the tempeh, and I didn't want to have tofu in its place, and I wasn't ready for anything but. Tempeh. And then, like rain I heard it, because it was a rush like a waterfall; like a thousand grains of wheat; like *plenty* it sounded.

And I turned and looked straight at Jimmy's back, watched him fill the bulk bins: bulgur, barley, rye, and quinoa. I swallowed hard when he turned to reveal he wasn't Jimmy. But between my staggering hunger and my cartoon-beating heart, I just froze and looked at him for *too* long. He smiled at me, his beautiful long face and big nose, and his scruffy unshaven chin, his unkempt blue-black hair, the lean lankiness of him—his skin as orange as a yam. But he didn't say a thing. Just smiled and held my gaze. For too long.

Then he walked away with his hand truck.

It had to come.

One day.

I was twenty-two.

My heart said run; my dick said linger; my mind said forty-ouncer (and do they sell them in such a place?); and my spirit—it just said: "Jimmy, what's this?" while I clutched Jimmy in the purple bag—my Linus blanket, my bunch of dried flowers.

And I thought of Jimmy's dick then. How we used to hold each other's, and gaze at each other. And it was like a hand, and like safety that way. As long as I had my hand around his, and he had his hand grasped around mine, we were safe. We could find our way in the dark. We slept that way all the time—me holding his; him holding mine.

I clung to him in the bag, standing there dumb as a boy on a platform, waiting for a train, a train that had left a long time ago.

And then he came back. Fully loaded. This time it was amaranth and spelt, couscous and long-grained basmati rice. And I watched him, couldn't seem to avert my gaze. "Pull, Seamus, pull."

A lit match.

Reminding me of how cold I'd grown—Zen monk with my lump of coal.

I salivated. He was food, calories.

Another horseboy. But a snakeboy too—the hooded cobra of his gangly slouch of a stance. And a bird, with that crow-black hair and shoulder blades like wings that protruded as he maneuvered the hand truck into place and lifted the plastic buckets of sustenance and poured them like all the endless miles I'd traveled.

Rain stick.

Whatever he was—horse, snake, bird—I wanted to fly, writhe, gallop with him.

He was the first guy I'd looked at in *that* way since Jimmy'd gone—and he'd even *been* Jimmy for a few anguished moments, from behind, in a backasswards kind of way. A thought that calmed me momentarily.

The reassurance of: *So long as it's backwards and includes Jimmy everything makes sense to me and will be A-OK.*

Then I just blurted it out: "Do you have any tempeh?"

He looked at me for a minute, impassively, but plenty too long. A knowing smile lit up his face, and his eyes shone with a strange impersonal kindness that unnerved me, made me want to embrace him and tell him everything all at once.

Pull.

He opened a refrigerator door for me and pointed, with a nod of his head, at the tempeh. Then he turned and went back to work on the bulk bins, making a racket, while I fumbled through the tempeh and started talking to Jimmy about how I didn't really want to ever meet another guy again. And I sought out Jimmy's face then in all its guises: on the platform; smiling; sleeping; laughing; coughing, ruined and haggard; then full, blushing, alive with the say-nothing smile and his index finger to his lips.

And then that mantra in my mind—*I don't know how to love you, I don't know how to love you, I don't know how to love you*—as I hunted carrots and celery, vegan cakes and cookies, wasabi chips, amazaki, and all things holy and nutritious for the repose of the soul of James Damon Keane. A seder for Jimmy. Jimmy, who had drawn all those red hoops on his map, and yet the angel of death had not passed over after all.

The angel of lust apparently wasn't going to pass over either.

I'm the angel of sex and death and I don't know how to love you.

And I remembered a threesome we'd had once on account of some guy who'd gotten hung up on me and kept coming around. Jimmy finally said: "Well, Shame, you guys seem to like each other, and I think you oughta get together, find out what it is."

"I know what it is, Jimmy, and so do you! Let's just forget it. He's another horny faggot. Like I need another one of those."

He rolled his eyes.

"Why you getting mad at me for not wanting to sleep around, Jimmy? That's backasswards."

117

He nodded and chuckled. "I don't know. Don't you think attraction is a message?" Jimmy challenged me.

"Yeah, and the message is: 'I want you.' Uncle Sam, the faggot." (Sounded like a good idea for my next painting: *Let Them Point and Demand Sex from Each Other*.)

He rolled his eyes.

But I wouldn't budge from my position, my rifle aimed and fixed on Jimmy's sweet horsey behind. "Why don't you do him, then, Mr. Jimmy? You can report back to me on what the message was."

He suggested a threesome, and so the three of us ended up swinging our little swords around for a few hours, spilling our half-baked chromosomes all over each other and recognizing whatever it is you recognize in sex—like old friends: *nice to see yas.*

"It's more than that, Shame. With gay guys, there's always a spirit baby that's born."

My face a question. "What the hell *is* a spirit baby—*really*? Where you'd find the money? Who and what are you, James Damon Keane?"

"Some things you gotta figure out for yourself, Shame." His smile.

And out went the light.

But what do I do now, Jimmy, several hundred miles and thirty-eight days into your death? Should I bring the purple bag with me whenever I trick? Threesomes with the dead? Naked boys wrestling on a bed scattered with marigolds?

I grabbed my tempeh and turned and almost ran into the boy as he steered his hand truck past me, lifting his chin, with just the slightest coy smile, as if to say "see ya later."

A girl in produce, with multicolored hairweaves and a plethora of piercings, was looking at me by then, since I was standing there frozen watching the bulk boy recede into the far reaches of the market. And she came right up to me, holding big red apples clenched in each upturned palm, and said: "He's mute, so if you want to talk to him you can—he's not deaf—but he doesn't say much, if you know what I mean," (she winked) "being mute and all. Just thought I'd let ya know."

118

I was a little taken aback, but she seemed friendly, and so I asked nervously, "Um, is he a friend of yours?"

She turned to place the apples in their rough wooden trough as she answered me: "Sure—I work with him. He's only been here a few months, and he *really doesn't* say much, believe me," she smiled, crouching down to grab some more apples from a box. Then she craned her neck to look up at me, "But sure, I like him alright." And she looked concerned suddenly, seeing something I was unaware of.

"Why are you crying?"

I didn't know I was crying, but I wiped my face to find I was. Just slightly. "Uh, allergies," I blurted.

She gave me the kind of sweet smile that said, *You're lying, but I understand, and it's okay.* "Do you need a hug?" *So* Eugene.

I did, but I didn't dare. I'd fall apart in the name of Jimmy.

I had to pull just then. "Uh, thanks, but not right now. Um, so . . . what's his name?"

She smiled knowingly, holding a large apple in her fist, moving her fingers over it like a baseball pitcher. "They just call him Eugene, 'cause he's here. But he has some Indian name he doesn't use. He'll answer to Eugene. You want me to go get him?"

"No! No, no, I gotta go. Thanks!" And I hurried to the register to wait in line. That's when I saw him coming toward me. He marched right up and put a little scrap of paper into my hand, smiling as he closed my fingers around it. Then he turned and walked away.

I stood dumbfounded, and then I opened my fist and the note and read what it said:

Want to hang out after work?
I get off at 7:00.
You can meet me here if you want.

29

I was the nurse and the janitor and the candy striper, bouncing around the room in just a jockstrap, hoping to cheer up poor Jimmy.

"I'm pullin', Jimmy, I'm pullin'!"

"You're a motherfucker."

The words of love.

But Jimmy had the libido then of a Zoloft droid, so I had to come up with something other than a sexy outfit.

I read him Rumi poems and put on Tammy Faye makeup.

You know my coins are counterfeit,
But you accept them anyway

But Jimmy lost the very things that gave him the strength to stick by me and stick around in general. Jimmy lost his humor and Jimmy lost his patience.

No good attitude for Jimmy. Shitting his pants and sweating all night was not for Jimmy. Jimmy was only patient while he was moving and independent. And he was past ready to go. Jimmy wanted morphine, and lots of it. And he wanted me to go get it for him.

"I can't do that, Jimmy."

"You have to," he said flatly.

I don't know how to love you . . .

I was close to blubbering tears. Killing him would be killing me.

"Otherwise you'll have to smother me with a pillow, Shame."

I just looked at him.

"Go find someone who will help me, Shame."

We both knew there were people at ACT UP who would help him.

"I'll help you, Jimmy."

But I didn't mean it how he meant it. I was his protector, his friend, and I was also selfish, scared, hung over with Catholicism. I needed Jimmy and I couldn't open the door for him, couldn't say goodnight.

"How about a massage?"

"I need Dr. Jack."

"I'm no Dr. Jack, Jimmy."

He looked at me, frustrated.

Then Jimmy got mad. And good. Jimmy was weak and unable, but he got himself up anyway, glaring at me sitting at the table. He put on his slippers—those sad little kung fu shoes—and his green army overcoat over his long underwear, his hair pitch-black now. Jimmy's roots had come in like death, they had. Black as a priest's cassock, black as carbon.

No pity. I can't pity him, but I doubted he'd be able to manage the stairs and thought to stop him.

He looked over his shoulder as he opened the door. "You fucked up." And he left the house.

I was nail-biting crazy. Annoying inane. I'm the caretaker; I'm in charge of Jimmy. I'm a heartless coward and a dumb, confused boy in way over my head. I can't kill Jimmy. I heard him slowly shuffling down those stairs. I knew I shouldn't have let him leave the house. Paralyzed until I wasn't.

I got up and ran after Jimmy, who'd made it all the way to the sidewalk. "Don't you touch me!" he snapped. I embraced him then, squeezed him. And he shivered as he fell into me. And his legs went out from under him, and he slid down me, pulling me. But I got him back up, noting the twins watching from the window, and then slowly I guided him back upstairs. Reassuring Jimmy all the while: "I'll go, I'll go." And once back upstairs, I helped him off with his coat and those sad slippers, both of which seemed to have grown huge around his withering body, and I settled him back into bed.

And all the way down to Sycamore Alley near the BART Station, where we first came up from underneath, to find Tony, who'd bring the morphine. But I hesitated with my thumb hovering over the buzzer. And I walked away. Jimmy will fall asleep, I told myself; he won't get up again. But I walked in circles all the same, orbiting Guerrero Street and lurking under the big acacia tree near the corner liquor store, just to be sure, watching to make sure Jimmy didn't come out. I thought of going to find Tanya. She'd get all the arrangements in order. But, unlike Jimmy, she wouldn't hear me out and she wouldn't collapse in my arms. Tanya was a warrior and would do the deed. So I didn't expand my orbit to Shotwell Street; I didn't want to get it started. I wanted to keep Jimmy right there for as long as I could. I wanted him to forget about death.

Selfish. Scared. Catholic. I was no Dr. Jack. No sir.

Jimmy was right. It was gonna take everything I had, and Jimmy *was* everything I had.

He did go back to sleep that day, but the next day I came home from the Y and there was a whole crew of ACT UP people there, gathered around Jimmy. They'd been talking, obviously, but fell silent as I swung open the door.

They gave me the whole solemn, do-the-right-thing talk, and I looked at the ground before finally saying, "You guys need to go." They who'd stood by me, and now I was kicking them out of my house. *Everything.* Them too, then.

They marched out.

But they'd left it sitting there on the table next to the bed. I looked at Jimmy and he looked at me. I noticed then how hollow his cheeks had become, how the bones next to his eyes, at his temples, suddenly looked as pronounced as his clavicles. I looked at his "good" tattoo and how big his eyes had become, dwarfing the third one.

"Take me back the way I came, Shame," he said quietly.

"Why do you always say that, Jimmy?"

"Road's the place for lost souls . . . promise?" I worried again about dementia.

"Where'd the money come from, Jimmy? I'll trade you my promise for your answer."

"Came from a book."

"Vague, Jimmy."

"Promise?"

"Sure thing." I longed for his smile, but his face remained expressionless.

"You gonna help me, Shame?"

"No." And I started to cry. He glared. He took a deep breath, watching me.

Jimmy had to inject his own morphine while I bit my nails near the window—behind me the corner liquor store, the tree, the buckled sidewalk, the fire escape—watching (unforgivable, inexcusable), wincing, his hand shaking, missing.

Again.

The blood. Bingo.

He looked at me, open as a flower. "Promise?"

I nodded vigorously.

Then I climbed into bed with him and made a pocket for him. Held him all those hours while he faded. Muttering and blubbering "sorry," and "please don't go," and "I love you, Jimmy"; "forgive me, Jimmy; I couldn't, I just couldn't. I'm so sorry for everything. I want you to stay. And I promise . . . I promise . . . I promise." Nothing left to do but promise.

And then I just hummed to him through my tears— *The Blue Danube* I think it was—as black eyeliner ran down my cheeks.

30

I ate the carrots and treats and amazaki—and even the tempeh raw—my sad little seder feast for Jimmy, sitting against the parking lot wall with Jimmy-in-the-bag and my bike under the big mural of Gaia and her cornucopias and prancing cherubic black children, swinging around fir trees, the big Cascade mountains looming like fairyland behind them. Eating through my tears. I wasn't going to be able to come back here. No sirree. No morphine, and no boys who don't talk, with secret Indian names.

But my emotions were like a crowd: give 'em what they want. Barabbas or the J-man. I *was* twenty-two. I couldn't be some old Pilate, washing my hands of it all. I was young and horny, widowed or not. Shadowed in grief sure thing, but my dick jumped like a Jack Russell terrier all the same at the sight of a boy like Eugene. Jumped up and down, tear-proof, grief-proof. People have dogs for a reason—and guys especially. They are exactly like dicks.

Jimmy'd even told me he thought it was good if I had sex with other guys once he couldn't anymore. But I'd only shook my head. Other than the occasional backroom blowjob when I was in a mood, I had zero desire to be with anyone else. "You're twenty-two, Shame. You gotta live."

Twenty-two, twenty-two, twenty-two. I was still twenty-two. And still alive. And I still loved Jimmy. So . . . *if I thought about it like a three-way?*

Only one thing I knew for sure: If I returned to that organic Jerusalem at 7:00 p.m., there would most certainly be a crucifixion, no two ways about it. Because, like I said before, the promise of sex with someone you're starting to like puts you smack dab in the center of time, history, and the universe itself. The birth of a new religion, and all the madness that ensues. Just like it had been with Jimmy. Jimmy of the platform and Eugene of the bins. Like saints.

More paintings to think about—but this time in the Byzantine style. Lust rose in me like sap. The kids were singing and dancing all over the wall behind me.

Fate.

Okay then, Jimmy. I'll come back. My shorts swelled a Greek chorus.

But first I had to find a place to stay.

I was in a city, so I wouldn't be able to find a campground or sleep in a park. Towns of a certain size are either dangerous or full of cops or both, and sleeping in parks is thus problematic. And Jimmy's hoops were never specific . . . perhaps there was a state park just east of town? I remember he had friends here; he'd likely stayed with them, but he didn't include names, addresses or phone numbers on the maps, so I was on my own.

I had an idea and hopped on my bike and headed toward the University of Oregon to find frat row. Jimmy's friend Sam had told me once that when in a university town, fraternities were a sure way to get free shelter. He'd been doing it for years, and it allowed him free lodging in almost any college town when he went to see concerts or whatever. Of course he was straight, but I figured I could pass when I really had to. According to Sam, all you had to do was say that you were a brother from the chapter at U of ABCDE, etc., and a year—say '91—and they'd say "cool" and let you sleep there. I figured in the modern world, considering, Jesus himself would have likely been born in a frat house.

I picked one with beat-up '60s-era architecture, too intimidated by the Colonial and Georgian-style behemoths, with their suggestions of

Biffs and Muffys within. I wasn't a good liar and I didn't need to make it harder by lying to someone who would consider me a freak or a loser.

I pulled up and leaned my bike near the door of my chosen domicilic prey just as some guy holding a bunch of books stepped out—on his way to the library, I guessed.

"Hi," I said, in my best, friendly, regular-guy manner.

"How's it going?" he answered, a little suspiciously.

"Well, I'm traveling cross-country on my bike and I'm a brother from U.C. Berkeley. I was wondering . . ."

But he finished my sentence. "Cool, dude, you can stay here if you want. Use the living room. There's a keg in the library." Then he added, looking a little perplexed: "I didn't know we had a chapter at Berkeley."

I didn't even know what fraternity it was, but I was quick to respond: "Uh, it got kicked off campus a couple of years back, right after I left. Real partiers, you know?" And we both smiled.

"Phi Delts are wild," he guffawed (thanks for the info). "Well, let us know if you need anything, man. The guys here are real cool. Just tell them you know me. Name's Jeff." We shook hands.

"Thanks, man. See ya!" And I dragged *Chief Joseph* into the frat house. An odd place for him. I stashed my gear in the corner of the enormous living room near a brick fireplace, behind one of the several threadbare couches. Then I got unpacked, took a shower, had a beer with the brothers, and told them lies about the guys at Berkeley and how they got kicked off campus for a drunken brawl (all while I washed my clothes with their free washer and dryer, stage left). You didn't have to be that creative to pull this particular con, I was finding out—but it helped—and I was grateful for that, since I had other things on my mind. If they'd only known what. But frat boys are easier to lie to than you'd think, and not half as bad as you'd assume either, so it was with a tinge of guilt—shooting fish in a barrel—that I told them my shameful lies in order to save thirty bucks.

I was back at the organic grocery at 7:00 sharp—sans Jimmy, the first time I hadn't carried him with me on this whole trip, and I was feeling kind of skittish. (I'd hidden him deep in the bowels of my sleeping bag back at the frat.)

I went and peered in the big front window, and there I saw his grin coming at me from down the aisle—that shy, crooked-mouthed smile on that handsome, unknown face. I had a feeling then he was gonna haunt me. And I remembered then what Jimmy had said: *Attraction is a message.*

Sure thing, Jimmy.

And Eugene had his hands and his brows up with all his fingers splayed, saying: "Ten minutes, okay?" He made me smile, and I felt my heart crack slowly like a pomegranate, showing its seeds. I nodded and went to lock up my bike on a parking meter, after which I sat out front on a bench watching all the hip people, just like in San Francisco, sitting and eating whole-wheat burritos or hummus and tabouli or some such, or lugging their full-to-bursting cloth grocery brags down the sidewalk back toward home.

While my heart beat like a piston.

At least the rain was gone.

The rain had stopped when I woke up that morning back in Roseburg, post-Ralph, and the sun was breaking through, making the whole city of Roseburg into a big steam vent, with rising mist, the still-wet sidewalks and trees and cars all shimmering like glass. It made me want to whistle as I strutted down to Denny's two blocks away. Every crack in the sidewalk was lousy with moss, and even the signs and the billboards were all rusty and molded, thick weeds at the base of them, growing mad and wet at the stems. It was unnerving after living all my life in California (it's only the golden state because all the grass is dead), and I didn't know whether to be reassured or horrified by all this green fecundity. I was used to plants wilting and being sort of perennially desiccated, but it looked to me that morning that if you were a plant in Oregon, you couldn't die if you tried. There was even a rainbow, and it was so close, I followed it to see what really lay at the end of it.

Turned out to be an on-ramp onto the 5. Place for lost souls.

127

Et tu, Roseburg?

Off in the distance, there were mountains with firs so dark, they looked like they led somewhere you could never return from. There were big evergreens in town too—they looked out of place next to fast-food joints—and they were the dark green of zombies, with trunks as black as Jimmy's roots. Not like the Trinity Alps, and Shasta, blasted as those places were with California sunlight and covered with pines, which were emptier trees than these dense firs, of a lighter green, with orange/red trunks—Kodachromic cheer. Because whatever California is, it sure is hopeful—sometimes annoyingly so. Even the redwoods, lurking in silvery gray mists, are the red of Chinese happiness and the green of good luck and everything's-okay suburban lawns. But these firs of Oregon, they were plain foreboding, gothic with darkness.

Then, as I rode whistling down the drying blacktop an hour north of town, there were suddenly big madrones everywhere with their barkless, smooth, orange naked wood—smooth and creamy as Jimmy's neck and belly and ass, sure thing. Only difference was that Jimmy wasn't orange. Jimmy was never orange; he was white-green from the Sicilian half of him, like lime.

I finally heard the door click and there was Eugene grinning orange as a jack-o'-lantern.

First thing he did was grab my hand and take me around to the back of the store where there were some cardboard boxes full of fruit past its shelf life, and he grabbed some apples and oranges and put them in his backpack, where he already had past-its-date tofu and yogurt. Then he motioned with his head for me to follow him out across the old, pot-holed, broken-glassed parking lot, rimmed with weeds. He led me into some trees by a little path that went down through maples and madrones to the river and the big cottonwoods along its banks. There was a lot of garbage lying around—cigarette butts, aluminum cans, used condoms draped like Christmas decorations over weed stalks—like any wild place within a city. We sat on a log and ate the fruit, watching the river, sometimes him pointing to things: leaves floating, a tree across the bank, a turtle rolling itself off a log, a fish jumping, strider bugs. It took me back to Ricky's oak groves in the hills, the creek beds on Mt. Tamalpais with Jimmy.

And I reached out with my hand to touch Eugene's shoulder, and he smiled and took my hand in his.

He pointed at me with the other hand, but he stopped when he saw I looked confused. Then he began to draw on the ground. First a stick figure of himself, distinguished by an *E* above it, then one of me with a *?* over its head. He wrote "where?" next to it. *To or from* I wondered. So I told him both: How I'd come from San Francisco and I was riding my bicycle across the country, just passing through—whens, wheres, whats, and hows, but no *whys*. He smiled with a sigh that pointed straight at that omission.

"I should probably get goin'," I announced. "I'm pretty tired and I gotta get up and go early, and, and . . ." But he just looked at me, and I heard the river, and me lonely—and the next thing you knew we were kissing hard and hungry.

We kept kissing—it was like thirst in the desert, like hunger and the food you craved most—tempeh. We gulped each other like starved puppies at a tit. Then we stopped and looked at each other, and I could see he wasn't afraid of my vague sorrow and its spilling. In his eyes I saw that he was somehow lost too, and something there said: "I want to hear your story, and I want to tell you mine."

Eugene pulled out the rest of the food then and we ate the yogurt, and big wet chunks of tofu, damp and cold as Jimmy's lips in the San Francisco fog. We laughed in the eating of it.

Then he urged me up, anxious to show me around. And off we went down the river path, among the deathless damp flora of Oregon, the golden and brown loam of leaves thicker than any carpet. He hugged a tree; he kicked a stone; he found a little dead mole.

I watched the way he moved, how he looked around—hooded now in his black sweatshirt—the way he noticed birds, insects, the wind.

The way he'd watch me move and look. I didn't need to say anything, and soon I realized that silence was just part of how you talked to him. It even started to feel rude and sort of rough when I said yes or no, so I just nodded or shook my head. The river was our voice—well, along with the wind and the traffic, I suppose. And maybe we were talking with our feet too—in where we went, how we stood. And his eyes, enormous and green-gold, were a kind of voice as well—in a way bashful, and yet piercing and direct: when they looked, they really looked, and they spoke in the looking.

Pretty soon we saw a green steel bridge arcing over the river and Eugene led me right under it, where he showed me some graffiti art, shadowed by the bridge—and then he pointed to his chest and smiled, proud of his work.

I raised my eyebrows, and then I climbed up the rocks piled there to get a closer look.

It was a very involved Hieronymus Bosch allegorical kind of thing with people crawling around on the pavement, drunks in doorways, twisted trailer homes—and in the big empty sky above the miserable scene were a few stringy clouds, along with big vertical eagle feathers. And underneath everything too, lying near some bum's dropped wine bottle, and under the cinder blocks of teetering trailers, were broken arrowheads and buffalo skulls.

"It's beautiful, Eugene." But it was more than that. It suggested something I couldn't quite put my finger on—something unknowable, something Jimmy. It was colorful, shadowy, pretty, sad, dark, light, everything all at once. Sublime is what it was. I grabbed his hand and squeezed while I looked at it, the rhythmic thumping of cars above us making it seem almost as if the picture were alive and beating like a heart.

I pointed to the feathers and arrowheads and buffalo, and he pulled out what I learned later was his medicine bag, which he wore on a string around his neck, and he held it then in his fist with a firm kind of strong smile on his face. He touched it to my forehead and put it back under his sweatshirt, and I wished then I'd brought Jimmy-in-the-bag to share with Eugene the same way.

"Hey, hey, Eugene." And I held his shoulders and couldn't not kiss him with everything I had.

Invigorated, he pulled me along, over the riprap stones abutting the underside of the bridge as we made our way further down the river, the big cottonwood boughs rolling like waves in the sea of the sunset sky, which was streaked with long drawn-out clouds, all purple, orange, and golden, dappling the trail with sepia light. I breathed deep the dusty-leaves-scented late summer air, and I wondered about Eugene, and about my own heart's strength. I figured he was either desperately lonely, or he really liked me. True for so many gay encounters, I'd given up ever knowing which it was, or if there was even a difference. But I hoped Eugene was just lonely. Be a lonely boy, Eugene. My heart's too full up and scarred for anything more.

I threw my arm around his shoulder. My buddy. And Eugene, he sort of became his own red line after that, and I stopped all my ruminating and just followed it; I followed him along that river, as he pointed out moss on stones; three-foot-high dandelions in tiny meadows between firs and maples; huckleberries, blackberries, salmonberries like red hoops. Which he fed me.

He found a salamander that moved like a baby walking, its eyes locked on us as intensely as Eugene and I looked at each other right before we kissed. And Eugene grinned big and crooked.

He took me up to Skinner Butte. The hillside going up was dense with undergrowth and fir, but at the top it opened up into California, all dead golden grass and oak trees. There was a sign at the top and Eugene placed his hand over the *r* and the last *e*. "Skinny butt," I read out loud, and patted his.

I thought of Jimmy then on Mt. Tamalpais, where he'd once read me Rilke poems:

. . . And sometimes in a shop, the mirrors were still busy with your presence . . .

131

Actually the whole world was. I stifled a tear.

Eugene took off across the grass then, running for the overlook. And I ran after him all the way to the edge, where, breathing heavily, we looked out over the whole town, heard and saw the train whistling down by the river, passing the big grain elevator (is that where all the bulk-bin couscous, amaranth, and spelt comes from?), and out beyond it the freeway with the people on it always going, going; circling, circling.

I kissed him while my chest still heaved, wanting to breathe his air, and him mine.

There were squirrels in the oaks that made me want to play, and I kissed Eugene more passionately and groped him, but I kept pulling back the minute I started. And he seemed to understand, and again grabbed my hand and onward we went—down the other side, through the smell of wood and dirt and the sour milky scent of just-cut blackberry stickers.

Then Eugene showed me the whole town—for hours we walked—never saying a word, either of us. He was expert in gesture and smile and eye. He made me see the shapes of things. He showed me more green bridges and pointed out the lumber mills stinking of sulfur and sawdust.

Near the university, there were coffee shops full of students amid somebody's idea of wisdom—always gothic towers and big elm trees. And there were strip malls that didn't bother looking smart; they were completely unselfconscious in fact, downright ugly and undignified as if to assert: commerce is stupid. There were gas stations and their machine thirst; bars and neon hunger; cement walls with names of juvenile delinquents and Fortune 500 companies all over them; markets full of the humility of vegetables—poorly shaped sweet potatoes, knobby squash, deformed carrots and turnips—and other things trapped in their tiresome sales pitches of packaging. We walked past chain stores lit up brighter when closed; saw cop cars and semis, eyes heavy-lidded in lizard-sleep behind the bowling alley; there were lost-looking high-rises scattered about, and little houses rotting in the rust and mold of decay. Eugene was like any small American city, only a darker green, full of the stains and residues of puddles never quite dried; the earth's face puffy from crying and whimpering—like the grief of America, unscabbed-over, an ulcer that never completely heals and can't dissolve and dry up like it would in California, where the sun erases everything.

Cremation's for California, I thought. This place wants the body, the soil. *What if we'd spent our year of love in Eugene, Jimmy?* I'd have had to lug the whole body back from where it came, in a shroud—in a little trailer behind the bike, I suppose.

It grew late in Eugene, where the days do not disappear but pile up like timber to rot or grow fungus—or maybe just remember. And it began to rain again, though only lightly. And we kept on walking— even though we were dog-tired—because we were a kind of river by then. Eugene pulled up his sweatshirt hood, wraith-like, and then we found a boarded-up shop and we sat there on the sidewalk under its awning, watching the rain and the darkness commence. He sat as close to me as he could, pressed up against me, and I heard him hum. Just like that, saying nothing, humming and looking out into the rain. Then he rooted around in his pocket and pulled out a little wooden pipe, packed it, and in the Oregon rain, we got stoned.

Eventually he took me out of the rain and into a drag show at some little gay club. It was funny and entertaining in the way men are when they have nothing to prove. There were tired, beat-up blonds, whose hands were way too big, singing Abba songs—"Dancing Queen" and "The Winner Takes It All"—and overweight brunettes with puffy hairdos attempting to mimic Madonna or Kate Smith, or both. The freedom of nothing left to lose.

One of the drag queens came up to us. She had an enormous hawk-like nose, and with her cheap banged-up heels, stood well over six feet. "Ooooooh, child, you got yourself a little white boy again," she chided.

Eugene and I both smiled embarrassed, and then the drag queen turned to me and said: "You know Sioux means 'little snake,' and his ain't, so I guess he isn't. Ha, ha, ha, ha, . . ." Then she disappeared into her bitchy reverie of laughter, preparing for her act, while I tried to square the riddle of what she'd said.

Then thin, gangly Eugene put his arm around me, and I felt that special high school date feeling I'd never known but always longed for as we watched Cherrie Kee lip-synch "I Will Survive" (with all its heartbreaking dramatic pauses)—adding, when the music faded out: "—in spite of the white man!"

Eugene gave me a little kiss as the crowd scattered toward the bar and tables. And then he put his finger up to signal for me to wait as he went off to the bathroom. I headed over to the bar to get a beer and was tapped on the shoulder from behind by Cherrie Kee. "Hi," she said with a big smile. "Where are you from? Don't get me wrong with all that white-boy stuff—I'm a performer." She smiled coyly.

I was always cheered at the sight of a drag queen, and I grinned like a chimp. I complimented her on her act and then told her I was up from San Francisco. She asked me if I'd met Eugene at the market, and I said I had, and then she asked me if I knew he was only nineteen and shouldn't even be in this bar.

"People feel sorry for him because he doesn't talk, and not talking he hasn't offended anybody yet. Unlike me," she added sardonically. "We're both from the reservation. I've been taking him up here since his father died when he was fifteen. A mean, motherfucking Klamath alcoholic who used to beat the shit out of him." Ow. I felt a pang that made me wince. I lit Cherrie Kee's cigarette, acting the gay Bogart, and she puffed quickly, continuing: "Wasn't actually his father though, it turned out. Long story. He was a real prick." She laughed. "Me and Eugene used to fuck around back when we were just kids, and his stepfather caught us once. I can laugh now: 69ing in the back of his pickup truck. Ha, ha, ha." She glanced over her shoulder and saw Eugene coming. "Anyway," she hurriedly continued, "be careful. He's a heartbreaker, honey. He lives in his own world, always has, always will. There was a time when he even talked. As a little kid. Don't get caught up in him." And she looked at me with a mournful sigh, like she knew it was more than I could handle, but that it was probably going to happen anyway. She communicated all this in a microsecond, as Eugene was soon upon us.

"Hi, Eugenee," she suddenly blurted, smiling broadly now and hugging him and giving him a kiss on the cheek.

His story. Just the beginning.

I panicked around then (either from the pot or the confidences, I don't know which), and excused myself to go to the bathroom—never a good place for peace or reflection in a gay bar. Everyone's watching: the big trough of a urinal, filled with bar ice, like a model runway for dick—everyone's member in full view. I wished suddenly I could meet someone for fast, cheap sex, and we could slip out the back door and I could be done with the hold Eugene had on me. Get on my bike and go. Oh, Blessed Mother, I prayed, find me some *other* lonely boy. And sure enough, walking out of the restroom, I spied a dark, lanky boy and loitered to catch his eye. He smiled and I walked toward him, and then I sat next to him on the bench he occupied. And the usual questions, and how tired I was to answer. And I couldn't help searching out Eugene in the middle of it all; he sat waiting for me quietly, looking patient and sure I'd be back.

"You okay?" the dark boy inquired.

"I gotta go." And for some reason I hugged him, which confused him but touched him somehow too. These places were so cold, and yet so warm—fire and ice, and even the hardest hearts could shatter in an instant. And I thought just then: they're much better broken.

So I gathered up my weak-skinned collapsing pomegranate of a heart—gathered it off the beer-stained, cigarette-lousy floor I did—and smiling humbly, walked back toward Eugene, transfixed by his gaze. And when I reached him, I just let myself fall into him. And we kissed in a way that made those around us notice.

I wanted to make him then in the worst way, and I wanted Jimmy to be with us, and thought: *Let me just run home and get the bag.* Or better yet, maybe we should go back there to the frat. What better place for gay sex?

So we left, but Eugene wanted to go back to the river. After all, there was a full moon out and the rain had ceased. We went down by another path this time, all wooded and really smelling northwest soggy-leaves dirt-fresh after that rain. Eugene pointed out several slugs and, laughing, prodded them gently. Even their reaction to danger was glacial, and I marveled at how they survived at all, wondered how they managed to get up the energy to do anything.

There were the same rotting logs, but in the moonlight they didn't look the same. The logs weren't rotting—mushrooms were being born. And Eugene isn't a horse *or* a snake—he's a bird. The owl of him, nestled away inside that hooded sweatshirt.

He took my hand then and we went back along the path to the place by the river where we'd been hours ago eating the fruit, and he sat down there and pulled out his pipe again and lit it up. I shook my head no when he offered it to me as I was still plenty stoned from before. He took a long hit and pocketed the pipe, looked out at the river, exhaling, and then turned to me and kissed me deliciously. And we got our hands in each other's shirts—and the warmth there. The rain and dark had driven everyone away from the river, and though it was a bit cool, together we were warm—all the while our hearts beating, knowing our penises throbbed with the same warmth and rhythm. Wanting to confirm and see it happening, I pulled at his clothes, and we pushed ourselves together, shoving our hands into each other's pants as we discarded our shirts (and the air cool from the rain made our skin goose-fleshed, which just made us cling all the tighter, rubbing our chests together, back and forth).

And his eyes following mine, never losing contact with them. He was already way inside me. I tried to do the same back but my eyes weren't like his. They were somehow lost and always looking, confused by words said or unsaid.

Off came our pants, and we let each other pull down the other's underwear before we reached for the cocks and held our fists around them as we kissed. And how we kissed and shared the innocent boyhood of nipples, biceps, bellies, thighs, flanks, and hands. I marveled at his skinny orange physique (a rust being?), and at the extreme blackness of his hair in the three places on the Y of his male body. Him all black and orange like Halloween and night fire and the day when the veil between the worlds is thinnest. My own private Great Pumpkin—but a skinny little pumpkin, in his case. A sweet potato.

And his eyes: big white moons behind the green, green spirals that never looked away from me while we worked the pleasure up and out of each other. The smooth gnarled hardness of his slender, silent cock, the furious aggression in lips and a tongue that never spoke. We worked like well-oiled, heavy-geared, high-horsepower machinery together, laboring to produce the same thing: the want and the giving, the violence and the peace, the work and the play of it, all mixed up and become enormous in affirmation, like of course the universe is expanding, and this is the center—our shooting cum a birth of stars across our bellies, cooling and thinning and reminding us that entropy trumps it all in the end. *Eh Jimmy?*

Because Jimmy was there too—up in the branches of the cottonwood tree. The moon.

Jimmy wanted me to live. And living is what me and Eugene just did—the gravity and the entropy of it, the warping of space and time, the Magellanic clouds of our hearts cracked wide open and spilling stars.

Eugene held me close and hard, smearing our seed together on our bellies, his hands on my buttocks, my hands on his. We fit. And we held each other a long time like that, nibbling each other, smelling like the heady pollen of chestnut trees. And I didn't want to let go; I wanted to stay with him. Eugene, who wasn't afraid.

"Come back to the frat house with me," I implored.

Eugene laughed at that, and I explained why I was staying there. And then we got dressed, Eugene beating the dirt and pine needles from his discarded sweatshirt. I saw the smallness of his orange butt then as he struggled into his jeans. I wanted to fuck him next time; I wanted to fuck him until his tongue spoke again. I wanted to climb inside him; I wanted him to climb inside me; to fuck me until the heaviness and grief shot out of me—I wanted to make love with Eugene in that divine gay way that makes a Möbius strip of love. A kind of love a straight person can never know.

I grabbed him and kissed him again once we were dressed, in gratitude. And he pulled me close to him. And for a while there was just that and nothing else. No sound, no nothing. Just him holding me, me holding him.

Then we started up the hill, out of the trees—up from underneath— and into the parking lot. At my bicycle, he kissed me and smiled, and then he climbed onto the handlebars, while I tried to balance and get the bike moving. He couldn't talk, but he could laugh, and his laugh was as low as the groans of the bad plumbing on Guerrero Street.

We weaved crookedly down the empty streets of Eugene back toward the university.

Fortunately, back at the frat, it was late enough, and a school night, so there was no one in the TV room where the kegs were, and we were able to steal into the house undetected, have a few beers, and make out on one of the ratty couches. In time, I showed him my little encampment. We sat on the sleeping bag, and that's when I told him I wanted to show him something. And out came Jimmy in his pretty little purple velvet bag with the gold tassels. I unwound the ties and told Eugene, as he peered into the darkness inside: "This is Jimmy."

And then I spilled the whole tale. Well, the short answer anyway.

He put one hand on my shoulder and looked at me and nodded. I started to cry a little bit and fell into him, and he held me like a friend.

And Eugene had condoms, and more pot, and we stripped again because we knew what we needed to do, and we didn't care about any frat boys. We only knew we had messages for each other—messages that we delivered enthusiastically for the next several hours with our mouths and eyes, and with our penises: me inside him, and he in me, sharing the Möbius magic. How he looked at me when he came, his eyes penetrating to the back of my skull where he drew his graffiti in bright colors right on my bones. He didn't need to speak any words and I didn't either—and that was a first. Chatterbox faggot, I'd never really had anything to say. What really needed to be told was communicated in silence.

And dozing off, I thought about my father, forever silent, and the erasure that was Jimmy's embrace, and about my mom. I'd never been able to get her to say anything of real import. I knew her through the records she played in her grief, hummed to me over the bars of the crib—the voice of my father:

La, la, la, la, la, la . . . la, la, la, la, la. . . .

When the light of the white misty morning woke me, I startled, for Eugene was gone. And I had no idea when he'd left. Granted, the sleeping bag was awkward for two, and he likely woke up feeling confined, but I was dismayed to think he'd gone without a goodbye. I was leaving, after all. Forever. The thought that I'd never see him again and hadn't even said goodbye made my heart sink.

I hurried to the bathroom, but he wasn't there. And then to the kitchen, where I came face to face with four frat boys drinking coffee and eating corn flakes.

"Anybody seen Eugene?" It came out before it occurred to me that they'd have no reason to know who he was—or for that matter, who *I* was, or whether I was referring to the town or a person. They just looked at me; I smiled disarmingly and retreated to my camp.

Pull.

I remembered then Jimmy's words about giving love and not asking for anything in return. We'd had a wonderful time, me and Eugene. Be like Jimmy, then; ask for nothing in return. I'd lost my father and Jimmy—I could lose a boy I'd just met. I could pull.

I packed up quickly, yanking a string off the threadbare couch and pulling a strand of the carpet up as well for good measure, tying them both to the bike. And when I had my rig all ready to go, down on one knee I went, Catholic blessing myself, thanking the Buddhas and saints for this campsite just like Jack Kerouac taught me to via Japhy Ryder in *Dharma Bums*.

And I thanked Eugene too. The place and the boy.

Hell, he couldn't have said goodbye anyway. And what's goodbye besides? Jimmy never said it either. Goodbye's just a bag of dust.

31

I had to call the morgue and his family both. The Government Pages, I guess? Sure enough. I took a deep breath.

"City Morgue, County of San Francisco. May I help you?"

"Hi, uh, my boyfriend died . . . and uh, . . . I don't know what to do about it."

"Are you his power of attorney?"

"No . . . I don't think so."

"Who is?"

"I don't know about that stuff."

"Hmm, I see. Are you in contact with his family?"

"No."

"Do you know how to reach them?"

"I can try."

"We'll send someone out. You work on locating his family. In the meantime, give me whatever info you have. His full name?"

I wanted to say: "Chief Joseph. He's like the most famous Indian ever and he didn't want to fight no more forever." I pulled instead: "James Damon Keane, and he's from Buffalo, New York, and that's where his family is. And I have his credit card and all that. He doesn't have a license or anything. Just a credit card."

"And what's your name?"

I wanted to have his then; I wanted to say I'm Seamus Keane, his widow, or maybe Ms. Joseph, his number one squaw. "I sure loved

Jimmy," is what I said. "I sure loved him." And I came apart right there on the phone.

"How old are you, honey?"

She ended up coming out with the guy in the morgue truck, and she sat there with me and listened. Sweet Monique, a big black lady who did the pulling for me, until I could get ahold of the rope of this life once again and do it myself.

Like a barge, life. Pull, pull, pull. Where are we all going? Where are we going, Jimmy?

Back the way we came.

"You want me to deal with the family?" she entreated consolingly.

"No, that's okay, but we gotta cremate Jimmy; he's gotta be here with me for a while. I'm gonna have to talk them into it."

Monique looked worried. "Did you say he needs to stay here?"

"Yeah."

"He can't stay here. We gotta take him in. It's the law."

"Can I visit?"

"I don't know. I suppose. No one's ever asked me about visiting the morgue unless the police are doing it, or somebody has to identify someone. You already know who he is."

I got a worried look on my face, pleading. "You just gotta keep him there at least three days. It's like a Buddhist thing with him."

She was starting to look like I'd run the limits of her compassionate largesse. She got up. "He ain't goin' anywhere, once he gets there. Not until the power of attorney decides otherwise. So, you need to talk to them."

"Okay, thanks Monique." She gave me a wan smile.

Jimmy's family. What did I know about Jimmy's family? Well, plenty actually, from the poems, and his late-night, book-on-the-lap reminiscences.

Jimmy was twenty-nine when he died. But he'd left home a long time ago. He only went skulking back to Buffalo when he learned that his mother was dying of a long, drawn-out illness: lung cancer. He hadn't seen her since he'd left, which was ten years or more. She chastised him when he walked into her hospital room, and he looked at the floor and he took it.

"She said awful things to me. Called me all sorts of names. She'd always been tough just like I used to be—we respected each other for that. But it wouldn't have been fair to fight back with her there flat on her back. We were tough, but we fought fair. Which is to say we were proud." Sighing Jimmy. "So I just endured it, tried to tell myself to just go the distance. I hadn't cried in ten years either, but after three days of her insults—and while my two born-again sisters sat by sniffling silently and with satisfaction—I broke and finally yelled back at her: 'Stop it, stop it, you bitch.' We yelled at each other back and forth for maybe ten minutes while my sisters lowly wailed in prayer from the corner. Somewhere in there I'd begun crying, bawling through my hurled words, and she had too—you have to understand, we never cried, ever." He huffed a big exhale of a sigh then. "I climbed into the little bed with her then, and you know what she said? 'I bore you . . .' She was right, but it seemed a strange thing to say, until she finished and it made sense. 'I bore you . . . you are my fruit.' And she fucking wailed, and I knew then we were the same. She died two days later, spent, but more like horrifically resigned, not so much to death as to regret."

Jimmy didn't cry then. He came close though, I could see. He shook his head out like a wet dog.

"Are you full of regret, Jimmy?"

"No. We're the same, me and my ma, but I don't gotta end the same."

"Tell me the story, Jimmy—what happened next?" I insisted.

Jimmy thought to do what anyone in Buffalo would do in terms of getting a new start. He went to California. "But I didn't just go; I couldn't just go, like I used to—I don't know. I had to go in a certain way. The railroads and airplanes and cars—they all travel in circles, and I'd end up back where I started. No sooner would I set out for St. Louis

143

than I'd end up in New Jersey. Once I went to Texas, and by the time three months had passed, I was in Florida. I actually headed for California twice before, but never made it past Denver. And then I was in Minneapolis. It was weird; it was like I was attached to some kind of tether. Maybe I slept wrong, in the shape of a boomerang or something."

"Maybe you loved your mom." The question that was my face.

He rolled his eyes.

"Maybe . . . well, of course . . . but I think it's more the circle of things."

"A closed loop. I know all about it, Jimmy," I said with my nods of assent.

"I got tested in that hospital. I'd walked by the sign for it three or four times and the day she died, I bit the bullet since I'd been avoiding it for years. After that . . . well, something was over, you know? I had to leave and never look back. At first I thought I should walk, but I knew I'd never make it. I'd end up hitching a ride or a train, and then I'd be right back in the old pattern, looping all over the continent like some pinball. I thought of walking because I knew I had to make it hard. I had to earn my passage somehow. I had to climb here. Climb out of something, get born, you know?"

I know now.

I called information, searching for his father, who he'd said had left them all years ago, but was still lurking around town somewhere. I didn't dare call the born-agains.

"Keane. Jack Keane." There were three J. Keanes listed in Buffalo.

"Hi, I'm a friend of your son's." But the first one had no son. Or was he just saying that, since it was the common response of so many fathers of gay sons? The second number was disconnected. I breathed deep for the third, but got an answering machine. "This is Jack, leave a message." That's when it occurred to me that Jimmy's voice was still on our machine. That seemed tacky, having a dead guy's voice taking messages from people who didn't even know he was dead yet. Tacky, macabre, cruel even. But there was no way I would erase it, because it was Jimmy's voice. That being the case, I decided against leaving our number for the final Jack.

Instead, I started going down to the corner liquor store and calling Jimmy.

"Hi, this is Jimmy and Seamus. We're not here." *Beep*. Music to my ears. In a Buffalo twang. Mr. Understatement. Jimmy.

The twins started watching me, wondering, pointing. Once they came over. "You don't got any phone anymore?"

"No, it's not that. Listen." And I handed Michael the phone. Arched brows. At which Marcus became overexcited, jumping up and down for his turn, so I had to dig for more quarters and dial again so they'd both get it. They got it. Big smiles and nods—they knew who it was. "Diarrhea boy!"

"He died," I told them. But I think they knew; they'd seen him fading for months. Their faces dropped all the same to get the news. But then they wanted to listen some more.

They'd run over whenever they spotted me there after that. To listen to the dead.

I think they had some idea that the message would change. That he'd say something—like what it was like on the other side.

"It never changes," Michael said despondently to Marcus.

"No, it never changes," I concurred.

That was the last time they ran over. Their mother had already taken to screaming at them in Chinese, something, I guessed, to the effect that they shouldn't be bothering me or running across the street. I had no idea which. I only knew she smiled at me when I looked at her, indicating that I wasn't the problem, in her insular, nonconfrontational way.

32

The frat had a pay phone, and it was as good a place as any to call my mom. I made a point to call her at home instead of at her office, so I wouldn't have to talk to her. All she wanted was to know I wasn't dead anyway. What was the point of talking? Which made me feel sad, until I remembered that just last night I'd realized it was sharing silence with her that was best. Silence and a song.

I oughta just call her and sing. No more talking.

I heard the beep, and her faux-cheerful voice. "Hi. This is Karen Blake. Leave a message at the beep and I'll call you back."

"Hi, Mom. It's me, Seamus. Everything's great. I'm in Eugene" (and he's in me). "Today I head east. Don't worry—I'm great." Then I sang to her: "*La, la, la, la, la; la, la, la, la, la; la, la, la, la, la, la, Bobby McGee* . . ." I kept humming the rest of it till I ran out of breath and then signed off—"Love ya, Mom. Bye."

I gathered up my things and, after throwing a perfunctory thanks at a few of the frat boys (one of whom looked at me askance, having witnessed the impromptu telephonic serenade as well as my kitchen query), I set out, determined not to go anywhere near the organic co-op.

But the morning was all misty and I got turned around, and the only way I knew to get reoriented was to find the river, and doing that, I ended up right back at the market like I was living out some Greek play. I couldn't not go in. But I hesitated.

146

A kid out front, straddling his little stingray bicycle, watched me curiously. I like kids and I hate being stared at, so I made up my mind and dismounted.

"How you doing there, partner?" I said to the kid.

"Okay," he said rather seriously, like a little man.

"Glad to hear it. Will you watch my bike?"

"Sure," he answered, as if to say *why wouldn't I?*

And through the door I went. I needed something to eat anyway. And I figured if he were there, I'd say thank you and goodbye, but not with words. I'd kiss him on the forehead and give him benediction because what we'd shared was holy.

As it turned out he wasn't there, but the stock girl was, and she said: "You're back looking for Eugene?"

"Yeah."

"Well, you just missed him," she blurted as she hefted a box of canned beans onto her cart.

"Is he working today?"

"Eugene? Nah. Yesterday was his last day," she said as she ran a razorblade around the edge of the box. "He came shopping first thing this morning."

"His last day? He quit?" I must have looked a bit alarmed.

"Yeah, he left town."

My face a question. "Where'd he go?"

She stopped and looked at me. "I think to some Indian reservation. I don't know. Like I said yesterday, he doesn't say much—bein' mute and all," she wisecracked. Then she reconsidered, probably remembering my fragile state from yesterday and seeing it now returning to my face. "I'm sorry, that was rude. I wish I knew, but I don't."

"Yeah," I said, a bit startled and thinking to ask her where the Klamath Reservation was, remembering Cherrie Kee's mentioning it yesterday.

"How was the date?" she said coyly then, but I just looked at her. "Good, huh?" And she gave me that sweet, sad smile again from yesterday. "You gay guys put yourselves through way too much." And she shook her head back and forth. Then she patted my shoulder. "Wait here."

She came back with a bag of scones and muffins. "Here, these are day-old; you can have 'em."

"Thanks," I said, stupefied. There was something about that store: the kindness of its strangers, and the fact that I'd been there three times and eaten each time and only paid once. She put her hand on my shoulder: "You take care of yourself, okay?" She must have thought me one fragile flower. I nodded decisively—my A-OK—and she returned to her boxes of canned beans, one of which she proceeded to boldly eviscerate with the box-cutter. And that was that.

I went out the door, still in a daze, clutching Jimmy and the bag of food. And there was the kid on the bike who made me think of one of Jimmy's poems:

> Kids like dogs
> Watching and waiting for big news
> Periscoping from a blissful sea of ignorance
> Give them news while it still means something.

I thanked him for watching my bike and said, "You wanna see a dead guy?" And I opened Jimmy-in-the-bag. "Right here, all burnt up, this is a dead guy. Name was Jimmy." He peered in and then looked up at me with a "no shit" drop jaw.

"You got a mom and dad, and brothers, sisters, friends?"

"Yeah, I got all those." Again, the *why wouldn't I?* look.

"Be nice to 'em, K?"

"Okay then," the little man said.

And I rode away, leaving him one story the richer.

That made two of us.

A little more than a story in my case. Because it occurred to me then, with Jimmy and Eugene both on my mind, that I'd been knocked up and I knew right then what a spirit baby was. And I laughed . . . *Ha, ha, Jimmy. Some things you gotta figure out for yourself.* Okay then.

Go east, young man"—backasswards—but that's just what I did. Over the bridge, and the whispering river, and out of Eugene, into neighboring sulfur-stinking Springfield, where, for the first time, I balked at pancakes (since I had scones and muffins from the market) and pulled into a donut shop, where I ordered a big, bland, highly caffeinated Styrofoam cup of tired, burnt coffee. I found a plastic table in the corner at the window where I could watch my bike, and I began to sip and nosh my scones. There was a little girl two tables over who I smiled at because she'd been watching me from her hot chocolate and slouched jelly donut. She'd watched me pull up, watched me come in, and watched me order, sit, stir coffee, and eat my scones while her mother, pensive, stared out the window at traffic. It occurred to me that if that little girl had asked me what I was doing, I wouldn't have known what to say. But I knew if I showed her Jimmy, she'd understand. So I just smiled at her as I got up to leave, and when I was back out at the bike, I held Jimmy up in his velvet purple bag, and shook him around, and kissed him, and did a little jig, and the little girl smiled like a madwoman, giggling and squirming in her seat before her mother turned and glared.

33

I climbed up and over the Cascades—out the 126, which just happened
to be the steepest route across those mountains. Well, I'd promised.

And then the mist turned to rain again. So I pulled over and put my
ball cap on—that was Jimmy's too: Buffalo Freight & Salvage—and
draped the nylon poncho over my shoulders. I tucked Jimmy up inside
the zipper of my windbreaker, up against my belly—carried him like a
child, I did. In the pocket of me, like a marsupial. All the way up that
winding snake of steep highway, in the rain, cars tailing me around the
curves, stinking of wet metal and rubber, all mixed up with the smell of
dripping fir trees and drenched grasses because around us was just endless forest, great hunks of bouldered stone, an occasional cabin or Forest
Service shed, and the gray churning sky over forlorn, lonely meadows.

Up near the pass, the sun came back out and the birds all made a
racket the way they do after rain, and the meadows weren't sad anymore.
They were all pixie-giddy in fact, and I wouldn't have been surprised to
see little bands of faeries marching about celebrating the ceasing of the
rain. The whole scene filled me with energy, and taking a deep breath of
all the steaming fresh greenness, I stood up on *Chief Joseph* and, pumping
hard on the pedals, made a final sprint for the top.

And when I reached it, it opened like a big picture book to a vast,
weird landscape—a trio of black volcanic cones called the Three Sisters
(I made a wish on each of them) shimmered in the after-rain way out
across a blasted-clean, almost-empty wilderness of black lava. As if the
whole world had turned to ash. Only it was full of tourists wandering

150

about like people lost on Mars, way out there in the rocks, looking around, having abandoned their Winnebagos like spent lunar modules.

I was starving after the long ride and thought of begging snacks from the space travelers, but I wasn't feeling too social. I was hungry all the same and there weren't any stores—hungry enough to eat ash. Mystical mad enough to eat my dead lover for sustenance. Jimmy'd said once in a poem: *I ate the road, mile by mile, like a snake swallowing its tail.*

Hot damn Jimmy and the silences he wrought. The timbre of his voice.

I lolled along, getting my breath back, and spied two apples lying in the ditch off the shoulder of the road. *Manzana* from heaven or some such. I pulled over immediately to pick them up, and as I bit hungrily into them—the sweet juice quenching my hunger and thirst both and running down my chin—I thought I understood Adam and Eve and the whole sorry mess, and I couldn't blame them. Would have done the same. If I were God, it'd be a whole different story, dropping fruit at will. Let them eat apples.

I dispensed with my poncho, tied Jimmy back onto the handlebars and remounted, having boldly sinned, and with renewed vigor, I pedaled onward across the burnt wasteland, half-expecting to see Von Trapp children, cartoon-burnt in their gamboling, singing sad opera arias. But there were only dazed tourists discussing Armageddon and looking for flowers amid just a smattering of plants—withered trees of knowledge. Jimmy.

Soon I was flying, the wind at my face, the looming yellow sign ahead greeting me with its black truck poised on the hypotenuse of a triangle, reading "6% grade" and warning the big rigs. Might as well have said "Grace" for me. An invitation. To flight. The place for lost souls. Yippee!

Down through the wind I went, shifting into high gear and pedaling long slow strokes as I peeled away the miles, coming upon and passing those forewarned trucks and keeping up with a good number of cars as well. I zoomed down arcing arms of pavement under great tunnels made

151

by towering forests, whizzed by pastures that opened so wide I got dizzy watching the torporous cattle who, upon seeing me, startled and bolted away from the road, looking like flocks of birds, all in unison running. Made me whistle it did, made me sing: laughed like a brook.

What had taken me hours to climb dumped me down its other side in forty-five blissful minutes. The slippery slope of surrender. Down into the town of Sisters eventually, which I half-suspected was a lesbian settlement, but which turned out instead to be a jackpot of rangy young men, slinging pizzas, gasoline, and burgers—or shirtless, painting houses and carrying planks, lolling about on corners. Eugene had done something to me alright, and I wasn't so sure I wanted all that back. Hot damn. I went for pizza—and afterward, stuffed and lethargic, I considered finding a motel, but being that there were still several hours of daylight left and trouble brewing in my loins, I headed out of town, hoping to reach the Deschutes River, fifteen miles up the road, where I'd been told by the pizza waiter (man, he had a sweet Adam's apple) that the red circle on my map was actually a state park I could camp in.

I tried to forget the Adam's apple, tried not to think about Eugene, who had a fine one of those himself, along with his other attributes. And Jimmy's—I'd licked it often like the salt lick that it was. In my elation that afternoon, I so wanted to kiss him, to feel his scruffy chin against mine.

And speaking of which, that's what eastern Oregon was once I headed out of Sisters—scruff, sagebrush, stony, and only occasionally dotted with pines and solitary clumps of cottonwoods down in the creek beds. So my imagined idea of a river campsite in a forest dell was clearly delusional, so much so that when I did reach the Deschutes River, and stopped midspan on the bridge to view it, what I saw made me wonder if I wasn't right back in California: a red rock canyon chiseled into the flat landscape around it, dry and dusty other than the ribbon of water, and with just a single cottonwood tree and a few picnic tables. There was a chained-up gate to the right on the other side of the bridge and it was blocking the road that led down to the river, so I guessed that was the state park, which was obviously closed. I rode the rest of the way across the bridge anyway and then up to the chain-link fence, intending to climb over it and have a look around. I leaned the bike against the fence, but just as I began to climb, I heard a woman shout: "Hey, you there!" When I turned, I saw her at the screen door of a small house that sat up on the bluff overlooking the road, and she called out: "You can't sleep by the river tonight. The rattlers are shedding, blind and snapping." I paused, poised on the fence like a cat or a thief, mulling over what she'd just imparted.

She offered me her yard to camp in, but quickly closed her door the minute I assented and climbed down off the fence to take her up on it.

I walked my bike up and pitched camp on her vibrant green lawn under a little grove of birch trees, wholly anomalous to the dry barrenness of the surrounding landscape and somewhat an answer to my earlier wish. I unpacked and fell asleep while it was still light as I was dead-tired.

That night I dreamed of a big buffalo wandering around Eugene, getting honked at by cars and meandering down alleyways, sniffing around in dumpsters, before returning to the bridge and the river and Eugene's graffiti, where it curled up like a dog, preparing to sleep. And it looked at me then, and it had Eugene's green eyes.

Startled, I awoke, on my back and looking up into the stars, which could have been his green eyes as well. Venus all around. Resolving it was just my soup boiling in the night, I burrowed back into my sleeping bag like a little rat. But I couldn't get back to sleep, and then it felt to me like someone was there watching me. I sat up.

The moon was big and lit up the whole yard—*is that you, Jimmy?*—and I could hear the river whispering. I got up and hustled into my clothes. It was freezing cold, and I scurried down the road and up over the gate (I knew enough to figure that cold-blooded rattlers wouldn't be out at night) and made my way down the dirt road past the big cottonwood tree and the shadowy picnic tables to the rocks at the river's edge. The river flowed slow and shimmering in the moonlight, vital, as if it were bringing something—something welcome and abundant—before passing by, making me think it might be taking something too.

I smelled Jimmy then. What was it? I crouched down, shivering in the night air, and took a big whiff of a squat little bush, and sure enough I knew—sage. The kind Jimmy used to burn in the apartment on Guerrero Street and at ACT UP demonstrations. I looked around and saw it was everywhere. I sat on a big flat rock and held my knees close to my chest for warmth for a while, breathing in Jimmy, watching the river flow. I knew I had to jump in. Didn't know why, just knew I had to.

I stripped fast and scrambled up a reddish boulder that jutted out over the water.

I barked when I dropped myself in. Good God, it was cold. I climbed out immediately, muttering to myself that I'm either crazy or I'm not—same difference. Then I huddled on the flat rock like a monkey momentarily, feeling too cold to even dress, with my hands scrunched up at my chest, remembering Jimmy the same way that first day I'd bathed him. I shivered dripping and watching the cottonwood, big slow rollers of night wind undulating its branches and making a sweet night whisper of sound.

"I love you, Jimmy," I shouted, and after a quick calculation, "Day thirty-nine."

Finally, with one last shiver, I jumped up, and in a frenzy dried my skin, hopping about clumsily in the painful gravel as I got back into my biking shorts and piled on my clothes. Then I scurried back up the road, teeth chattering, climbed up over the fence, and made my way back up the road and into the yard and my sleeping bag, where I quickly nestled with Jimmy-in-the-bag, wondering if I should have left a bit of him down there in the stream. But he said "the way he came," which was from Buffalo by bike, and not from Oregon by water. Still, I got to thinking about salmon in a stream and all that, and then about how I took things too literally generally—or too metaphorically, or both, or neither. Arguing with myself, until I was so confused, I had to pull. Jimmy's in the bardo—drop it.

And when I dozed off, there were Eugene's eyes again, which woke me up.

And then that echoing sound of birds in the nighttime started up. Nightingales, I supposed.

Such a moonlit night wasn't about sleep, so as soon as I saw a hint of dawn on the eastern horizon, I figured I might as well get my start. I thought I should thank the lady, half-fearing she'd spied my little transgression, but there wasn't a sound from the house, the curtains still drawn. I got my things together, and once again like a Dharma Bum, I clasped my hands in prayer and thanked the lady and the place both—the moon and stars, the rattlesnakes, the cottonwood and the river too—wondering how strange it was that I'd never seen her eyes, but couldn't shake Eugene's, with all the snakes blind and snapping down at the river that smelled like Jimmy.

34

My friends kept calling to cheer me up, leaving invitations on the machine. Jimmy's friends, Julie and Sam, appeared one night after several unreturned messages. There they were, all in black, showered and beaming.

"We're taking you out to dinner and Uranus."

I managed a smile, but I knew I'd never be able to handle a night out with them. "Jimmy's dead, you guys—*we're* staying in." And I tried to close the door.

"No." Sam's motorcycle boot held the door open. "Come on, Shame." He pushed his way in and the two of them dug up an outfit for me and took me for Pakistani food on 16th Street, where I was overly fascinated by the blood-orange color of the tandoori chicken; it was the only thing strange enough to seem interesting.

We went from bar to bar; I gave it a go. It was great sometimes that in San Francisco you could go to queer clubs that welcomed straight people and that straight people weren't afraid of. But this wasn't one of those times. Because all I could do was scan the room for Jimmy, mesmerized by every dark-eyed gangly boy. Like some particularly tormenting obsessive compulsion, I kept searching, even though the minute I saw one I was full of regret for having even looked. I even hated them a little for playing at Jimmy. Couldn't they save that for another day? Be someone else?

Even when I wasn't looking for Jimmy, there was a huge empty mouth waiting inside the doors of all those clubs. It was in almost every face, and every heartless electronic song. Just because it beats like one doesn't make it a heart. I grew disgusted with the dumb same old dance, drink, blah, blah, blah, take home some sex like a doggy bag. Julie and Sam told me to cheer up, that I should have a better attitude. Great, I've finally gone clubbing with Dr. Pinski. I felt guilty, of course, for dismissing their good intentions. But not for long. Cheering someone up is like "What-Not-to-Do-for-a-Depressed-Grieving-Potential-Suicide 1A." I knew where those clubs would take me as I started to tear up and ask Jimmy, *why'd you leave me here?* I saw the ropes fray and break that connected me to Sam and Julie. All it took was one trip to the bathroom, one cute boy's drug-addled stare, and the hole in the ozone of human existence gaped open to full flower like the speechless, screaming mouth of God himself. I knew my feelings weren't original. Edvard Munch and a few others had beaten me to it, but this was the 3-D holographic version. I pushed through the crowd and got out. And when I hit the sidewalk, I ran. I ran block after block, all the way home. Like a little boy, scared, not knowing what to do—running the same route I'd run with Jimmy.

Home to his bike and the ritual space of our love, which was just four walls and a bay window, an acacia tree and a corner liquor store and a rickety, rusted fire escape, and the smell of Chinese food, and two little boys' too-loud screechings and TV volume, and those forever-blinking multicolored Christmas lights chasing each other all through the strings on *Chief Joseph*, lighting up the ceiling and its plastic glowing stars and planets. And I draped his clothes all over the bike—the battered army shorts and the Red Hot Chili Peppers T-shirt—surrounding it like a makeshift altar with a whole slew of Virgin de Guadalupe candles, which lit up the shelves of dog-eared books, and in so doing, conjured James Damon Keane, who whispered, as always, God bless him, "Pull, Seamus. You gotta pull."

"Can't," I whimpered, on my knees.

Pull.

And not ten minutes later, the lights and sound of an idling taxi yellowed the window, and the clump, clump, clump of Sam's motorcycle boots and the rap, rap, rap on my door.

"You okay, Shame?"

My red swollen face. "We're having sex, can you come back later?"

"Come on, Shame, we were worried about you."

Then a crescendo of Chinese erupts as the twins' mother cracks open her door. I'll have to let them in.

The candles quickly tame them and they sit down on the bed while I grab the bottle of Carlo Rossi jug wine and a few jars to drink from. But they shake their heads. So we just sit on the bed, the three of us, like monkey see-no, hear-no, speak-no all in a row—with me in the middle—and say nothing.

Sam scoots closer and I let my head fall in his lap. But I don't cry. I only cry alone, or with Jimmy, or out on the street. I just stare into the candles while Julie holds my hand.

They exchange looks, and Julie, ever responsible, ruins the silence: "I think we'll stay here with you tonight, Shame."

"No, Julie. Me and Jimmy, we want privacy."

"Shame, you gotta . . ."

"No, I don't."

"Julie, it's cool," Sam chimes in.

I clasp her hand, give her what little I got. If she doesn't understand, so be it. As for Sam, he's loyal, I'll give him that—he digs male intimacy, in a soldier football player kind of way. I snuggle into his crotch, purposely pressing against his dick. I don't want sex; I just want someone who isn't afraid. He pats my shoulder, and sweet heterosexual Sam passes the test.

I look up at Julie, who still thinks I gotta . . . *Pull.* Now I can. It takes two straight people, I realize, where it only took one Jimmy fag boy.

35

I rode into the sunrise, followed it in my backasswards way, since all the time it was sliding right over me, going in the other direction. A backasswards wise man looking for a star over Bethlehem. Bethlehem Steel more like, because I was going to Buffalo.

I came into the town of Redmond in the bracing cold desert morning, passing an old rusted Army jeep on the edge of town as I arrived—how long sitting there? What story untold? What soldier? Whose father? Rusting in peace.

The geometry of the town soon shifted my brain to the left of those endless and unanswerable right-brain conundrums. I rode down streets past curbs and mailboxes and houses all in a row, street corners at ninety degrees. There were traffic lights and stop signs, auto repair shops, feed and grain, markets, gas stations and restaurants, a guy at the Shell station watering his Astroturf—a high school with a sign about the Spartans' big game Friday.

I entered a Hardee's, joined the early crowd, truck drivers and locals jawing about weather, the Spartans game, and the tragedy of Californians moving in with their German cars and fences. I wanted to chime in that I felt the same way about Californians, but I *was* one, and a wacked faggot one at that, so I thought better of it. Besides, they didn't even acknowledge my existence. They're yammering, that's all, that's what geezers in small towns do.

Listen o nobly born . . .

I watched out the window as the sun rose and the town's shadows headed for cover. I was happy to be in a warm place after that ride this morning that woke me with its chill like no amount of caffeine ever could. Out on the street, I could see the old men in their pickups holding their coffee cups, looking cozy, lolling down the main street at 10 mph. There was dew-soaked sage growing in the lot past the parking lot and bright-eyed green signal lights over the intersection, swinging in the morning high-desert wind. I'd been delinquent about pancakes, so I ordered two plates of them to make up for yesterday. The father, the son, the holy ghost, plus Ralph, Eugene, and the spirit baby—a pantheon of male love.

I left the waitress a three-dollar tip, imagining she was the woman by the river who'd put me up for the night and saved me from the snakes. And I headed out of town past a couple more big cottonwoods and through the sagebrush, scrub, and sand-diamond-sparkling-something in the pavement on the shoulder of the road. *The garbage and the flowers.* Looking ahead into nothing because the sun was blinding me. I could just see a gradual rise in the road, a gray strip leading into sagebrush nowhere, smelling of Jimmy. I heard a truck bearing down the grade before me, but I couldn't see a thing, just a blotch in front of the bright ball of the sun. I knew that soon enough I'd hear the chugging wind-down of the hydraulic brakes as he slowed down to enter the town, huge and blind as the future, carrying a full load of whatever was in store.

Jimmy came to California.

36

I went to visit Jimmy, but they wouldn't let me in. I gave the flowers to the security guard, who sort of held them out in front of him like a soiled diaper.

"What am I supposed to do with these?"

"They're for Jimmy, the guy in there." I motioned with my head.

"This is a morgue, sir."

"Well, you can give them to your girlfriend if you want." Hot potato. I wasn't carrying them home.

I assume he threw them in the trash, as marigolds aren't romantic enough for your girlfriend. She might think you're dumping her.

So all I really had was the pay phone.

Other than those hourly phone calls, I just stayed in bed, staring at Jimmy's bike. Or rather, it stared at me.

I'd promised, but I stalled, stayed in bed, grief-frozen. Waiting. Waiting for Jimmy. To tell me what to do. Even though he already had. Though the last thing he'd asked of me I hadn't done. I hadn't killed the man I loved.

Jimmy's father never called, of course, but Monique finally did.

"Mr. Blake, I have some news for you."

"Yeah?"

"Uh, Mr. Keane—your friend James—?"

"Yeah?"

"He actually did the paperwork. You don't need to call his family. He's got it all taken care of. He filed all this six months ago." And she read: "'In the event of my death, I hereby request my body be disposed of by cremation.' And he paid the fee." Doing what needs to be done.

"How much?"

"Eight hundred dollars, Neptune Society."

"When you gonna do it?"

"It's done."

"What?"

"Don't worry. Day four. I held it up for you." Dear Monique and her sweet subterfuge of the big ugly acronyms of county government.

"Oh, thank you, thank you . . ." And I kept thanking her to stave off the tears.

I hung up before she shattered me with the sweet honey of her voice.

Monday I had to go get him, the dust of him.

Jesus Jimmy, to dust you have returned.

You *ou didn't take me with you, Jimmy, but I can still take you with me.* Chattering away, my soup and me on the bus with Jimmy in a cardboard box on my lap, like the sweet baby Jesus.

I sat in the bay window on Guerrero Street with that box in my lap for a long time, looking out at the pay phone, the corner liquor store with its comforting, constant golden light at night and in the rain, and at the acacia tree next to it, buckling the sidewalk. Too big, and I knew one day they'd come for it. They—like the collective God in Genesis— and their giveth-ing and taketh-ing away. They got Jimmy, and they're gonna want the tree and the liquor store one day too—and they'll come for the twins, who'll soon get big, fearful, and opinionated; and they'll come for this big bay window on Guerrero Street like they'll come for me.

162

37

I reached the Ochoco Mountains within an hour, rising up east of town into pine forests. So much for my dream or delusion of sagebrush forever after my previous delusion of Douglas fir forever. One delusion leading into the next like Biblical begetting.

It had gotten warm, almost too warm, and fast. But I felt a breeze as the pines thickened and the elevation increased, and I looked at them as if I were passing cattle or milling people and I wondered about them and what the future held. They might end up as baseball diamond benches that only really bad players get to know, or as coffins, forging a lonely intimacy with some stranger. I hoped that they appreciated that we didn't put Jimmy in a pine box. Which got me wondering about the fuel they used for the incinerator. Probably gasoline, not pine planks. Jimmy, my Vietnamese Buddhist monk. Imagine if all those downed by the acronym burned themselves like monks in the street. A new kind of Gay Pride parade. Floats of burning monks. Even Ronald Reagan would have had to have said *something*. But the acronym is forever a symbol of how the kindness—let alone the attention—of strangers is a rare and special thing indeed.

The pines thinned out in time, just like my friends had done. And my father's friends before us. And back into the rocky desert I went, with its post piles of orange stone, deep canyons cutting into the flat plain, clefts of shadow, and those ubiquitous yellow flowers growing in the gravelly silver and pink dirt. Hardly anyone on the road but me and the bugs. And it was warm and quiet and very empty, and sometimes—a lot of times actually—in the middle of all those sad musings, in all that vastness, I felt strangely happy or peaceful or something.

You were right, Jimmy—*road's the place.* . . .

38

Looking over at Jimmy-in-the-jar on the mantle, I realized I needed to find something to put him in for the journey. I remembered he had a velvet sack, Jimmy did—purple as I recalled—and I rooted around for it. He'd kept his drug paraphernalia in there: a bong, roach clips, pipes, papers, rollers, all that. I had an inkling it was big enough to hold Jimmy.

But I couldn't find it, and I was knocking over boxes in the closet, which was filled with all our junk. Even though Jimmy and I had almost nothing in the way of possessions, we had boxes of crap: papers, art supplies, books, I don't know what—clothes. The past. I knew that bag was in the closet somewhere, in a box. Buried. There really wasn't anywhere else it could be. It was a studio after all: one big room and one big window and a fire escape. Otherwise, we just had a mattress and box springs up on cinder blocks, scavenged bookshelves, my folded-up easel in the corner, a stained round table and reject café chairs with missing legs from dumpsters (Jimmy hammered on two-by-fours and got them to stand). All our kitchen stuff was from thrift stores: random knives, spoons and forks, bowls and tumblers, mismatched pepper and salt shakers. Our clothes lay in piles.

Because the closet was full of boxes.

Frustrated, I ended up with my back to the wall, my knees up, face in my hands between my legs, about to lose it.

Pull.

I gave up on the velvet bag, and went out to get a cup of coffee. Where I ran into Lawrence.

"Hey, Seamus." Lawrence's gratuitous hug. "How's Jimmy?" The faux sincerity, eliciting my passive-aggressive response.

"Dead."

"Wow, I'm sorry."

"Yeah," I sighed.

"You wanna talk about it?"

"No thanks," I offered, as nicely as possible, before turning and ordering a coffee from the cashier.

But Lawrence insisted: "You gotta make it into art, Shame."

"Nah, Jimmy's too big for that," I said, handing over my money.

He looked at me, vexed: "I'm serious, Shame." I didn't respond, walking over to cream my coffee. I knew he meant well. He believed in art as the solution to everything. But I'd never painted Jimmy; I'd never photographed him. Jimmy'd always been uncontainable—he'd gotten loose in my life like a toxic cloud, bled through the window casings between my dreams and waking life, between thoughts of him and thoughts of every mundane thing from peanut butter to a bar of soap. Jimmy'd put Cristo to shame because Jimmy was art on the scale of creation, and that's why I had to take him back and out on the road. He was an unfolding story still, an ongoing dynamic event between my psyche and the world it called home: a genie out of the bottle. I had to go find him. What could I say? *I'm taking Jimmy on a trip. He's taking me. We're going off traveling together.*

By now Lawrence was pulling the front of his pants down a bit so I could see his underwear's elastic band: *Wouldn't You Really Rather Have a Buick?*

I didn't smile. "You being careful, Lawrence?"

He nodded impatiently, too quickly.

"Be careful, Lawrence." I hugged him.

166

"I'm having a show . . . ," he informed me. But it trailed off as I barked, "call me," knowing I'd long since stopped answering the phone, interested only in the message machine's refrain. Of course *he had a show*, of course he likely wouldn't call anyway, of course none of it mattered. San Francisco was over.

I went home and decided to clean, which meant all those boxes—and my remaining Marie Antoinette paintings—ended up on the fire escape. And after I'd gotten them all out there and the coast was clear, I dropped them one by one onto the sidewalk, knowing that in San Francisco it would all be rifled through and scavenged within the hour. The last box hit a previous box, lurched, and completely spilled its contents onto the street. And out popped the purple bag.

"Jimmy!" I shouted, and down the stairs I ran.

I was almost too late. There was a punk girl pilfering already as I careened out the gate and bounded down the three steps. Even the twins had emerged.

"Don't touch the velvet bag!" I shouted.

The twins stood back, excited at my urgency, while the punk girl just looked up at me, mid-rifle, holding my zafu against her chest like an algebra book as I hopped over and grabbed the bag out of the box she'd been scrounging in. I emptied it of its drug paraphernalia, which clattered onto the sidewalk. But something big wouldn't fall out as I shook it, and when I reached in, I found a hardback book: *Bury My Heart at Wounded Knee*.

Strange title, like it was talking to me. *But where's Wounded Knee? And why are you asking me?* And then I thought of Tony Bennett and how he left his here. Where was Jimmy's heart? Upstairs in a mayonnaise jar. Now that I'd found the bag, maybe I could cremate the book too and take them both?

I opened it then and all crammed in among the pages were Jimmy's maps—the ones he'd shown me that first night together—with their red highlighter squiggles marking his route and circles for where he'd stayed. And something else too. There was a hole in the book, shaped like a dollar bill that went all the way through it so that it was as if . . . as if . . . someone had already taken its heart and replaced it with—money?

But the money was gone.

Where'd you get the money, Jimmy?

Riddle solved.

"What is it, what is it? Let us see," screamed the twins, hopping up and down like rabbits.

"It's a treasure map, boys."

And I headed back upstairs with the book and maps, the twins hot on my heels, pleading, "Can we come? Where's the treasure? We'll get a shovel." Silenced to muffles by the slammed door.

39

Eventually, I reached a small town called Prineville, and I was back in sagebrush high desert with its grasses and occasional pines. I found a diner, and while scarfing a burger and fries, I noticed a banner across the street announcing that the Prineville Public Library was having its annual sale. As I always liked to walk around a bit after eating, I headed over to look around.

It was pretty much what I'd expected: bin after bin of cheap trade paperbacks and best-seller-caliber hardbacks with glossy jackets: Danielle Steel, Judith Krantz, Tom Clancy, Michael Crichton, and Jackie Collins. What a world.

Then I saw something I didn't expect: face out, once again as if talking to me, was that book that had asked me back in San Francisco to bury its heart. I'd never considered reading it, and couldn't besides with that big hole in the middle of it, so I'd ended up burning it in the fireplace and had put it in a little stuff sack and packed it, with the vague notion of granting its wish if I ever came upon Wounded Knee.

I picked up the book and flipped through the table of contents, and it was like Dorothy waking from the dream of Oz. There was Chief Joseph and Crazy Horse, and Sitting Bull and the Sioux and the Klamath that Cherrie Kee had mentioned in reference to Eugene. I bought it for fifty cents.

And I sat down on the curb next to my bike and started to read. *Listen O nobly born to what I tell you now* . . . Yet another book of the dead.

I'd never been particularly interested in Indians. I didn't like those old movies. The Indians were always running around too much, chasing people and making annoying war whoops. They made me nervous. Of course, I knew vaguely they'd been screwed royally by a Manifest Destiny–obsessed acronym that I was a member of—but I'd never been curious about the details. Like my mom that way. She didn't know a thing about 'Nam or what the father of her child died for. Better not to consider what God and country were capable of.

I leafed through the Edward Curtis photographs. Wow, those Sioux were hot; I mean they had some presence. A bunch of dandies with a lot of confidence. Fabulous outfits, with seashells for armor and lots of feathers. They even called themselves birds, and they called themselves something else too . . . a horse people, a horse nation.

And I sat there for two or more hours, on the curb, in the shade of a little tree, reading about the Sioux, about the broken treaties, the subterfuge, the greed for gold, and the killing of the buffalo. It had the makings of a seriously tragic opera from the start, with a final aria by Custer, or Crazy Horse, or Sitting Bull, or all three. The Sioux were nobody's fools, and over a series of years they won not just battles but an actual war against the acronym, burning down all the American forts in the Powder River country and forcing the acronym's army to retreat and even sue for peace. And here I thought Vietnam was the first war they lost.

The Lakota's (the Sioux's real name in their own language) world seemed to be the greatest expression of freedom—a way of life that was in no way limited or confined by others. In battle they counted coup. It wasn't about murder or annihilation or genocide so much as making a hit (coup) or getting the enemy's horses and women. Almost like a kind of sport, but a lethal game. And even the bluecoats acknowledged they were the best horsemen they'd ever seen.

And then Custer came. In the nick of time. So as to ruin everything once and for all. A sort of backasswards Jimmy, complete with blond dye job. Because after he died, it really came down on the Lakota, and

Crazy Horse and Sitting Bull and all the rest of them were on the run and eventually killed or corralled onto reservations, which led to starvation and, of course, Christianity. Same difference. A people who'd only hunted buffalo and gathered berries and talked to the sky were told to farm and go to church. Red Cloud even tried to be conciliatory, but in so doing his people soon became victims of propaganda in the press, the greed of agents and politicians, and the needs of the disinherited from all over Europe. (To think that these people had everything in common, and they killed each other anyway. Pawns in someone else's game. Same as it ever was.)

And then the appearance of the ghost dance from a Paiute who came from out west, and how the dance spread like a crazy religion: paint yourself white and dance, and the white men will vanish and the ancestors will return—and what's more, while you're dancing, you'll be invincible and no one will be able to kill you. All of it ending in a ditch in the snow, the white men gunning the ghost dancers down. That place was Wounded Knee, and they say that's where Crazy Horse's heart is buried in an unmarked grave.

What happened to the Indians sounded a lot like what had been happening in San Francisco. And the grandfather in Washington—yet another—with all his hosts of acronyms, and not a one of them cared. Let 'em eat ketchup; let 'em eat pills; let 'em live in the Badlands (no matter whether it's a not-very-interesting gay bar in San Francisco or an uncultivatable South Dakota desert of clay, rock, and sandstone—and not a buffalo in sight). And all those gay clubs—just a ghost dance.

I next read the story of Chief Joseph, who was Nez Perce. A once upon a time: the quiet little valley and the peace-loving people, the ugly fag medicine man who scared the whites, and the whites getting all hot and telling them to move away from their ancestral home, and the Nez Perce saying no, and the whites getting threatening, and the noble Chief Joseph saying, "Okay then, we'll go." And the soldiers saying "you got ten minutes" or something ridiculous, and it wasn't enough time, and so the people hurried, but the soldiers attacked them anyway—and then the long thousand-mile, three-month pursuit and all the clever maneuvering by Joseph, and finally the speech in the snow: Chief Joseph said, "From where the sun now stands, I will fight no more forever."

I crossed the street to a minimart for a forty-ounce bottle of Crazy Horse malt liquor—a gesture of respect in my strange backasswards way. But I looked twice at the twenty I handed across the counter: the face of a man who spent a good deal of his time killing Indians—including the one who had saved his life—glared back at me.

Blood money.

I jammed the forty into my left pannier and unfolded my map, hoping for a campground, my mind on the Sioux and Eugene and Jimmy and Crazy Horse, all of them mixed up in the muddled opera of my head—the soup of it.

The book had said Crazy Horse held out till the bitter end (not even a photo), for in his vision this world was a dream, and in it he could endure anything. And I remembered then what Jimmy had said when I'd asked him how he got interested in Buddhism.

"Crazy Horse."

I'd thought it another of his enigmatic answers then. Which it was. *Some things you gotta figure out for yourself, Shame.*

Well, I figured out this much—Edward Curtis would have done Jimmy justice. Handsome motherfucker. We needed an Edward Curtis for death by acronym. The San Francisco *Bay Area Reporter*'s little passport obit photos just didn't cut it.

And something else too: I knew where Wounded Knee was now, and when I looked at the map, I saw I was heading straight for it.

40

I hadn't the heart to tell my mother Jimmy was dead or even that I was leaving. The last time I'd visited, she'd made us Russian tea and snickerdoodles. Comfort food. All wrapped up in paper and bows, sitting on her little entry table, where she'd always put my sack lunch when I was a little kid.

"Mom, he can't keep this stuff down. He'll throw them across the room just like last time."

She looked slighted. But she'd never even met Jimmy; she wasn't "ready," she'd told me. And not because of the acronym, she assured me. No. It was about him being my queer lover. White lie.

"And when will you be ready?"

"Oh honey, think of your father." And she'd reached to uncork a bottle of Chardonnay.

"What about him? Was he homophobic too?"

"No one's homophobic," she'd snapped.

And she wasn't. I knew that. Thing was, Jimmy was "short." And she'd done short. She wasn't doing short again. That was the reason; I knew that was the real reason. But she couldn't say it.

When Jimmy had been hospitalized with pneumonia—*he'd* said plenty and how he'd moaned. "This sucks. I don't want to do this hospital thing." Horses are supposed to be shot, after all. Jimmy was right to be mad at me; horses shouldn't have to shoot themselves.

173

"Seamus," he muttered, "I wanna go home; take me home."

"No can do, Jimmy. Not just yet. Soon, Jimmy, soon." And he'd already fallen asleep by the time I'd finished speaking. And there I was in an ugly white, antiseptic room with its plastic and its steel and its utter emptiness and un-hominess—like some public bathroom or a BART station. That's when it first hit me that I felt abandoned by my mother. My mother didn't do sorrow—not this kind; not again. She just put on a face, smothered by a sorrow that didn't even have its teeth anymore. All bottled up—pun intended—signed, sealed, delivered. Soldier's wife. I could have used a friend then, but she'd have none of it. I was forever a kid to her. That was final too. And kids don't have adult problems. It occurred to me that if my mother called while I was in that hospital, her message might have been something like: *All done, honey?* Like Jimmy was my steak and potatoes or something.

Yeah, I'm done alright. And I'd cried then in earnest, and that attracted a nurse, and God bless her—the nametag said "Jill"—she did what was needed. And she took me down for a cup of coffee and we didn't say much—just small, sad smiles. Blanche Dubois can say what she will about strangers, but it's the kindness of nurses and political activists and small children that I counted on.

"Where are you going?" Jill asked.

"I'm gonna go home."

"Is someone there?"

"Oh yeah, lots of people." And I faked a smile, because it was a white lie. There were only our spirit children at home: Little Joseph, Elmer, Genevieve, and Victoria. And the acacia tree, of course, the buckled sidewalk, the golden light at the corner liquor store, the screech of the little twins, the rattle of the window when the bus passed, the emptiness of the fire escape in the big bay window, and *Chief Joseph* sparkling in Christmas lights.

41

It was already dusk when I finally left Prineville; I couldn't stay there. In the book, Indians had called paper "talking leaves," and something about that image and Andrew Jackson on the twenty and all those books was nightmarish. I watched the loosed golden leaves of cottonwoods blow across the road in front of me, whispering, creepy—an old, old song.

There wasn't a car in sight, in either direction. And eventually, five or so miles down the road, I came upon an old drive-in movie theater, the pavement all turned up and full of weeds and brush. A ruin. I bet they'd shown some westerns there. The speakers still stood like skeletal parking meters, and the screen too, enormous and singular in the flat surrounding landscape of sagebrush and yellow clumpy flowers. It was peeling, and looked to me like a great unnoticed and unrecognized portal to some other world—like that big black rectangle in *2001: A Space Odyssey*. Because other than it, there was nothing but silence, and just a small breeze playing in the weeds among those scattered speakers, now and again rippling the big white screen. An ideal place to camp. It looked like any world but the one I just came from.

I leaned my bike against a speaker and laid my sleeping bag down where the pavement had deteriorated to dirt but was still nice and flat. I sat there, holding Jimmy, propped up against another speaker, and looked up at that old tattered screen, wondering if it had anything left to say while I nursed my bottle of Crazy Horse like a self-satisfied infant.

Enormous in its silence, white as a ghost, the wind made it dance to a hollow, forlorn song. I looked at it until I was nearly blinded by its blankness and sleep both, and that's when Jimmy's face, like a mirage, filled the screen in those moments between wakefulness and slumber. Vivid he was too with the big brown eyes and say-nothing smile, the dark scattered chin scruff, the Adam's apple and turned-up nose, the tattoo for good in front of his ear, the third eye and the golden angel's hair. And then Jimmy morphed into crow-black-haired Eugene, and then Eugene into sighing stoic Chief Joseph, and from there all the rest of those chiefs from the book: Red Cloud and American Horse, beautiful with their mouths set and their chests bejeweled with shells (I'd seen men like that—Jimmy, his chest covered in pearls); Dull Knife and Sitting Bull; Spotted Tail and Hump, with their set, dignified frowns. And all of them with Cherrie Kee's hawk nose and Eugene's penetrating eyes.

Finally, a painted horse came flying off the screen in 3-D and I startled awake, knocking over my forty-ouncer, knowing then I'd come to Crazy Horse—the screen a blank because he never allowed anyone to take his picture.

I got up and climbed into my bag, and when I fell back to sleep I dreamed the monolith was an enormous tree with white leaves, moving in the wind. Talking. But I couldn't make out a word.

Next morning, I couldn't ignore it as I packed up. Kept my eye on it, I did. Riding away too, looking back over my shoulder—kept my eye on it like I had the Campanile Tower at U.C. Berkeley and Mt. Shasta. A pillar of salt. The truth and the past looming and leaning down over me, the heavens on bended knee—God wants to make love, the old lech.

Or is it death who's horny?

Well whoever or whatever God is, he gets his man. Every time. Same difference.

The holy ghost.

—dance.

42

My mom and I went out for lunch and I told her I was leaving. She gulped a rather substantial swig of her Chardonnay, picked up her napkin, and dabbed her lips before responding.

"Is that a good idea right now?"

"He asked me to, Mom."

"He asked you to leave?" She looked perplexed, but in fact she just wasn't listening or was arguing in that odd way she had of turning everything she wanted to challenge into a question.

"He asked me to take his ashes back home."

"Is that reasonable?"

I took a deep breath. "It's not about reason, Mom."

She sighed and gave me an annoyed look. "Well, Seamus, it should be. You're a man now, you're not a boy."

"Actually . . ." But I wasn't going to take the bait. I had brought her here to tell her, not to ask her, not to explain even—and not to argue about everything else. It was a courtesy as I saw it. I was still mad at her for never having bothered to meet Jimmy, for failing me as a friend. "Yes, Mom, I'm a man and can make my own decisions."

"Do you have the money for the flight?"

I didn't need to tell her I'd lost my job. Fortunately, I'd be getting Jimmy's deposit back for the apartment or I'd have been too short to go at all. "I'm not flying."

The question of her face is not the question of my face. Hers is more of a vexed and suspicious, almost fearful, *what-are-you-talking-about?* face.

"I'm taking his bike."

"His bike?"

"He asked me to."

And she said carefully, looking at her salad, "Well, honey, he may not have been in his right mind."

"His mind was very right, all the time. He was never demented. And you'd know that if . . ." I stopped myself.

She didn't take the bait either. "Oh, well I just think that's an awfully complicated way to do it."

I wasn't going to say the road's the place for lost souls. "Well, I'm complicated, right?" Then, seeing she was in no way reassured, I smiled and reached out my hand to touch her arm. "I'll be careful, Mom, don't worry." I'd always done what I wanted to do. She knew that about me. "I'll call you every few days."

"I would like that."

I smiled and she gave me a clipped smile back. And then I chanced it. "What did you do when Dad died?"

She inhaled and then drained her wine glass. "I was pregnant. . . . I couldn't really think about it. . . . It was probably good you came along. I had something to take care of." She gave me her small clipped smile again, which meant "enough." Okay then. We paid the bill and stepped outside, where I hugged her goodbye, tried to give her a Jimmy squeeze, but she cut our hug short. She'd raised me is what she'd done. Doing what needed to be done. Like Jimmy that way, I suppose. Never thought I'd see them as in any way alike.

"I love you, Mom."

"I love you too. Be careful, Seamus."

And off she walked to the BART train to disappear under the bay. I watched her in her gray overcoat. The booze had aged her. To think she

178

was a sixties girl once. Oh well, she'd survived. I wondered if I would. Jimmy hadn't. My dad hadn't. Lots of people didn't.

If my life had been a music video, I would have belted out a tune from 1969 . . . *Take it . . . take another little piece of my heart, now baby . . .* We could have sung it as a duet.

But my life wasn't a music video.

She was so hard to reach. And I couldn't do what she'd done. No way, no how. She'd put her whole youth away when my father died. Boxed it up—literally—and put him in a frame and mythologized him, went back to church, became a mother, and settled in for the long haul. She'd held on to only the music. Well, that was something. That I could understand and appreciate, even though my mom and I hadn't sung to each other since that fateful thirteenth year.

As for me, I had no church to go back to; and I had only dolls for babies—no, what had been born in me called me away, not home. And Jimmy wouldn't let me make him into anything but what he was. He wasn't a war hero or Chief Joseph—he was a nobody like me. He wasn't a myth—he hadn't died for anything or anybody.

Jimmy was just a promise now.

But I could sing for him, sing of him. Like my father, he too was a song:

I've seen fire and I've seen rain . . .

43

The next day I saw Jimmy crucified in a church in a town named Dayville. It was dark in there, and I mistook the J-man for sweet Jimmy up on the cross. One more skinny, put-upon man, out to save my soul.

Dayville was a swell ruin of a town in every way, in a little glen of cottonwoods where the road jogged up and over a small hillock before twisting down into the one-street burg, past a defunct and oversized Odd Fellows Hall, and a couple of four-story brick former banks or hotels, much too grand considering the town's size. But more important, there were those giant bough-heavy cottonwoods, splattering shade all over the road, and promising the little river that flowed somewhere beyond. I knew Jimmy'd been here because he'd circled it in red on the map and written a poem about it too called "Places Named for Time":

Not a where, but a when.

The sweat cooled on my face as I hit the shady spots because Eastern Oregon was all sun in September—three days running of cool mornings and blasted hot afternoons.

I ate at Ellen's Diner coming in and going out. In passing. Through. Where I tripped the bell that hung from the top of the door as I entered that hot afternoon of my arrival, jonesing for pancakes, which I was now eating for dinner as well—albeit with Coke instead of coffee on account of the heat. There was a counter and stools and four or five

180

tables lined up on the opposite wall. The single customer, a husky man in his midforties, was drinking coffee on one of the stools. He put his cup down and said, "Howdy there," while a woman I presumed was Ellen said, "Good afternoon," expertly produced a full smile, and thrust a menu across the counter at me where I'd decided to seat myself, two stools down from the man, who then barked, "Where you from?"

I had that sinking feeling that he was going to be one of those small-town characters intent on getting the skinny on me as if that were his and everybody's business. I didn't mind so much, but he wasn't giving me a ride, and I was tired and had a bad shoulder ache that day and a crook in my neck. I took a deep breath and answered that I was from California, which was almost as shameful as being queer to some of the Oregonians I'd overheard in the past few days.

"I was in Sacramento once and Frisco too, back when I was in the service." I looked at him to gauge his age, so as to place him in whatever particular war before responding. He looked to be my father's age.

"Were you in Vietnam?"

"Yup. You ride that bike all the way from California?"

"Yup."

"What are you doing a fool thing like that for?"

I wanted to answer that I *was* a fool so it was in character, but I restrained myself, saying instead, "It's the best way to travel—not too fast, not too slow."

"Not too slow?" he raised his brows incredulously. Then he craned his neck to look out at my bike parked at the plate glass window under Ellen's arcing red name. It arced the opposite way that her smile did when she looked at you, and I wondered suddenly if she were a sad woman. "How fast can that thing go?" he persisted, again incredulously.

"Fifteen miles per hour max, I'd say. I move along at about ten or twelve most of the time, so in a ten-hour day I can cover just about a hundred miles."

"That's a fair distance, but no competition for trains and trucks and airplanes, and . . . you know—whatnot," he guffawed, before taking a sip of his coffee. He turned to Ellen then. "Ellen, would you agree this boy is crazy? Ha, ha, ha." He laughed heartily, in a friendly way. If he only knew.

"Yes, Carl, I'd agree," she said with a clipped, uninterested smile, as she wiped the countertop and asked me, with just a hint of sarcasm at Carl's expense: "So what will our crazy California man have for supper?"

I smiled and ordered pancakes. She raised her brows, and I smiled.

Carl turned toward me again and asked: "Why are you having pancakes for dinner, and why do people do these fool things?" But before I could answer he went on to say that Ellen made great burgers and that he saw no reason to leave home. He'd left Dayville once. "Just once," he lifted his finger, "to go to war. That's when I was in Frisco and all that. After my tour, I came right back here and haven't left since. I don't understand why people don't just stay home."

I felt it would have been presumptuous to answer him really, and it was all rhetorical besides. But he looked at me then, and I formulated an answer, which I didn't give him: *I'm more or less crazy, I'm a homo and Jimmy died, and I promised him.* Instead, I nonchalantly answered that I guess I just liked to travel.

"You ever been to Vietnam? That'll kill the travel bug. Hot and humid, bugs, damn fungus and disease everywhere, cold in the mountains—lot of people don't know that—and all around, just plain unpleasant. And ugly as hell," he guffawed again. "Maybe I'm just lucky to be born in the most beautiful place on earth. Wouldn't you agree, Ellen?" He raised his voice since she'd already disappeared into the kitchen.

"What's that, Carl?"

"Dayville's the most beautiful place on earth!" He smiled at me as he said it loud enough for her to hear.

She came out with my Coke. "It's beautiful here, yes." She seemed tired. And I wondered what she really thought; what her dreams were; where would she rather be? I felt for her that she had to tolerate his banter. Not that he was a bad or rude guy. I was even sort of enjoying his chatter—once I'd gauged it was really more about him than me. But

Ellen had probably gotten tired of his manly bullshit months, years—even decades—ago. What was pleasant for a morning cup of coffee at Ellen's, knowing you were moving on, was just not the same thing day after day over a long period of time. Then again, this was a small town, so I supposed people had to put up with each other somehow.

She raised her eyebrows. "Refill?" I'd just quaffed the giant plastic bucket of crushed ice and Coke in two or three gulps. And after I nodded, she added, "Pancakes'll be up in just a sec."

"Thanks," I muttered, my cheeks filling with air as I subdued what would have been a resounding, even echoing, belch.

There was a lag in the conversation, which naturally caused Carl to look again outside at my bicycle.

"You rode that thing all the way from California?"

I nodded sighfully. "Yup, and I'm going all the way to Buffalo, New York."

He whistled. "Just for the heck of it? What's in that bag?" He looked at it lying on the counter next to me.

I sipped my Coke and sat back. He really wanted to know? Maybe I *was* hitchhiking, since this was Carl's diner on some level—his town—and I was gonna have to pay in chitchat to sit in it. I'm only a white liar, and I didn't want to bring up Jimmy, so I stuck to death instead.

"My dad died in 'Nam," I said, with some reticence, dumping the conversation back in his lap. It was always risky to bring this up, especially with a vet, as the ones I'd met either felt very protective of me on account of my dad, or else they'd go off on fucking gooks and tell endless tales of macho prowess. Either that or they were traumatized, in which case they'd not say another word. I could have told him I was a lost soul and that I was transporting the dead. I could have told him I had no idea what else to do and my heart was broken. Instead I dodged him with my dead daddy. And I immediately felt guilty for it.

"I'm sorry to hear that, son," he said quietly, respectfully, sitting up straighter. "It was hell over there." Now, he got thoughtful. "I got lucky, spent most of my tour in supply. Where'd they get your daddy?"

"Some place in Quang Tri Province," I answered.

"Jesus Christ. That place was hell. I'm real sorry, son—Ellen, I'm gonna pick this up." And with that he yanked out his wallet. Say what you will about Oregonians' dislike of Californians, I was being given a lot of free food there. I thanked him. And he quickly changed the subject.

"Well, what did you do before you got on this bike?" And he indicated it with a gesture of his head.

Who are you, and what were you before?

I wasn't about to tell him I took lousy photographs, painted irreverent Marie Antoinettes, fucked a lot of boys, met and took care of Jimmy until he died, and tutored small children—between visits to my shrink and slinging coffee. "You know, the usual stuff."

"What line of work you in?"

"Uh, . . . teaching."

"What age?"

"Little kids," I said softly.

He nodded, "Well, I'm a handyman myself. I can fix just about anything, and I'm still as strong as a young man. My back's in good shape. I'm lucky. That's my Chevy half-ton out there. Just got it a few months ago. A beautiful vehicle."

"It's nice," I muttered, peering out into the street at it (big and beige and typical).

"So you're gonna ride that bike all the way to the east coast? That's amazing. I don't get it. Ain't you got a girl or something back there in California?"

"Or something." Would my mother count? Jimmy-in-the-bag?

"Ah ha, so that's it!" And he laughed, leaning back on his stool. "You're trying to mend your broken heart out here."

I just smiled. You don't know the half of it, Carl, and I can't tell you for fear you'd run me down with that half-ton of yours, dead daddy or no. Either that, or he'd be one of those small-town queers, or not-queers as the case may be, as he took me home and plowed me with expletives through the night in his doublewide trailer. My next question would answer that.

184

"Is there a campground around here?"

Carl started describing some place by the river (relief)—a jumble of "left at the mailbox, then right past the old barn . . ."

But Ellen interrupted him and said, "You can stay at the church—they always put the bikers up there. We're on the route, ya know."

"Well . . . ," and he shrugged, surrendering his effort to answer my question, and looking husbandly put-upon as she proceeded to go into detail about how to find it, and who to talk to once there.

I had an urge to ask her if she remembered seeing Jimmy last year on his way through here. I was wearing his clothes after all—the same Red Hot Chili Peppers T-shirt, the same army cut-offs and hightop shoes. And I wondered if he'd stayed at the church. I tried to remember the poem and what it mentioned: *Dayville, Weekville, Monthville, Year/ Gravity, Einstein, I'm a queer* (or was that just my doctoring and Seussing of it?).

Ellen continued, rousing me from my poetic reverie. "Dayville is on the Bikecentennial route. We get bikers every single summer."

"Bikecentennial?"

"It started in '76 as a bicentennial celebration, and it's kept up since. 'Course the season's pretty much over." And she smiled, adding, "You're a straggler." Sure am, I thought, grinning at her. I could have hugged her.

Didn't dare.

I thanked Carl again for picking up the check as he said, "See you in the morning." Was that an invitation? Then I picked up Jimmy like a purse and went outside and walked the bike down the street to where Ellen told me to, spying the small steepled chapel on a hillside above the road, surrounded by trees—elms and alders, and those ubiquitous cottonwoods. As I walked my bike up the gravel drive, a short, thick little lady came out, with a *what-do-you-want?* scowl on her face. I told her Ellen had mentioned that bikers sometimes stayed nights at the church and asked whether that was true. She nodded her head suspiciously, sizing me up, and turned around to lead me toward the church, without a word. Christian charity, I thought. Thank God for it or a person like her would never help me out.

She started pointing things out along the way: "That's a mulberry tree; that's the cesspool valve; that . . ." And then she turned, and looked at me sternly. "What's that on your shirt?"

"Uh, . . . it's a cross. Of sorts." But she wasn't gonna buy that. "A rock and roll band," I admitted sheepishly. She shook her head, clearly disgusted. I thought about how bad it smelled too and hoped she hadn't caught a whiff and that the church had a sink to wash it out in.

St. Andrew's Presbyterian Church was a small white A-frame with a blue slate roof. Next to the church, connected to the side of it, was a meeting room, where we now headed. When she got to the door, she pulled out her keys and, putting one in the lock, turned to look at me again, suspiciously, as if I'd transgressed somehow.

I just smiled. "You seen this shirt before?"

She glared, but didn't answer me.

Inside the meeting room were tables and a countertop with a coffee-maker, foam cups, creamer, a stapler, some scotch tape, and assorted coffee mugs—and bingo, a sink. The room was decorated like a class-room, with the usual Christian art: 1970s-era macramé, children's drawings, paper construction, lots of nature calendars with innocent scenes of butterflies and rabbits, and sometimes children with butterflies and rabbits—and crucifixes of course.

The lady looked at me and said: "You can lean your bike on the counter there and sleep here."

I rolled my bike across the linoleum-tiled floor and leaned it up against the counter before asking her, "May I see the chapel?" She looked at me as if to say *what for?* Then, overcoming her hesitation, she led me through a darkened doorway into the shadowy little church with its tall, column-like stained glass windows on either side. Three wishes coming right up. But would they count in a Presbyterian church?

Same difference.

"You got the Lord?"

It sounded like another disease, in which case it should be rendered in all caps, with periods in between: L.O.R.D.: the acronym. I wanted to say I got Jesus-Jimmy-in-the-bag.

"I was raised Catholic," I answered. Trying to pass. But Catholicism isn't much better than Satanism to some Christians, and I suspected too late that that might be the case with her. She just stared, and led me back out of the chapel.

"You been born again?"

"I was raised Catholic." Not taking the bait, not going to be bullied. I could go sleep outside, down by the river where Satan was blind and snapping like the rattlesnakes of Redmond.

I took a deep breath.

"You oughta read the Bible," she said, pulling one out of the drawer and placing it next to the coffee machine. "Gotta get right with God."

I inhaled again and held my tongue. She was putting me up (or rather the church was), so I'd cork it until she left. C.H.R.I.S.T.I.A.N.I.T.Y.: it's not so much the thing itself, but the side effects that kill you—the opportunistic infections of misinterpretation and politics—and the parasites that come with it.

She kept right on looking at me, and that's when I thought that maybe she was mentally slow. "I'm glad you found something that helps you," I feebly answered.

"Helps me?—I'm saved," she exclaimed confidently.

"Well, I'm doing my forty days and forty nights," I answered her.

"You read the Good Book there. It'll help you." On a whim, I pulled out *Bury My Heart at Wounded Knee*.

"You ever read this book?"

"I only read the Good Book."

"This is a good book," I insisted. She looked at it perfunctorily. "This is a book about faith too. Faith in the U.S. government."

"Well, we all suffer for our faith," she said dismissively. At least she got my meaning.

"Well, we suffer with or without it," I added.

187

"And no point in suffering for nothing," she replied. "For the faithful, there's a reward."

"Didn't work that way for the Indians."

"They had faith in the wrong thing." True that. And she pointed to the Bible again. "That's the word of God, not your silly Indian book."

"Well, I like history."

"The Bible's got history in it."

"But it's not mine."

"It's everyone's history."

"Not the Indians'." And I wanted to add: "not the queers', either."

"Sure it is. God's story is everyone's story."

"Well, now, that we can agree on." I smiled and thanked her and turned toward my bike, hoping she'd get the hint that the formalities were over.

"You have a good rest," she concluded, looking severe. She then headed back over to her little house nearby, sheltered by a clump of trees, looking back frequently. But I felt lucky I didn't look like Jimmy—his tattoos and piercings, the dark eyes and dyed hair. I wasn't clean-shaven, but I hardly even had a beard—and though I smelled carnal, and the shirt was a bit disturbing, I was just not a scary-looking person.

I resolved that I had to sleep in the church, just had to. So I pulled my sleeping bag off my bike rack and took it into the chapel, where I laid it boldly out on the altar like a picnic blanket. That's when I spied the minister's vestments hung up in a closet half-opened in the far corner of the chapel. As I neared it, I noticed a single gold thread hanging off the bottom of the black one, and I went to pull it. But I stopped and thought I'd check the bike first and see if Jimmy'd already done so—and if so, I'd know that he'd been here.

I went back out into the meeting room and searched the bike frantically, and after a few minutes, sure enough, there it was! On the center column, under the seat. He was here! He'd grabbed a thread off that very vestment. I'm sure she remembers the shirt! I'm the second coming. Full circle. A closed loop. Jesus Jimmy.

I heard a knock at the door then. Quickly, I gathered up my sleeping bag, hauled it out of the chapel, threw it down near my bike, and ran to see who was there. But it wasn't the little lady, as I'd feared. Instead, an old man stood at the door, with a long beard, wearing sunglasses and a baseball cap with crystals and precious stones sewn into it, forming a sort of shimmering garland around his head.

"Hello," I said. The question that was my face.

"You on a bicycle?" he asked.

"Uh, yeah . . . the, uh, lady said I could stay here." But he pushed past me into the rectory before I could finish.

"Let me show you something," he said earnestly.

"Okay," I answered, at a loss.

"My name is Woody." And he quickly sat down at the biggest table, opened his backpack, and pulled out a box of gemstones and Indian arrowheads.

"I'm Seamus." But he didn't seem to care about that. He was a man on a mission.

"Sit down here," he ordered me. He explained, as he dug through the box, that he was a prospector by trade. He proceeded to tell me story after story involving old mines he'd unearthed, crystals he'd come upon, Indian burial grounds he'd discovered—secret places no one knew about except him. And now me. And—I was beginning to suspect—all the other thousands of bikers who came through this town.

He gave me three buffalo-bone arrowheads, and then he stood up. "Don't lose these." And he held my hand in both of his. "They will protect you. Why, if it weren't for these arrowheads," referring now to the whole box, "I'd be a dead man. There's kids around here who shoot at me. They always miss, of course, thanks to the arrowheads."

I didn't know if he was talking crazy, but I had a sense it was all at least *based* on fact. He was eccentric enough to be one of those old-time prospectors, and kids did run around with guns out here (my count of gun racks had surpassed my trip-long pancake count in one afternoon). Having been a kid, I could immediately see the reason why kids would harass a man like Woody. He had that outsider-freak-homeless look that kids, in their own insecure way, liked to make fun of, as if to test the powers of their success at human mediocrity. Likely, they used BB guns, but who knows? I wanted to tell him that I was crazy too—that it's okay, I understand. But what was it that Tolstoy could have said, but didn't? *All sane people are the same; all crazy people are crazy in their own unique way.*

He let go of my hand, wished me luck, and slipped out as fast as he'd come.

I looked at the arrowheads, remembering Eugene's medicine bag, and the mural he'd drawn under the bridge. I wished then that I had a little bag to hang around *my* neck. Well, I had Jimmy-in-the-bag, best luck I ever had—but way too big to hang around my neck.

I put the arrowheads in there with his ashes—*good luck charms from Woody and Eugene for the both of us, Jimmy. Good luck on day forty-one in the bardo.*

Then I thought about him here in this room as I pulled off my shirt and filled the sink to rinse it and wring it out. Thought of him sitting at that table, looking at Woody's crystals with his big brown eyes, his brow furrowed with interest.

I hung the shirt over the back of a chair and took my sleeping bag back into the church and spread it out on the altar again and crawled in. And I wished I could hold him; I wished he had a body still. My hands grasped longingly at the velvet bag. And I thought suddenly how morbid it was to be arriving in all these places where Jimmy'd been—with him but not *with him*, separated by time and space . . . *the mirrors still busy with his presence. . . .*

Disembodied. A ghost.

I thought of Eugene then, who did have a body. Indeed. And it made me feel guilty, but I wished I could hold his; I wished I could hold somebody. As full of people as it is, the road's an awfully lonely place.

I dozed off, but when I awoke in the middle of the night, that church was solid black, not a smidgen of light anywhere. So dark, I wondered if

I'd gone blind. I fell back to sleep and dreamed I was in a confessional. "Bless me father . . ." And then I recognized the silhouette through the screen. "Jimmy?—I'm sorry, Jimmy; I'm sorry for letting you down." He pulled back the screen—looked hot in that collar—and blessed me in Latin: *In nomine Patris, et Filii, et Spiritus Sancti.* And for penance? *Better luck next time.*

I woke with a start, and it must have been getting close to sunrise, because I could see the inside of the church emerging from shadow all around me, the stained glass coming to colorful life. When I looked up at the cross, I saw Jimmy was on it. I sort of startled then and got up to make sure it was Jesus on the cross and not Jimmy. Upon closer inspection, the long shoulder-length hair gave him away. But I got up on my toes and kissed his feet anyway.

I heard the church lady at the door then, and I hurried to get my things out of the chapel as I heard the lock click. She'll think it a sacrilege for sure that I'd slept on the altar.

We met as I entered from the chapel and she from the door.

"Where'd you sleep?" She eyed me suspiciously.

I cannot tell a lie. "Uh, in the church." I fished for words. "It was warmer in there—I mean cooler." She stared at me suspiciously, and then past me toward the darker recesses of the chapel. I almost wanted to share with her how I'd seen a beautiful boy named Jimmy hanging from the cross. But it was so ironically difficult to share a Christian moment with a Christian that I just sighed.

I was still shirtless and felt obscene, so I grabbed my T-shirt and yanked it over my head, disappointed it hadn't completely dried.

"Hope that Woody didn't keep ya up." She kept looking past me toward the chapel—expecting what? The refuse of my satanic rituals? The burnt offering was right there in the bag.

"I should have warned you," she went on, "he always comes around when there's people staying here."

"It's okay, he's a nice man, and I enjoyed talking to him. He gave me some arrowheads."

"Poor soul," she stated.

He'll be inheriting the earth, I wanted to tell her, but I wasn't going to get back into all that. She was already glaring at the unopened Bible as I tied my shoelaces. My cue to say adieu. So I thanked her and wished her all the best and got out of there. And she stood with her hands on her hips as I pulled out of the gravel drive on my bike, calling after me, "The town of John Day's just over that next hill there." She pointed, adding, "God bless."

So Jimmy'd been wrong about Dayville. It must have been named after this John Day character. But perhaps he too was named after time. Like most places, as it turned out, Dayville was named for just another john. The earth's a whore and the conquerors are all johns—sounds like something someone once said, but I don't know who. Me perhaps.

I wondered then if there were a town named Jimmy or Seamus somewhere. There certainly was a Eugene.

I went for pancakes at Ellen's and made small talk about the church.

"You meet Woody?"

I nodded.

"Poor soul."

Et tu, Ellen?

She looked off into the middle distance. "He lost his wife, and his mind went with her. Used to be a regular guy."

Death will do that, I wanted to say. I thought of the arrowheads then—gifts from a crazy brother. Three bones, three wishes—I'd never need the services of a church again. And I thought of Jimmy then too, up on that cross—winced at how it turned me on. I contemplated how he'd look and I enjoyed seeing his body in my mind: the limestone-green paleness of him, the dark hair in his open armpits and at his waist, the vulnerability of his nipples, his torso stretched. I thought of how I got turned on to a crucified Jesus once in a church and had asked my mother why he was so scantily clad up there.

"Well honey, it's hot in Israel . . . and it was a different time, they wore different clothes . . . and they'd been beating him, so even if he had a robe or something, it would have fallen off."

"Don't you think that his loincloth probably fell off too, and that he was probably really naked when they crucified him?" I persisted.

"Well, I don't think so, honey. You shouldn't think about such things. God doesn't walk around nude."

In nomine Patris, et Filii, et Spiritus Sancti. I gobbled my trinity of pancakes, gulped my coffee, and listened to Ellen talk about all the other bikers she'd met while she stared absently out the window as if waiting for some half-ton that would never come. "Church groups, family reunions, biking clubs, people raising money for cancer . . ."

. . . lost souls?

I asked Ellen then: "Where's the Klamath Reservation?"

She motioned with her head. "Out by the coast. They're salmon people." *Et tu, Klamath?* This was getting weird.

I pulled out my wallet then, but Ellen shook her head. "Carl's already out on a job, but he wanted to get this for you."

I nodded. "Please thank him for me." Her sad smile.

A dog followed me out of Dayville. I shooed her, but she wouldn't let up, and after I'd left the town a half-mile behind me and nearly reached the river, I stopped and tried to send her back home. Not that I knew where that was, but I figured she must live in town. Who knows how big a dog's territory or wanderings got out here. But she just wagged her tail, having made up her mind she was going with me. So be it, I thought, and told her I thought she was acting like a dumb dog, disgrace to her species, all that. When I reached the river, she stopped and stared at me as I crossed the little bridge, and then I felt bad for scolding her. She'd known where her stopping point was all along. I left her there, and she watched me for a long time. And I wondered if she recognized the bike, the shirt, wondered if maybe she'd remembered the scent of Jimmy.

44

If it was time for goodbyes, then I owed the kids at the Y a visit too. I'd neglected them, which is a rotten thing to do to little kids. I hadn't even explained, and kids don't sit around surmising on death and taxes, so they probably just thought I didn't like them anymore.

Nothing could be further from the truth.

There'd been calls of course from Mandy, the coordinator of the Afterschool Program, when I'd stopped showing up. None of which I'd answered. I simply listened to her messages and then waited to call back at 3:00 a.m. a week later when I knew she wouldn't answer.

"My boyfriend died, Mandy. I can't deal with the kids right now. Sorry. I'll give you a call in a while."

I hadn't heard back from her, until the very day I decided to go visit. On my way out of the house, I checked my mail, and there was the envelope in Eustacia's perfect script. Inside, condolences on some cheesy dime-store card decorated with white flowers. All the kids had signed the thing, which read something like "In your time of grief, know that you are in our hearts . . . yadda, yadda, yadda." There was Eustacia's beautiful script again, Ivan's name misspelled "Ovan" for old time's sake; Miguel's scrawl; Win's frustrated *W* and *I* connection in cursive; Mo's enormous (each letter of a different scale), moniker with first, middle, and last name, taking up half the card.

Why'd you go and do that, Mandy?

I had to go back upstairs. On the floor, back to the wall, my knees up, face in my hands between my legs. *Pull.*

But there was no way I could go visit after that card.

I didn't dare.

Sorry kiddies. Better luck next time.

45

Carl was right. It was the most beautiful place on earth. All morning I rode through rolling hills with big orange rocky cliffs off in the distance, the sun bright and rising toward noon. I'd lucked onto a good road with little traffic, and the pancakes and coffee and warmth had cheered my mood, so it was just me and Jimmy and the world waking up, bleeding out into the endless empty places that stretched so far in every direction around me, I'd get dizzy in the looking. But something sad trailed in my wake too—my mind on how these were all places Jimmy had passed through and left behind, never to see again. I was running back across it all, erasing them for good, like some old words left behind on the blackboard of Jimmy.

I thought about him, looking down at my legs and feet as I pedaled: his dark hairy shins, dirtied with grease from the bike chain making these same motions. He saw all the same beautiful places, smelled the same sage and juniper, felt the same sun, heard the same hawks crying out in the sky. I felt then he'd given me this. This whole world out here, like a parting gift.

Two hours later, I was pumping up a rise, having reached the high red cliffs I'd been watching in the distance, when ahead I saw a blue pickup on the shoulder, with its hood up. Stalled, I supposed. As I got closer I could see a long-haired man working on the engine. And then—I couldn't believe my eyes: what looked like Eugene came spilling out of the passenger door with a wrench in his hand.

"No way!" I said out loud to myself, stopping my bike abruptly a hundred yards away. It can't be him—that would be like Jimmy smoke rising right out of the bag like a genie. Genies, like churches, who offered three wishes: Eugene, Eugene, Eugene.

I coasted forward toward the truck, like a wary dog, my heart banging around like how it had the day I first set eyes on him. He didn't see me at first, as he'd hopped around front to give the wrench to the man working on the engine. But then his head popped up, and looking like a dog himself that could see movement in the distance, he walked out into the road eyeing me as I slowly approached, still nearly a hundred yards down the road.

"Eugene!" I called, uncontrollably smiling, and that asymmetrical grin of his erupted across his face as he recognized me and came running down the yellow line in his clunky army boots and the same black hoodie from our night together in Eugene. I pumped harder on the pedals so as to reach him—and when I did, I nearly spilled myself off the bike, braking abruptly and throwing out my arms. We hugged over the handlebars, Jimmy right at our crotches. And I felt Eugene bleed into me. I didn't want to let him go; I wanted to tell him about the dream where I saw his eyes and the buffalo and about him on the movie screen and how sorry I was about Custer and all them; actually I wanted to say nothing and just take him over into the ditch and make love there for an hour. Let my body tell him, let my mouth and eyes and hands and feet and arms and legs and cock tell him everything I had to say while he did the same. Not a word.

I loosened my hold though, considering he wasn't alone, and I was mystified besides at what he was doing out on this road in a broken-down truck. This was *not* the way to the Klamath Reservation.

"Where you goin', Eugene?" I asked, perplexed. He pointed east down the road, and I smiled then—I guess because we were going the same way. And then he held his medicine bag to his chest, and what that meant I couldn't say, other than wherever he was going it must be somewhere good and meaningful to him.

197

I got off the bike and walked it up to the truck, where I leaned it on the back fender. Eugene grabbed my hand then and took me up to meet the other man, who was just out of sight, working on the engine and obscured by the open hood. I was a little nervous and tried to disengage our hands, not sure who this man might be. But Eugene just clasped my hand tighter—and though skittish, I was glad.

The man came up from underneath, like from right out of the engine, when we approached, grease on his hands and grease on his forehead. Looked like Ash Wednesday to me, and I had half a mind to ask him if he were Catholic in my nervous wacked way. He looked to be in his forties, clearly an Indian, with long hair tied back in a ponytail, a bit of a paunch, and wearing an old blue T-shirt and Levis.

"Hi," was all I permitted myself to say, wondering how to explain to him how I knew Eugene.

"Who are you?" he said bluntly, with an expressionless demeanor.

"I met Eugene in Eugene," I answered, aware as I said it of how stupid it sounded.

"Good place for it," he said with a clipped smile. I wanted to add that Eugene and I had fucked each other silly in a frat house, and that I couldn't get him out of my mind—and that I was awfully sorry for history, and all that—

"And what are you doing out here?" he interrupted my racing thoughts.

"On my way to Buffalo."

"Ha, ha, ha." He laughed heartily. "You and me both." I didn't get what was obviously a kind of joke—I was more focused on hoping it was true. When I looked at Eugene, he didn't seem to be in on the joke either and just stared blankly. Then there was a silence, and the man went back to work.

So I offered: "You need any help?"

He lifted his head again, and this time, with a bit of surliness, said: "Why, you knowledgeable about Dodge straight sixes?"

Of course, I hadn't a clue, and it apparently showed. "Uh, no, not really."

"Not really, huh? But a little bit?"

"Well, actually . . ."

He finished the sentence for me: "You don't know shit." He paused long enough for me to feel insulted. Then he began laughing: "Ha, ha, ha." He slammed the hood down, brushed by me, and opened the driver-side door. But before hopping into the cab, he paused suddenly and looked intently at my bike, then briefly at me—at first with suspicion and then with a faraway look in his eyes. Then he hopped in and turned the ignition, and after a *chee, chee, clump, clump*, the engine caught and roared.

"Hop in, Smoke," he called to Eugene, and I saw the man's face framed in the rearview mirror staring at me.

It was a look of mistrust. And why was he calling Eugene Smoke? What's Smoke? Is there a town called Smoke around here, and will his name change from place to place? Will he be John Day by the time he reaches the next town? Austin by suppertime? When they call him Buffalo, I guess I'll know my journey's done.

Eugene or Smoke, or whoever he was, kissed me quickly on the lips, grabbed hold of my bike, which was still leaning against the soon-to-be-departing truck, and held it out to me. Then he ran quickly around to hop in the passenger side door, as the truck began rolling through the gravel. There was a clunk, a backfire, until finally the engine roared to life again.

And then it was Eugene's face in the back window, smiling his crooked smile, getting smaller and smaller. I thought momentarily to hop on my bike and ride like hell to catch up to them. But that would be futile. As it was, they were a portrait: the faded, creamy blue truck on a little rise in the highway under big pink and orange cliffs, with shadows slashing across the road in front of them. Two orange men in a blue truck in an orange world scattered with gravel and dusty little blue and yellow flowers, flat sandy stretches, and a sun bright and searing, the rosy rocks spreading out for miles and forever around them. And those blue-black manes of theirs like two black crows perched on their heads.

I realized I'd once again obtained no information, was just as unlikely to see Eugene again as the last time. Which made me suddenly angry. Like he was playing with me. But it wasn't that, and I knew it. He just didn't say. Plain and simple as that. He was the boy who just didn't say.

And I felt pathetic on the side of the road with my dead Jimmy, having been laughed at and mocked and stared down by Eugene's friend or whoever he was. Maybe it was his boyfriend, and he'd been jealous of me. And now he'd taken Eugene away for good.

Am I a jilted bride? A jilted widow? Both?

I'm carrying his baby! I wanted to call out.

Pull.

I felt like that dog back in Dayville, but with nowhere to go back to. Or maybe I just hadn't reached the end of my territory either. That would be Buffalo, thousands of miles beyond.

Pulling meant moving, and fast. So I rode hard through those canyons, which were heartbreakingly beautiful. They even looked like a broken heart, all orange/red and falling apart, creviced, full of flowers and sometimes little trickling streams. One step ahead of my soup—or one pedal rotation actually. And when I finally got to John Day, I found a café and ate a sandwich, and on my way out of town, picked up two forty-ounces of Crazy Horse (my brand from here on out) and gulped the first while I pedaled, sans hands, as I headed toward Jimmy's red hoop, up and over the Blue Mountains, which rose, but not too steeply, over the lonely sagebrush desert ahead. It was unwise to drink, of course, midday in the heat, but I was feeling wacked and unsteady.

I felt a jumble of emotions about Eugene, hence the drowning measure taken. I was shell-shocked by his sudden appearance, and I wanted to know where he was going; I wanted to spend an hour with him at least, a day, a month. I wanted to make love to him; I wanted to talk to him, but how could I? How had I let him get away? I was mad, excited, sad, surprised, grateful, even frightened. Like I'd conjured him. Or maybe it was just that spirit baby, kicking like mad inside me.

And into the great empty quarter of America I went. Like a bottle of malt liquor or a boy's asshole, America is. Sing that, Walt Whitman. *My country 'tis of thee . . . Oh, bountiful.*

Slowed down by the drink and the ruminating, I still pedaled on, eventually coming upon a campground at a place called Unity Lake, just short of Jimmy's bull's-eye, which was up the road ten or so miles in a town called Ironside. Good God, must be rusted to hell, I thought. "I couldn't take that tonight," I muttered. "Fuck it, I'm staying here."

Unity Lake was obviously some kind of reservoir, as it was this enormous flat body of water in the middle of a plain of scrub and sand. The campground was a parking lot surrounded by golf course–like grass, all heavily watered by sprinklers. There were even solar showers. It was like a paved platform in the middle of nowhere (like the *2001* slab again, but this time fallen flat on its face), and it was lousy with geriatrics in Winnebagos.

I found a spot as close to the lake as I could, which wasn't very close since the campground was set a good hundred or more yards back from the lakeshore—the green, green grass in between. It must be a drinking water reservoir, I guessed. The lawn looked inviting to sleep on, but the sign said "NO." I crossed it and sat down along the lakeshore a long time thinking of Eugene and how odd it had been to see him, and wondering if I ever would again. Maybe they'd break down again. It was an old truck, after all.

I heard the familiar honk of geese and watched a group fly over in their V formation, always one of them straggling or off to one side. It meant an early winter, I vaguely remembered from a TV show or somewhere. It made me a little nervous being that I was traveling by bicycle and still had most of the country ahead of me.

As the sun dipped, I re-crossed the lawn and looked toward the highway off in the distance. And I'll be damned, I saw the blue Dodge truck floating there on the horizon, moving east fast. I must have passed them somewhere? I couldn't believe I'd passed them and not seen them. Where? In John Day? While I was buying my Crazy Horse malt liquor?

That'll teach me not to steal shadows. I was full of a sudden yearning, and a huge disappointment both. All I had left was to watch and see if they'd slow down and turn in here—but they flew right by. My elation sank, considering the idea that it wasn't likely I'd see them again at all now. If I'd only obeyed Jimmy and his red hoops I'd be up on the highway in Ironside and maybe even having dinner with them. I had half a mind to hop back on *Chief Joseph*, and with the sound of a U.S. Cavalry trumpet in my ear, pursue them into Idaho and beyond up into Canada.

Backasswards.

Pull, Seamus.

I drank the other Crazy Horse instead, and when I pissed on the lawn in the last rays of the setting sun, it was a stream of blue diamonds over the green.

"Hoka hey," I muttered. And to think they'd reduced him to a forty-ounce bottle of malt liquor. The alchemy of America at work: turning a good man to booze. Product that moves. And how many people purchase these forty-ouncers with just that intention: *as good a day as any.*

Eugene was awfully skinny. Maybe he was carrying the acronym too.

But he was just so orange, nothing peaked about him.

He looked starved, though. And why was I so attracted to that? That precarious look of being right on the edge between life and death—a weird vitality that seemed to speak against the evidence. They may not be here tomorrow. Skinny boys always got my attention.

Perhaps I just liked bones. And I thought of Jimmy's bones, his pronounced clavicles and handsome chin, his brows and cheekbones, his knobby knees and elbows, his long fingers and knuckles, and how he had one rib that stuck out—all of them did in the end, but this one was bent and protruded from the start. He'd told me once as he got thinner that we couldn't have sex for a while. When I asked him why, he said that we were both so skinny that our bones banged together and he was bruised. "Like two skeletons having sex," he'd said.

And what's a bicycle but a skeleton—this one wrapped like a mummy with untold stories. Shadows.

That night the stars came out thick in big bands like they had once over Mt. Tamalpais when Jimmy and I had camped out there in the oak trees, drinking beer and reading Baudelaire.

He was somebody to talk to, Jimmy was, and that's why I kept on talking to him even after he was gone. I held him in my lap and out loud told him how the hills above Unity Lake looked like black velvet under the starlight and how the lake's rippling waves were silvery. I told him how cool the grass was now that the sun had gone, and how enormous the sky. I told him how much I loved the night air, how it tasted like his kiss after drinking cold water. Like a promise. I told him I missed him and I told him I thought it had been a good thing to make love to Eugene. That it had made me feel close to him again in the doing of it. That he was right: there were messages in attraction. And spirit babies.

And then I thought how I'd never see either of them again and how the road is indeed the place for lost souls. And I thought of what a lost lake that was too—lost in place and time. It seemed like it needed someone to help it find its way back home, to where it came from—like Jimmy and that Indian book's heart. Where *did* this water come from anyway? Had those geese carried it all drop by drop from some tundric plain up in Canada? Had they inadvertently dropped the whole sorry thing one fall? Maybe the geese would come back for it in the spring, take it back to where it came from, drop by drop. And maybe it didn't matter. Didn't matter that things were lost. They're just as well lost as found—so what? Same difference. Everything's lost, and everyone too, and that's as it should be. Jimmy never meant to put me down by calling me a lost soul—he was just saying I was someone with potential. It was a compliment. The only good soul is a lost soul, and only a lost soul can find its own way home.

And all that night, the geese passed over honking their forlorn call, the lake unable to call back up to them, mute as a boy who doesn't talk.

I counted them like winged black sheep as I lay there, massaging the crook in my neck, unable to sleep—named them even, one by one: James Owen Blake, Jimmy, Eugene, Sam, Julie, Tanya, Lawrence, Ralph and Carl, Karen Blake, Ellen.

The last thing I did was make shapes out of the stars, which turned into me and Eugene having sex—Orion's belt unbuckled, Orion's cock spurting shooting stars like fireworks—until I dozed off and the sparkling heavenly bodies sprouted wings that led to dreams of birds. Not migrating birds, but birds of prey, soaring and diving, landing, silent and watching like hawks, perched on fence posts out in Oregon, the wind ruffling the feathers on their heads ever so slightly. Watching, watching, somehow watching over—in the way of birds.

I woke up to more birds—sparrows and larks, busying themselves around the campground. The seniors weren't yet stirring, the curtains on the campers all pulled closed, while beyond them in every direction, emptiness spread until it ran into mountains. Above, a sagebrush sky— the kind of sky where all the clouds are just tiny and clumped and scattered in a random kind of order, going on and on.

It looked like forever.

And it felt like Jimmy. Jimmy, who was never forever but made me feel what that was. I opened the bag and ran my hands through his ashes. He's like an instant universe. Just add a little water, and we'd have a big bang right here.

I cinched up the string on Jimmy-in-the-bag and gathered up my gear and headed out, warming up as I reached the highway. In no time at all I was in Ironside, where there were screaming kids in a schoolyard on the edge of town, swinging, looking like pendulums or oil pumps, all out of unison, but in some kind of utter harmony. Kid power.

The town was also loud with wind, and dogs and chickens and birds and kids, their voices blown about and disconnected from them. People raised their voices to shout across streets, and big rigs applied their hydraulic brakes, slowing down as they came into town. A cacophony of strange birds.

I ate pancakes in a saloon.

Beyond that town, everything changed. There was suddenly big agriculture: immense green swaths watered by enormous pinwheel-like irrigators, and lots of brown people doing the heavy lifting and picking. Distant water tank trucks lumbered about down the dirt roads among the fields, and I could see that without the water being brought in (and the Mexicans), this place would be absolute desert, as it became, abruptly, at the very point the fields ended. But the sagebrush sky didn't end, and neither did Jimmy—nor the road. All I had to do was look up, look forward, or remember, and it would all blast outward like a neutron star and take me away.

The highway connected with another highway, and then things speeded up and crowded up considerably as a big billboard loomed, welcoming me to Idaho. The road became a parade of trucks full of potatoes and onions, and Mexican farm workers in old AMC Hornets and Oldsmobile Cutlasses and Chevy Monte Carlos. It felt like California. Even the requisite big houses began to appear on distant hills, high above the shacks that housed the laborers. Then Nampa with its rail yards and thrown-up chain motels, the land plundered, nature pushed aside—you could see the neglect in open, littered lots. It was the usual American scene: once the city comes, nature goes from a glorious and beautiful young creature to an old bag lady or hobo, wholly derelict, neglected and spit upon. Urban gravity sucks everything down, sprouting acronyms and poison in its place. So much for my own private Idaho—this was a public bardo.

I was suddenly overwhelmed with anger, ranting to myself about how wrong it all looked. Like, no wonder we're obsessed with child molestation. Maybe the earth's our daughter, or son, not our mother at all. Not Gaia, but Gai-ita or little Gai-ito—Guyito, a sweet little Mexican kid with pesticide cancer and a whole phalanx of white power-mongers denying him medical benefits while fondling his innocence because his parents are crooks for being illegal even if they are working long hours for low pay so everyone else doesn't starve. Used up and thrown away. Death isn't a tragedy necessarily, but a trashcan for a coffin is. My father got a Hefty lawn bag with a zipper, Jimmy got a box, then a jar, and now a velvet bag. The Sioux got a ditch in the freezing snow. Guyito—what'll he get? He'll end up some robber baron's piñata.

And thank God for my revitalized libido or I would have spiraled into further miseries as my soup roiled and boiled. But all those Mexicans out in the fields were actually making me horny and got me thinking about Eugene. The way they stood around, or looked at me from the backs of pickups, silent, watching—like birds.

I kept an eye out for the blue truck.

And trucks there were, long lines of them, bearing down, blasting their warning honks and whooshing by me. I felt like raising a fist—little old Woody of the road. Damn kids!

All the way into Boise like that, haunted by Jimmy and Eugene both, as the farms turned to houses in rows, and then into boulevards of strip malls and motels, not seen in such profusion since California.

I found a liquor store, a pizza parlor, and a Motel 6, and with my bike on my shoulder, hefted my gear up the stairs to room 206, showered and shaved, turned on the TV, and then climbed into clean, cool sheets and belted back my Crazy Horse while jawing on a pizza, wishing Jimmy was in that bed with me, or that Eugene would knock on my door and we could fuck away the emptiness and forlorn loneliness that all highway motels are so swollen with you can see why murders and suicides favor them.

I dozed with the pizza box full of crusts sliding off my lap, and I dreamed of those AMC Hornets and Monte Carlos out on the road. I'd come up on them and pass them and look inside, and one would be full up with Edward Curtis Indian Chiefs from the book: Red Cloud and American Horse and Sitting Bull and Chief Joseph, all wearing baseball caps and work clothes, crammed in together, off to find work in the fields. And one guy way over in the corner, his face shrouded by a sweatshirt hood—Crazy Horse, sure thing. The next car would be bursting with boys I'd slept with: Alejandro and Tran, Lawrence and Sage. Then a Cutlass riding so low to the ground, there were sparks.

And inside that one: Eugene and Ralph, Jimmy and my mother. When I looked in the rearview mirror I saw my father's face and startled awake. It was 5:00 a.m., too early to start out, so I sat and watched the highway for a while from my window like my mom and I used to do while waiting for the bus or someone to come and take me somewhere. She used to tell me: "Just listen to it, Seamus:

Whoosh, whoosh, whoosh, vroom, rattle, whoosh, buzz, vroom, buzz, whoosh, whoosh.

"Sometimes you can hear a song, Seamus. If you listen real close, there's a song in there."

46

I put Jimmy in the purple velvet bag, hammering on the bottom of the second mayonnaise jar to get him all out. Then I tied him to the handlebars upfront where I could watch him—and of course, talk to him.

Jimmy masthead, like the prow of my ship.

I'd been slowly giving the furniture away, but there was still a bookshelf and a dresser full of clothes, which I lugged piece by piece to the curb. *Our little world sure went fast, Jimmy*—and I had to wipe a tear.

I kept just the clothes I'd need, and I wadded them up to cram them in the panniers—half of them Jimmy's, including the baggy shorts and the Red Hot Chili Peppers T-shirt he was wearing the day I met him. Because what I needed was Jimmy, or to be clothed in him anyway. Jimmy fit me, and I fit him.

Clearing the mantel, I came upon the envelope with the pictures in it of Thomas and Franco. I looked at them again with young, black-haired Jimmy. I thought of Jimmy having sex with them, what it would look like. They'd touched his beautiful body, they'd held him, caressed him, kissed him. They'd known what I'd known, and so I thought then that they were my brothers. And those were the only pictures I had of Jimmy besides, so into a pannier the old stained envelope went.

47

I owed her a call. So after pancakes and a good dose of seven or eight cups of overcaffeinated Denny's coffee to give me courage, I dialed my mother at home, where I knew she wouldn't be. Some courage.

"Hi. This is Karen Blake. Leave a message at the beep and I'll call you back."

Every time I tried to tell you . . . all the words just came out wrong . . . so I'll have to say I love you in a song . . . "Boise, Mom. All is well."

Click.

I'm sure I was irritating her, but at least I was checking in.

Lying too, because Boise was a terrible place for a bicycle, as are most cities. And it had the added distinction of having only one highway out of town heading east. An interstate, which after two miles and a flat tire, I decided was something I'd never attempt again. The shoulder was a mess of broken glass and litter, chunks of truck tires and car parts, because the speed of the interstate produces a shrapnel all its own. Garbage, but no flowers. And if the wake of wind behind a truck is bad at fifty miles an hour, it's plain unnerving at seventy or eighty. I pulled off at the first exit and set myself up to hitchhike at the on-ramp.

A wheat farmer in a spanking new red and silver Ford F-150 picked me up not long after. He talked about the Basques in the area and how he "dickered" with them in selling his wheat.

"Dickered?" My imagination ran wild.

"Yeah, with whiskey. Means negotiating a price." I'd done that. Dickered with the spirit of life (that's what whiskey means. I'd learned that in Health Ed.—some old Scottish word, I think).

"What are Basques doing way out here in Idaho? Aren't they from Spain?"

"Not if you heard them tell it. They got a whole nationalistic thing going. I believe they consider themselves the first Europeans or something like that. Their skulls are shaped like Neanderthals or some nonsense. I can't follow it. Anyway, they know their wheat."

I looked at him a little suspiciously.

"First Europeans, eh?—like the Indians of Europe?"

"I don't know about that."

There was silence for a while and then I asked him: "Isn't Chief Joseph from around here somewhere?"

"Not actually, no. Nez Perce are from Washington originally, but they've got a reservation up north" (and he gestured with his head) ". . . near uh . . . Lewiston, Moscow—up that way. And there are a couple reservations east of here." He looked tired in the telling, but also like the kind of guy who liked to be thorough.

"What are they like?"

"Poor."

"It's tragic, isn't it?" Two white guys talking.

"They played their cards wrong, as I see it."

"In terms of dickering?"

He grinned. "They didn't dicker very well. They were better at fighting."

"Well, what about all those treaties? No one dickered fair with them."

"Don't start in on all that. Where are you from?"

I knew saying California was an admission of guilt, so I pulled one out of the hat: "South Dakota."

"The Dakotas, eh? Good wheat country."

"Yup."

"Whereabouts?"

"Uh, Rapid City."

I hoped he wouldn't start asking for details.

"Then you know all about Indians. You got them Sioux out there."

Shaking his head with bitterness, he was.

I just looked at him, my face a big question.

"I used to work for the bureau years back."

"FBI?"

"No, BIA." *Here we go again*, as our moronic ex-president liked to say. The dance of the acronyms. I hummed Tchaikovsky to myself while they flowed like water from his mouth: AIM, USFM, GOONs, DOI.

Holy acronyms: Sorrow and grief seem to follow in their wake. He was at Wounded Knee II, not to be confused with Wounded Knee I, which I'd read about. He filled me in on the second one: the occupation of the historic site by the American Indian Movement in 1973.

"Didn't they kill the ghost dancers there?" He just looked at me. I tried again: "What's a GOON?"

"Guardians of the Oglala Nation. They were on our side. So don't get me wrong—I like plenty of Indians. It's like how Sherman said" (and he smiled with self-satisfaction), "'the only good Indian is a dead Indian.' Well, let's qualify that: the only good Indian is a Christianized, proud-to-be-an-American, probably a veteran . . .'" (dramatic pause here) "Indian."

Oh brother. "How long did it go on for?"

"Months. An Indian finally got shot—two actually—and one of ours. They eventually called the whole thing off. Mostly it was about starving them out. Just like how they killed all the buffalo last time."

I knew about that from the book. They declared open season on the buffalo and people shot them from trains. Dead buffalo scattering the plains so there'd be no herds for the Lakota to hunt.

I turned and looked out the window. All that ugly talk amid all that beauty, the landscape big and flat, spud-brown and gold. Green fields appeared out of nowhere just like near Unity Lake, like carpet laid out and up to the distant mountains, rocky and mottled gray. Jimmy was beautiful like that too, even when he was mottled gray. The only good faggot . . .

"It's gonna be an early winter," the farmer said. He pointed out a cow, saying, "You can tell from how heavy the fur is on their backside."

I nodded, and as soon as there was a fork onto a smaller highway, I asked him to let me off.

"Thanks."

"Be careful," he barked and waved goodbye.

All kinds of people and all kinds of skies. Today, the clouds were like snot smeared across the horizon. But I was blessed with another empty road, and it filled me with elation. Off I went. Just me and Jimmy forever in every direction. No Christians, no BIA, no interstate truck wind and car shrapnel. Idaho opened up, and it was as if there was music in the silence of it. Sweeter, vaster music than I'd ever known, opening like a multidimensional funnel that pulled me wider and wider out into it.

In time, the green fields gave way to hay fields, all harvested now, with big giant bread loaf–looking haystacks dotting the stubbled fields. Beyond the hayfields was grazing land and cattle wandering about. Those close to the road would stop, chewing their cud, and watch me pass. A bovine nation.

Then there was just grass and rock all around in a deep stillness, and the highway rolled along softly like a big wave far out at sea, just rolling along, over each little hill, each of which made me sweat going up and then cool off in the breeze as I coasted down the other side.

Then up ahead, I saw something all scattered in the road. I couldn't make it out at first—I thought maybe it was clothes or some kind of freight that had fallen off a truck. It was vaguely red and black and brown. When I got up to it, I was shocked to recognize it was meat, flesh. And it was spread for about two or three hundred yards, in chunks.

A massacre? My throat caught. Then I saw a hoof. A friggin' cow. Or it had been at one time. The biggest roadkill I'd ever seen, and it wasn't pretty. I had to dodge, slalom through it, the chunks were so big. Any one of them could have knocked me off my bike. I recognized a shin, a shoulder. When I got to what was left of the head, my stomach turned. An eye stared at me. Someone had hit this thing and then others kept hitting it, I guess, or maybe a truck dragged it to pieces. I just couldn't imagine it would get so chewed up before someone stopped and dragged it off. Though it was too late for that now. It didn't seem right just leaving him there, but it'd be a mighty big job cleaning him up at this stage of the game.

That's when I saw the vultures. Watching from some rocks. There were flies too. A lot of them. Filling the silence suddenly. A different kind of music. A different vastness. A regular charnel ground. That was some big death. Too big even for the vultures and flies. The way it looked to me, it was going to just get ground right into the pavement by cars and trucks or be carried on tires going who knows where, until the body of this cow would literally be spread like mustard all the way across the country and there'd only be grease spots left here. In the meantime, it'd be feasted on by flies or end up in the craws of vultures, brought to their young, the next generation feeding on death.

At the end of it, on a rise, I stopped and stared a good long time back down that long gray line of road through the golden hills of grass, under the distant mountains, the meat sculpture all spread down the length of it. Sublime. And me with a bag of death on my handlebars. And the beauty of that place was just suddenly so profoundly sad, time dragging it at the speed of light, all of it blooming and vanishing on speeded-up film, like the seed of death ripening. That Eugene holds and me too, and even the twins back on Guerrero Street, and the farmer and the waitresses in Denny's—and Jimmy is the flower of it all. The grief just came right out of the road and whacked me with its pavement palm. Ouch. Grief bleeding out of the landscape in colorful images of mountain and stream, pickup and gun rack, plowed field and fallow field, green mountain and gray, dead cow and living—and under it all the bones of Indians and soldiers and pioneers and buffalo and God knows what else. Squashed flowers. The grief, spinning out of everything everywhere all the time, fast and sure as the spokes on my wheels because I was suddenly pedaling madly, not so much to run away as to ride the grief wave, to spend the feeling, to spill it, move it, give it its due. Because you couldn't stand still for sadness. I knew that from my endless walks. Couldn't frame that landscape and put it on your TV. You had to ride it. You had to bark, or wear down your knuckles. Maybe that cow was the flesh of God's knuckles that he'd run down the road, wacked as a mad faggot.

I rode fast for miles like that, all the way past the interchange to Ketchum and Sun Valley, where Hemingway blew his brains out.

I'd done another hundred-mile day, caught up with Jimmy's red hoops, which indicated tonight's destination as a campground just beyond Carey, Idaho. Carey had looked like a small town from the map, and it was, but the place was anything but quiet. It was Friday night, and kids were caravanning down the main drag in pickups and jeeps, hooting and hollering, with pennants waving and red, white, and blue jerseys on their backs. Some kind of big football game. Everyone was in on it, and not just the kids and the cheerleaders who sped by in an old Mustang, squealing around the corner. Even outsiders and posing tough guys loitered smoking on street corners, watching.

It almost seemed strange, seeing people in groups suddenly. I hadn't seen any more than a couple people together since Boise—and even then, there was the loneliness of urban anonymity. Before that, through Oregon and now Idaho, mostly I'd seen lone individuals in empty places or the strange hollering zombies of Ironside, the invisible geriatrics behind their curtains at Unity Lake, or just silhouettes speeding by in cars, not really people at all. Shadows. They all could have been shades—the dead—for all I knew. Weaving their way back and forth across the country, sewing a great death shawl or mask over the bones beneath. And the trucks, like great lumbering animals, herds of them like buffalo (they killed the buffalo, only to reinvent them in their own image), migrating, back and forth, crisscrossing the country with the fungus of commerce that makes of the land, slowly but surely, a foul moldy bread.

How many of these same trucks, waitresses, service stations, and tough guys loitering, Carls and Christian ladies, and shadows and weavers, had seen Jimmy? And none of them ever knowing that the ghost of him had returned, passing through again like a dusty wind.

48

My last night in San Francisco, I snuggled up in the sleeping bag and put a candle in each of Jimmy's mayonnaise jars so as to burn up whatever was left of him and wish him well. They burned all night, and in the morning I tossed the jars out the window to shatter for the twins to find and marvel at—a deadman's glass bones.

I was gonna miss that sad little bay-windowed apartment, with the bad paint in the halls, the grimy gum-pocked stoop, the sidewalk where those twins were always up to something. I remembered them from a morning last winter under darkening skies, Jimmy in the hospital with pneumonia. Their father was loading his truck and they were standing shoulder to shoulder, their heads cocked back and their mouths wide open, catching the first drops of rain.

Little pullets.

I could've stopped. Part of me wanted to.

I didn't dare.

I hoisted *Chief Joseph* up on my shoulder and down the stairs I went.

I saw the broken mayonnaise jars on the sidewalk, the labels holding some of the broken glass together. "Best"—and he was. I'd held him here when he fell into me in his old army coat—so, so thin—the day before he died. I kicked the glass off the sidewalk and into the gutter. Sorry, Jimmy, but it's probably not safe for the twins.

Doing what needed to be done.

49

From the map, I knew that Craters of the Moon National Monument was twenty miles further on, and in the setting sun I decided to press on through the chaparral to reach Jimmy's red hoop, knowing there'd be camping there. I left Carey to its lively American reveries—no place for the dead, or a wacked faggot.

Though I knew there were both everywhere. And I looked for them. The dead were fairly easy to spot, lined up in rows in cemeteries—and I'd read in a book by Balzac once that something like the top twelve inches of all the dirt on earth was basically just the dead: animal, plant, and other. But queers were a little trickier to spot—the living ones, that is. More of a game. Like spot the ghost, because like ghosts, only some people could see them. That guy at the service station loitering, for instance—he hadn't quite fit, had he? A tad too James Dean. And he thinks the bullets can't get him if he paints himself "straight," strikes that pose and dances "straight."

The sun went fast and the shadows lengthened out big and ominous below gnarled juniper trees, twisted and forlorn—and even below the squat sagebrush and chaparral. I pushed on because there was clearly nothing between Carey and the park. Then the black scar of it appeared on the horizon, like a big splat of burnt blackberry from some enormous pie. A pie in the sky that had finally fallen.

Before long, I was winding through one of the strangest places I'd ever seen, though it was so black I could barely see it as dusk rolled into

217

night. It was just a solid scab of lava, miles in every direction, with a gray road running through it like a gray stripe on a black rock (good for wishing, as I recall). There were little sections where grass grew, a few bushes, even squat trees near the bathroom, which was nothing more than a glorified concrete outhouse, but substantial all the same because it was the only building anywhere in sight.

I pulled in at the restroom, as it was the entrance to the campground, and plopped my bike and gear down when I found a flat patch of dirt. It was warm out still, so I dug around for my flashlight and climbed among the rough black rocks to see if I could get up high and see a view. Eventually, I reached a little promontory and was able to see the road and the running lights of trucks way off in the distance, and even Carey, a faint glow on the horizon.

But I was more interested in the stars, looking for Jimmy and Eugene and the pie shop nebula where this black rock must have been long ago hurled from.

It wasn't until morning—the birds singing me awake—that I saw the blue truck. Up above, parked at an angle, up on a dirt patch full of shrubs and flowers, right in the middle of that chunk of black stone. I couldn't believe it. And I thought that must be some shitty truck if I'm keeping up with it.

I sat and stared at it for a long time, anxious to spot Eugene. But I was hesitant to approach on account of the other guy. So I watched and waited, and finally I scurried up the hillside to their camp, where I found only the remnants of a fire in a pit full of ash. Neither of them were in sight anywhere, but I could see the dirt roads now that led to the other little brush and dirt campsites among the rocks, and my eyes followed them, searching. I climbed up a nearby butte to get a view and still I saw neither of them. It occurred to me it might be someone else with the same truck. But how many blue '64 Dodges are on the road? It had to be them. So I sat and waited, trying to warm myself in the sunrise, thinking how Jimmy's hair was as black as this rock when he died, the blond all grown out and shorn away.

I looked around and saw flowers—brilliant yellow and white against the black. All flowers for Jimmy that I'd never pick—and wouldn't need to either as the world was Jimmy now, and he already had them growing all over him like his own private cosmic platinum dye job.

I don't know where he came from, but suddenly there he was, right next to me. Like a bird. It was his shadow I saw first. "Eugene!" I turned. His crooked smile. And then he crouched down and he kissed me. And he took me by the hand, hurrying me along, up over some nearby rocks and down a gully that led to more rocks and more gullies, far back into the scab of earth and down inside of it to where there was an actual stream that disappeared into a cave. And before it did, there was a big sandbar of a beach along the stream with a black rock jutting over it like an awning, hiding it from view, and it was there that he stopped and turned and he pulled off his dirty white T-shirt and then his boots and dusty blue jeans, his baggy checkered boxer shorts, and holey socks. And smiling then, he pulled me close and his tongue was so hungry, his penis so eager and straight up like a dog barking for a walk or dinner. He tore at my clothes and I helped him rid me of them. And I understood completely in that moment why people destroy families, ruin friendships, and generally make a mess of their lives for sex. But I'd consider that later.

"God, you're starved, Eugene. Me too. It's so good to see you." And we accosted each other through our grins (his threatening to tear his whole face apart, which was so thin, it could barely make room for it). And thank God for our tongues. If we didn't have them, we'd have used our teeth and torn each other to pieces. As it was, we gulped at each other's bodies, using all of our mouths, *except* for our teeth. Hungry and thirsty both.

I guess it was pheromones—or was it grief? I knew so little about him, and he so little about me. We only knew we needed to be inside each other with such urgency, as if our cum belonged to the other and we had to get the book returned to the library and fast. Could love be late? Nah, just imminent, and always in the nick of time.

We wrestled, groaned, and ached, guided by our penises and our hearts, and once we looked directly into each other's eyes, and without saying anything, acknowledged we weren't doing this really: it was happening; we were riding it. It was like the road that way. We were guests, the two chosen special guests, two blessed lost souls.

And also like the road, I had a sense I'd never see him again. We were a time and a place. In passing. How I liked it best. Or so I'd told myself. But not with Eugene. No, Eugene made me want to stop and stay forever. Right on a giant black scab in nowhere Idaho. Center of the universe. We splayed our bodies out like stars, our spidering limbs everywhere and all of us inside out—armpits open, the undersides of our cocks and scrotums turned toward the light of each other as we came together—atoms splitting—at the center. A backasswards big bang as we vanished into absolute zero. Before space and time. An original moment.

Our seed then everywhere, flying all over, splattering the black sand with little white flowers.

And then it all came rushing back: the big bang on speeded-up film, right up to that giant splat of black lava, sizzling and pulsing in Pleistocene Idaho, and then cooling and cooling. And it kept cooling. And it was cold by the time the universe caught up with September 15, 1991. Naked, we had to hug each other close as the goose pimples rose on our skin.

We said nothing because Eugene never did. I hardly talked at all anymore myself, come to think of it. All these "rides," they just talked *at* me. And I only talked to myself now mostly, or to Jimmy.

I looked around at the black, black stone of the cave we were sitting in, huddled together on a sandbar of dark gray sand, soft and bracingly cold. I heard him strike a match, and before long he was inhaling. When he coughed, it echoed, and he hopped up then, and putting out his hand, pulled me up. We kissed some more because whatever it was between us, it was that rare thing that keeps spilling long after the spilling is done. A river.

We climbed into our clothes: his left foot got caught in his boxer shorts on its way through and he hopped and laughed, its echo filling the cave. And then I laughed too, and the place boomed with us. Him and me, and how big the thing between us was.

He indicated he had to go with his hands pointing, so I followed him out of the cave, along the stream, over the black rock and through the gullies, and up back toward the truck, where the hood was once again open and the other guy under it.

Which made me momentarily nervous. I hesitated, and Eugene looked at me inquisitively just as his buddy's head popped up, having heard our approach. The guy looked at me for a minute, and then he said, "Painted Horse." And he eyed me suspiciously. I looked at Eugene for an explanation. He motioned with his arms and legs like he was riding a bicycle.

I looked back at his buddy and answered: "Blue Truck."

He gave me a small, quick smile that indicated friendliness, but also that he didn't completely trust me. Then he bent down to pick up a wrench from his battered red toolbox. "You learn anything more about straight-sixes since we last saw you?"

"Sorry, no," I smiled shyly.

And then Eugene did something funny on my account. He stepped away from his friend and did a little cheerleading routine and spelled out L-O-U-I-S, like an acronym.

"Louis," I said.

Louis was smiling, and so was Eugene, and so was I. And Louis had a good hearty laugh, looking at Eugene fondly. And I could see he loved him in how he looked at him. Which made me wanna cry—because the last time I'd seen that look on a man's face was when it was James Damon Keane's and it was aimed straight at me. Something brotherly.

I felt uncomfortable and emotional—all happy and sad at the same time. I sort of wanted to leave, but I also wanted to stay—because I felt close to Eugene again, and because his friend Louis seemed nicer this time, even if he was a bit brusque and I couldn't quite figure him out, nor the nature of their relationship. Eugene headed over to some scrawny brush to piss, and I asked Louis, "Where you guys going?"

"Home," he replied.

"Where's home?"

"Pine Ridge."

"Isn't that where Wounded Knee is?"

"Yup. You know about that?" And he looked at me directly.

"Yeah, I read a book about it."

"A book, eh?" He nodded his head slowly; then he dipped back under the hood.

"What's wrong with the truck?"

"Carburetor problem. But I think I can jerry-rig it and get us to Idaho Falls." Jimmy's next red hoop.

Eugene returned and I looked at him, half hoping for an invitation, but I also suddenly felt the need to flee. "Maybe I'll see you guys there," I said. But Louis wasn't listening anymore, working his wrench, contorting his face in the effort. Eugene just smiled. I kissed him quickly, just a peck, and I hurried back down across the rocks to my camp below. When I got to my bike, I looked back up the rocky slope and there he was watching me. He lifted his hand in a forlorn wave.

Ask for nothing back, Jimmy said.

I needed to pull. I wanted to be with Jimmy then. Gone-Jimmy, who I still didn't want to go.

I looked up to wave again once I'd gotten on the bike and moving, but Eugene was no longer in sight. Hoped he'd understand. I thought then if I rode hard today, I could pass Idaho Falls and cut south on a smaller road and I could be rid of them.

Because Eugene was going to take Jimmy away. *Don't go, Jimmy. Not just yet . . .*

I headed down the empty road, back into the sagebrush, distracting myself with spices, wracking my brain (spice-racking?) for the right one that would describe him. The essential spice. Something orange: turmeric, cayenne, cinnamon. Another name for Eugene. He who had many; he who had none. The same engine-grease black hair as Jimmy too, but with a hint of blue. On account of the big sky over my head, perhaps? The big sky with its snotty clouds or its endless sagebrush, or today, its high, remote cirrus like eagle feathers, like what Eugene had drawn on the underpass way back in the city named for him. He wasn't a horseboy: not with that nose; not with those shoulder blades like truncated wings. Eugene was a birdboy. Horses that run and birds that fly. I loved the fleeing things, I suppose. The going things. I was just a mangy lost dog, loping through an empty lot.

A green highway sign said "Arco 2 miles." Wasn't that a gas station or an antidepressant or a boy's name back in California? In the thicker growth of sage and willow-choked creeks on the road leading into town, I scared up pheasants and a couple of antelope, who bounded off away from me into the brush, white butts upended—gayer than geese, which would likely fly over any time now.

And then I entered Arco, and there wasn't a car on any street I could see, or a person out anywhere. It was like a ghost town at the end of the world. Like that town in *The Andromeda Strain*. All the buildings were whitewashed wood in high WW2 style. It had a big welcome sign, calling itself the first atomic city, having been completely powered by nuclear energy before any other place on earth, or so the sign said. I didn't get it at first, but as I entered town I saw more and more signs (but still no people) commemorating the milestone. Eventually I found a large information kiosk in front of city hall with all the details: A complete timeline of the development of the "peaceful" use of nuclear power and the numerous experimental reactors that were built in the desert east of town in what is called INEL (Idaho Nuclear Experimentation Laboratory). Great, another acronym.

I continued along the main drag until I found a place for pancakes. I sat in the window, but with my back turned purposely to it, in case any blue trucks drifted past. Other than the waitress, who was ghoulishly pale, I was the only one in the place, my imagination conjuring up all

223

manner of horror about how her bed must glow, and about the unseen townsfolk, shut-ins all, in various stages of radioactive decay.

I looked at Jimmy perched next to the ketchup where'd I'd put him, already vaporized to nothing, post-nuclear, with nothing to fear from Arco and its radiation. *How's the bardo today, Jimmy?* Day forty-five.

No answer.

I looked out the window then and craned my neck down the road, wanting to see one thing: the blue pickup. Wanting to, not wanting to. Not wanting to.

50

It was 6:00 a.m., so Guerrero Street was more or less empty, fog-enshrouded—all the better to make my escape. But so beautiful too. San Francisco was a maddening city, hard to leave, a place where nostalgia could set in thirty seconds on the back of an image. Every place else took years, but San Francisco was beautiful like a curse. It wouldn't let you go. "Left my heart" and all that. Platitudes with an iron grip.

I pulled, took a deep breath, and reminded myself that despite all evidence to the contrary, I *was* in reality. San Francisco may be covered with Victorian sugar, but the biscuit under the frosting is the same as anywhere else. You've got to keep reminding yourself of that. Otherwise it's the city of promises never quite delivered. And that could be anything from a sunny day to the fabled Oz of homosexuality, which was chipping away like old paint as so many of us died.

Sometimes I plain hated San Francisco, the way it dissembled and seduced.

The acronym closed in on Jimmy just as soon as he arrived. He was sick within two months, after having been asymptomatic until he reached our fair city—our fair, enchanted city, shadowed by the angel of death that no one sees until it's hovering over you like the fog and you can't get out from under it. Trickster city. Black widow with a pretty Victorian hourglass on its belly, and we're all crawling around clueless as fools on its web.

And it wants your heart, so don't doubt it'll ask.

51

I rode out of Arco, and into the sagebrush nowhere, as empty as I was. One hundred miles of INEL, which just goes to show you how deceptive a short little acronym can be. This particular acronym looked like the rest of the grass and sagebrush high desert of the Great Basin, other than the occasional cement bunker in the distance and a lot of fences protecting—from what I could tell—pretty much nothing. And the sound of gunfire, of course. I'd soon learn it was coming from gunnery ranges far away, as apparently the sound of a gunshot will travel hundreds of miles if there's no sound to drown it out, or nothing else to obstruct its travel. And there wasn't. Just like grief that way. I kept an eye on my tires.

The place had a hugeness that overwhelmed me. There was one rest stop, twenty miles inside, chock full of seniors who, I ventured a guess, were just in from Unity Lake. Geese.

I pulled in for a drink of water and to rest my left knee, which had grown stiff and was starting to swell. The place was fenced heavily and plastered with signs warning NO TRESPASSING, $500 FINES, US MILITARY RESERVATION (Is that for Indian veterans?), HIGH SECURITY AREA, and all kinds of things like that. There were military vehicles there as well and one stereotypical U.S. Marine in flight glasses and a crew cut who walked right up to me and asked me what I was doing riding a bicycle out here. He said it with the kind of arrogant self-confidence that deserved a punch in the nose for good measure. But I was a fag and he looked official, so that wasn't going to happen on two counts.

"Just passing through," I answered him.

"Not a good choice, soldier. You can't stop and camp here. You have to ride the whole thing today. You won't be allowed in here after dark." He had his sleeves rolled up and was clearly not any kind of guard or MP. He was just flexing his bantamness.

"I see. Well, okay then. How far across is it?"

"One hundred clams, soldier."

"Clams?"

"Backflips, footsteps, jump ropes, hop-skips, pancakes—miles, pardner."

Pancakes? "I see. So what's the big deal out here? Why is it so high security?"

"You bet it is. The fuel rods from Three Mile Island are out here." He grinned like a Cheshire cat.

I wanted to say, *Whoopee, you learn something new every day*, or *You don't say*, or . . . *So what?* Something about him annoyed me, the way he smiled about something like that. It was that "you're gonna die, sucker" smile. He looked like the kind of guy who would really enjoy something like Three Mile Island, would want to get in on the action. I wondered what his euphemisms for fuel rods might be: dildoes, fannywackers, chopsticks, bones?

"But the security, I mean. After all, we're in the middle of Idaho. What are they afraid of?"

He explained that there were four hundred and fifty—and he'd didn't say "about" or "approximately"—known nuclear terrorists in the world. "You never know when Colonel Qaddafi might ride out here on his white horse." He winked, and laughed.

Or Crazy Horse or Red Cloud, I thought. I got on my bike then. I wanted to get it over with. I winced as my knee throbbed, but once I got going the pain seemed to ease.

Cars passed now and again, but it was an empty highway generally, until someone pulled up right behind me and slowed down. I didn't look, but pretty soon they were pulling up alongside me, and I prepared myself for more Halls of Montezuma lectures when I saw instead his orange arm on the open window of the door, and then his green eyes and his blue-black hair: Eugene, leaning out the window, smiling big as ever. I could pretend I didn't see them, mind my own business, whistle, look off into the sagebrush nowhere.

"Would you like a ride out of this evil place?" Louis called out, leaning forward and looking across Eugene from the driver's side.

It was windy and there was no food or drink for a hundred miles, my knee hurt, and in my rush to escape the Marine back at the rest stop I hadn't filled up my water bottles besides. And, and . . . *I'm not asking for anything back, Jimmy, see? But they're offering.*

But I reconsidered. No, I'm not going to be able to sit next to him for a hundred miles, and then be able to say goodbye again. No sirree. I must have looked morose because Eugene smiled and looked at me with a pleading-teasing look.

I relented, sighed right back at him, and watched the truck pull past me and brake into the gravel. When I reached them, I followed, waiting for them to stop, but they never quite did. Louis leaned out the window and called back to me: "We can't take a chance on stopping, the engine might die. You gotta get the bike in there somehow while I'm moving."

My last chance to wave them off.

Eugene hopped out the passenger side door then and came to help me. I quickly untied the velvet bag and tied it to my belt and then we lifted the bike together and ran after the truck, tossing the bike into the truck bed with a bit of a crash, which made me wince and Eugene laugh. Then I followed him as he grabbed the door and hopped in, with me close on his heels, my perineum aching as I ran, and my knee too. I shut the door once inside and off we zoomed, looking over my shoulder to make sure nothing had been lost on the road when we'd tossed the bike truckward.

Eugene was still scooting over to the middle of the seat to give me room. He was in a real good mood, it seemed. He put his hand on my thigh and smiled big. He was happy to see me. And it felt good to be crammed in next to him, our thighs flush. I wanted to drop my sadness like a stone and just kiss him. I wanted to watch my bike slide right out the back end of the truck and bounce itself into screws and bolts, scattered clothing, and a book that told a story you couldn't bury anyway—one more piece of roadkill. I clenched Jimmy-in-the-bag, resting in my lap, the one thing I wouldn't wanna lose.

"Sorry about that," Louis said, pulling back onto the road, his eyes in the side mirror.

"No problem. Thanks for the lift."

Nobody said anything for the next several minutes while I absorbed the hot lava of Eugene through my thigh, making my frown warble and begin to rise. Then Eugene grabbed my hand and I tensed.

"It's okay, Blue Truck. You're winkte, I know," Louis mentioned with a clipped smile, his neck back, eyes in the rearview mirror.

I looked at him, my face a question, not knowing what a winkte was, or why he called *me* Blue Truck.

"Uh, what's winkte?"

"Two spirit."

I nodded and arched my eyebrows.

I'd heard the term before somewhere in San Francisco. Some artist friend of Lawrence's used to do these scrotum portraits and each ball had a different inlaid photographic face: one a man, one a woman, and always 1950s people, like Ward and June Cleaver, with titles like "Two Spirits Have Twice the Fun" or "Two, Two, Two Spirits in One." And long explanations in the program about how Native Americans believe gay people have two spirits, which is what makes them queer. Which meant there were five of us in the cab of that truck if you did the math—maybe even six.

"So who are you?" I asked him. "Are you like . . ."

"I'm his uncle."

"Oh."

"You thought I was his lover?" And he laughed. "Ha, ha, eh Smoke? You and me. Ha, ha, ha."

Eugene grinned.

"Isn't his name Eugene?"

"Nah, he's not Eugene. His name's Rupert No Wind. And I'm Louis No Wind."

"Rupert?"

"Yeah—you wouldn't use it either, would ya?" And he winked.

I looked from Louis to Eugene, and he shrugged shyly, a little embarrassed at the exposure of his geeky name.

"So what's Smoke?"

"Another name for him. Smoke That Came Back to the Lodge. That's a vision name."

"Vision?" He looked at me like I was stupid, which I was, considering. "I don't really know about stuff like that."

"But you know about Wounded Knee? I thought you said you read books? Didn't you read about Crazy Horse in that book of yours?"

I nodded.

"You remember what his vision was?"

I racked my mind and remembered something about it. "Well, he . . . uh . . . couldn't be killed except by his own people? And his horse was sort of like his medicine or whatever?"

"That's it. Painted horse. A warrior . . . he served his people that way. Vision is about how to serve."

I nodded.

"Smoke's winkte; he serves in a different way. Everybody has a place."

I didn't say anything, but I thought about that for a while. Everybody with a place. I sure didn't feel I had a place . . . *road's the place* . . . I guess I could see how a lot of fags found a kind of gay place: hair-dressing, florists, fashion design, nursing, that kind of thing. But it wasn't my place and I doubted it was Eugene's. San Francisco had been a place once.

"What exactly is the place of a winkie?"

"Wink-*te*," he corrected me. "Well, being a two-spirit person is powerful medicine. Depends, but it's usually a ceremonial role. Or you become a medicine man, that kind of thing."

"Sounds cool." I nodded again.

"It's more about service, Blue Truck, than cool."

"Oh. Well, I just meant it's nice to hear that, because I've never heard anyone say much nice about being queer."

He gave me an understanding look then. "I'm just learning about it myself really. Most Indians don't treat the winkte any better than white people do after all that's gone down. So many traditions are lost or barely alive." And he looked off to the mountains. Then he patted Eugene's thigh. "Maybe Smoke can bring some of that back."

After a few moments, he turned to me and said: "So tell me again where you're going and why."

"Well . . ." And I looked at Jimmy in my lap. "My boyfriend died . . . this is Jimmy, here, in this bag." I held him up. "And I'm taking him home."

He looked me in the eye. "Buffalo?"

"Yeah, Buffalo."

He looked at me again. "And where'd you come from?"

"San Francisco."

"A lot of people dying there I guess."

"Yeah, a lot. Lots of uh . . . wink . . . ," and I hesitated, stumbling on the word.

"Winktes. Well, I'm taking *him* home." And he patted Eugene's thigh again. "Eugene's mother died," he continued. I looked at Eugene then, who'd taken out a sketchpad and was drawing with a black pastel crayon. He looked up and sighed. "But that was a year ago, and they buried her back there in Oregon." And Louis told me the whole story, while I watched Eugene draw a face in black charcoal. It emerged along with the story. How she'd been sick for a while, and how after she'd died, Louis had decided to come out to find his nephew.

"I'd never known him. He's my brother's kid and my brother died in 'Nam."

I perked up and he looked at me. "So did my dad."

"He an Indian?"

231

"Oh no, I'm Irish." Chance for a choice white lie lost. But that would have been just too white of a lie, pardon the pun.

"Well, Rupert's mom hadn't been on the rez for years. She'd been dead set on getting off the rez since she was a kid. Well, that's what Frank told me anyway. He'd always liked her. So much so that he went looking for her. Her and her sister had gone to Seattle—through the relocation program. They used to pay Indians to leave the rez. It didn't work out. Usually doesn't." And he sighed. "But they weren't about to turn tail and head home. They fell in with the local Indians up there. Got involved with men—you know, the usual. Somewhere along the line she reconnected with my brother. Before he shipped out I guess." He took a breath and looked out across the sagebrush before continuing. "In all the confusion, with his body coming back and everything else, and none of us really knowing what he'd been up to, we never heard nothing about her. She married someone else, a Klamath guy, and that's where Eugene grew up. She sent me a letter a year or so ago right before she died. I didn't even know I had a nephew." And he chuckled.

"How'd she find you?"

"On the rez. It's easy, man. You just send it general delivery, Wind Clan. It finds you. I was just getting cleaned up. Used to drink a lot. I figured I'd go out and meet my nephew, try to do right by him."

"What did she die of?"

"Lung cancer. Smoking killed her."

He stopped talking then.

We were all three silent then for a long time. There was just the wind, the emptiness, the distant bunkers like forgotten mausoleums.

Stories as yet untold. The road was made of stories, and there was no escaping stories, even if you wanted to. I thought then that what drew me to Eugene was that he couldn't tell a story. Or, rather, he told it in a different way. Without words. With his eyes, with his body and his hunger, with his smiles and sighs, with his seed.

Eugene pulled out his pipe and his lighter. Louis gave him a disapproving look but started talking about the acronym we were crossing instead, and how, contrary to popular belief that no one had ever died in a nuclear accident, there were in fact three Army guys who were lost right out here in an experiment gone awry back in the early 1960s. "It was a meltdown basically, but since the reactor they were working with was about the size of a toaster and they were servicemen, there was no need to tell anybody and no danger of it becoming a public disaster. But it killed three guys all the same, and they buried them in drums. The families wanted their kin, but the government said it was too dangerous. Shut 'em up with money, no doubt. They put the guys in those drums and left them out here and then they encased the blown reactor in concrete and put a fence around it a mile in each direction."

"How do you know all this?"

"I just listen. There ain't no secrets. It's just no one's ever listening."

The wind buffeted the truck in a gust. Stone silent Jimmy, maybe he whispered now on the wind. Or maybe it was those Army guys talking.

"I met a guy on my way out here when the truck broke down. He worked quality control. He told me a whole lot of stories—Enrico Fermi, where they almost lost Detroit. Someone wrote a song about it." He looked over at me. "Does it surprise you?"

"No, I guess not. I'm just surprised I hadn't heard it before." He looked at me again and I thought of Wounded Knee. Heard it all a hundred years too late like everybody else. "And what do you do once you know?" I ventured.

He looked at me then. "Not a lot you can do. Remember it. Tell everyone you see."

I thought about ACT UP then. We were having two different conversations, or we weren't. "So it won't happen again?"

"Oh, it'll happen again. It happens all the time; it's happening somewhere right now, you can bet on it." Oh yes. Well, maybe it was three conversations now, heading toward four, five, one hundred.

I thought of Sarajevo. "You don't think it'll ever stop, eh?"

He looked at me directly, and said nothing.

Eugene nudged me to show me what he'd drawn, and Louis looked over too. I assumed it was his mother's face, a mass of choppy, short lines, lots of shading. I couldn't tell if she were smiling or frowning, alive or dead. Her face was emerging from, or receding into, stone.

"Don't know how he draws in this rig," Louis piped up, "rattlin' and shakin'. These look different than the other ones." And he looked off the other way. "I call them Blue Truck drawings."

52

And sure enough, San Francisco made one last play for my heart, as once down in the station I encountered the same problem Jimmy had had when I'd first found him on the platform in West Oakland: NO BIKES ALLOWED DURING MORNING RUSH HOUR. Even though I was going the opposite way. Backasswards. And I had a sudden fear that I couldn't escape, that the Venus flytrap of San Francisco had me good, that I'd have to head back upstairs and wait for three hours in a coffee shop at 16th and Mission like some dumb fly on a web, and who knew where that black widow was.

Close. I marched down to the end of the platform where the first car always stops, and I figured I'd just plead with every train engineer. The first engineer I begged gestured me on without a fight, and I thanked him profusely until he tired of me and shut the window.

53

We drove the rest of the way to Idaho Falls in silence. Where I got us a motel room. Two double beds. I didn't know how that was going to work out until Louis climbed into one of them and said, "Do what you gotta do, but don't make too much noise." And he guffawed and vanished under the covers, turning his head to the far wall.

Eugene hit the lights and then sidled up to me and grabbed the hem of my Red Hot Chili Pepper (the garment, not the metaphor) T-shirt, and over my head it went. In no time, I was smothered in the silk of him. *What the hell's a winkte?* I remember thinking—somebody who winks? It sure feels good whatever it is.

He cupped his hand over my mouth at the crucial moment of meltdown.

And I spent the night holding Eugene, and dreaming that I was gathering up a parachute, folding and folding the silk of it, having flown and wanting to fly again.

I woke up early, to Louis's snoring and the whisper of Eugene's breath and the peace of his uncontorted face. We'd carried my bike up the stairs and into the room and it leaned against a dresser, all packed up and ready to go.

These men had been good to me. Some white kid, probably with ancestors who'd blasted away at buffalo and into that ditch at Wounded Knee Creek. *Ask for nothing back.* A bit late for that. My turn to vanish, Eugene.

236

It wasn't later than six and cold, and I had to pile on Jimmy's old ratty green sweater for warmth, his red windbreaker over that, and his long johns to boot. I yanked a string off the polyester bedspread and tied it onto the bike, and then I quietly rolled out the door. I fumbled with the map out on the street and found my way to the highway that led into Wyoming. I didn't even stop for pancakes—just wolfed down some god-awful sweet rolls at a minimart.

By the time I hit the Snake River, clouds had gathered and it started to rain. I pulled off and got out Jimmy's poncho, tucked him up inside the windbreaker, and got back on the road. They found me that way, pedaling along in the rain, a rooster tail of water behind me as the tires hummed their wet, revolving song—the bicycle waltz: one, two, three. This time they didn't bother asking, just slowed down, the taillights glowing red (one of them anyway). And out hopped Eugene. And the same routine as before got my bike into the truck bed and me up front, hand in his hand, thigh against his thigh.

They said nothing. Just the windshield wipers and their forlorn little squeaks speaking woe. We drove all the way up the Snake River like that, past pastureland and hillsides of beautiful chartreuse quaking aspen, on through the horror of Jackson Hole and its boutiques and faux out-west décor. Up through the Grand Tetons (they really are purple mountain majesty, but only Ray Charles knows how to sing that song with joy *and* sorrow) and on into Yellowstone, where we stopped at a big yellow lodge that was almost empty, scaling back services as the summer season had already waned.

I bought them gas, and while the tank guzzled it up and Eugene found a bathroom, Louis stared at the sky and its light, intermittent rain.

"Let's hope the thunderbeings aren't out."

"Why?"

"Because they might make you dream about them, and after that you'll have to do everything backwards."

I didn't recall dreaming of them, but that's how I did everything already.

"Really?"

"You become heyoka, a clown."

I looked at him, and he went on: "Because it all ends up funny. Like if I felt cold, I'd have to say I was hot. If something was serious, I'd have to laugh. Or, if I had a story I really needed to tell, I wouldn't say a thing."

"Are you talking about Rupert?" And I topped off the tank and replaced the nozzle in its holder.

"No," he said abruptly.

"Louis?"

He looked at me.

"How do you feel about white people?"

"There sure are a lot of 'em." He winked.

I wasn't sure how to take that. "Well, I've never met any Indians before, and after reading that book, I feel kind of bad about even being in this country at all."

"You didn't kill anybody, did ya, Blue Truck?"

"No, sir." In fact that was my problem. I hadn't killed the one person who'd asked me to kill him.

"Being Indian's a state of mind, Blue Truck. So is being white. Just don't be a wasicu."

"What's that?"

"Means 'takes the fat,' like those people down in Jackson Hole. More than they need. Way more."

The three of us went into the lodge for lunch, and other than a distant table with a geriatric couple eating, we were the only ones there. And while we sat there at the big picture window looking out across a huge meadow, the sun came back out and a mist began to rise. And way out there in the mist, we saw a buffalo grazing.

"Your destination." Louis pointed with a French fry.

I smiled.

Eugene and Louis were eating and both staring at me then. I sort of smiled back. It felt like they were having a conversation about me, but they weren't talking and they weren't even looking at each other. But it was like I'd just come back from the bathroom or something and it *felt* like they'd been talking.

"Thanks for the ride," I said.

"Thanks for the room," Louis replied, "—and gas, and lunch," he added, pushing the check my way.

"This one's on Jimmy," I announced, pulling out my roll.

American bison," Louis joked as we passed a park sign on our way back to the truck, warning park visitors not to hoist their infants onto buffalo heads to sit between their horns for photo ops. An honest mistake?

Twenty minutes later, we hadn't seen any more buffalo (if you see the Buddha on the road, kill him. Advice well taken by the white man a hundred years ago), but a wrathful jet of steam came bellowing out of the hood.

"Damn—Old Faithful," Louis reported dryly as he pulled over.

"Jimmy," I thought to myself, smiling. "He's everywhere." And I thought of his lovely member—how many times it had spouted like a factory steam whistle, signaling the end of the work day, or like the earth itself, putting forth crops and water, rain and river. Old Faithful. Osiris and the life-giving river, and the sky is our mother. I looked up and saw the Virgin's blue mantle, enveloping us. The earth, he's just a boy. And I tried to remember the last time I'd seen the life hop out of Jimmy like that. Like a spring rabbit.

He didn't want to stick it in me anymore toward the end. "I'm not that motivated," he'd quipped, "and besides, this thing" (holding his half-hard horsedick by its belly, as if it were a cat) "is lethal now." And then, admonitorily, when I'd frown with disappointment, "You ain't coming with me, Seamus. Place for you . . ."

"I know my place. Under you or over you. Heads or tails."

Jimmy and his say-nothing smile.

So, we were back to frottage mostly, which was nice, because we didn't need any condoms then. He'd rub against me, and I'd rub against him. Maybe that last time was when he was behind me squeezing it off between my butt cheeks, raining white stars across my back—Magellanic clouds. Or perhaps when he'd driven it, each vein in high relief, along my sternum, making love to my heart. I liked it that way best, my heart pulling Jimmy up from the roots. Jimmy throwing rice on the groom of my heart.

What was the *very last* time? I couldn't remember, and it made me panic. It suddenly seemed very important.

It was in Golden Gate Park, that's where it was. We were walking. He was never horny anymore, so when it came over him, we'd make sure to make the most of it. We went back in the trees and dropped our pants, our cocks bobbing like kids in a pool, bouncing. And he spilled all over my shirt, which I wore all that day, fingering the hard spots that no one knew the holiness of but him and me.

"Don't ever wash it. It's probably the last batch." He was kidding, or he wasn't.

"I love you, Jimmy." And I'd leaned over and kissed him across the table at the little Thai place on 9th Avenue we'd gone to after.

"And who wouldn't?" he replied sardonically, motioning for the waitress.

"Can't think of a soul," I'd answered him. But by then, he was talking coconut curry, and how hot, and did they have eggplant. And me, I was in over my head.

He glared up from his noodles five minutes later.

"Don't worry, Jimmy. I'm pulling."

Where's that shirt now? Probably went out into the street in one of those boxes. If there were a Jimmy Museum, it'd be in a glass case, the people crowding round, little kids pointing out the stiff parts you could barely make out: "Right there, Mommy, see?" The last batch.

Eugene wasn't much of a mechanic, and the clouds were clearing, so he dragged me into a meadow to let Louis handle the engine alone. I walked behind him, holding his hand, watching him, his thin hips and

240

wing-sprouting shoulder blades. And I worried a little that I was looking for Jimmy in Eugene, and that the beast that throbbed at my waist didn't seem to distinguish all that much. It was faithful alright, in a sort of impartial way.

But Jimmy and Eugene were nothing alike. Jimmy was all about making me pull, keeping things moving. Eugene, he seemed to be about just watching me and showing me things, staying in one place, even if it was but for a very short time. Like I say, he was no horse, he was a bird. He perched.

And inhaled.

He winked—is that why they called us winktes?—and exhaled. Soon we came upon a creek and he showed me dragonflies and water bugs, creamy blue lupine flowers dusted with rain and chartreuse green tufts of dew-clad moss. He found a little frog. And he winked again.

I sighed, thinking that since the weather was clearing and they'd taken me up the hardest part of the incline, and the truck was once again broken down, it was probably my cue to get back on the bike and go. But I didn't want to leave Eugene's side just yet as the two of us wandered further and further across the meadow and away into the woods. Eventually we came to a cliff, where the forest opened up into a huge vista, a river canyon below us. And it was like we were back in Jimmy, the big nowhere that expanded all around us. His whisper way down there far below in the water, humming I don't know what. A song.

Eugene turned and our mouths came together, and then the fury of it, the fire lit and he one landscape and me another, and our shirts coming off and our buckles undone, and we were birds flying over each other, his chest like a beautiful orange desert, and me some salt flat, and then we brought them rain.

We were the earth when we made love—or of the earth. We were with Jimmy when we did it, because he was earth and so it was like we made love in the palm of Jimmy's hand. I guess I loved Jimmy and Eugene all at once when I made it with Eugene. It sort of confused me, but it also felt just right. A holy trinity three-way: the lost soul, the birdboy, and the holy ghosthorse.

We loafed back through the forest, me saying "who are you, Eugene?" while he handed me things by way of an answer: a crinkled old leaf, a stick, a granite stone, a horse turd—once a robin's egg (he winked at the really good ones)—a butterfly's wing, a curled fern flute, bright orange lichen rubbed together in his hands and poured over my head like dust.

Multitudes.

Louis was sitting against the front tire when we made it back across the meadow. "I can't patch it; we gotta find a new hose somewhere."

"I can ride my bike back to the lodge," I offered.

"Nah, that's not necessary. We're in a national park, and they have rangers to come hassle Indians. They call it road service. They'll be along anytime now."

We all hopped in the cab and waited. And sure enough, Ranger Rick appeared within the half hour. He was the cop kind of ranger; he did it all by the book. The pulling over, the lights, the making us wait, while he probably checked the registration. "Do Indians register their cars?" I asked Louis.

"Not usually. We're exempt." And he ever so slightly lifted one side of his mouth, without averting his gaze from the rearview mirror. I wasn't sure what he meant, as usual.

"Hello gentlemen. You got car trouble?"

"Yeah, a radiator hose. Give us a lift?"

He looked us over, considering. "I'll take one of you," he offered.

Louis hopped out. "I'm the only one who knows what this rig needs, except for Blue Truck there," adding as he walked away: "He's an expert on straight sixes."

Eugene and I played cards and smoked pot in the back of the truck while we waited for Louis to get back. He had to teach me all the games, since I never played cards—my mom had liked Yahtzee and dominoes and Scrabble. He'd correct me by replaying the hand for me, or putting out cards all in a row and pointing.

"What's my incentive to win?"

He used his tongue against the inside of his cheek to mimic a blowjob, and grinned flirtatiously.

Real simple commerce, me and Eugene.

I liked how he put his hand on my knee to congratulate me, to correct me, or from time to time, to just say hey.

Cinnamon . . . Nutmeg . . . "Don't take your hand away."

He just laughed.

We sat out there for hours, with the smell of pines and grass wafting on the breeze from the recent rain, fresh and new, and we took deep breaths of it.

I started humming then, and they were songs from a sad place because that's where I'd been all morning.

Humming and playing cards.

And Eugene started to hum along with me, and I looked at him, thinking, "Well, he can hum. He can moan, he can laugh, and he can hum."

He was listening and picking up the tune, then following along with me once he got it.

So he taught me cards and I taught him songs. He knew most of them already, even if they were old songs, being of our parents' era. What I was really doing was telling him my story; we were sharing our lost fathers—our mothers too, I suppose. We did "Bobby McGee" and "Do You Know the Way to San Jose" and "Quinn the Eskimo" and "Hurdy Gurdy Man" and "Heart of Gold." And then he hummed some newer ones back at me: Tracy Chapman's "Fast Car," which made us kiss long and hard because I was on a bike and he was in a blue truck. And then "Don't Worry, Be Happy," which made us both laugh and whistle along.

I kept winning at cards.

243

Then we played a sort of charades where we had to guess the song, so it got a little more obscure. I tried out "Danny Boy" and "Moon River," neither of which he could get. And I didn't know the names of any of the dance tunes he hummed, except for "808 Skate."

Then Eugene asked me to get the book by holding his hands out like he'd just opened it to read. There was only one book he could have meant. I didn't know why he wanted it just then. But I leaned over and dug through the panniers until I found it and, pulling it out, handed it to him. He flipped around until he found the songs, and he hummed them for me. I'd hardly noticed them when I read the book, but it turned out all of them were Sioux. The first was "Prancing They Come," and it was all about horses. And then he hummed the one about the coming of the buffalo. There was a sad one toward the end of the book called "The Earth Only Endures," and then one called "In a Sacred Manner I Live." We sat beside each other, with the book between us, him humming and me trying to sing the Lakota words that were printed among the musical notes, or when he laughed too effusively, the English translations, which I tried to fit to his humming. He kept lifting his hands, trying to get me to sing louder, and we rolled our heads back over the edge of the truck bed and we sang together that way to the clouds (me with words, and he humming), which were now big fluffy white buffalo drifting by one after another like an enormous herd.

Eventually we stopped singing and just watched.

Groped around and found each other's hands.

We turned and looked at each other, heads rolled back. Smiled.

Held our hands tight, real tight.

Thanked each other that way. Shared gratefulness.

We kissed each other then, like how we always did, like we were ice-cream cones, creamy and dripping: 31 Flavors and then some — multitudes. He went for my waist and what he owed me from playing cards, and I laid back and marveled at his shiny, crow-black hair: licorice, beetles, Nigerians.

"I wanna stay with you," I whispered. Crazy shit. In a truck bed in a national park we weren't allowed to pull over in. *Stay where?*

244

Just with.

I was humming one last song, which if I'd had the guts to sing it would have sounded like this: *Black is the color of my true love's hair* . . .

And all the while the sky just lousy with white buffalo, silently lumbering over us.

54

Aside from a few dirty looks—me being a rule breaker and all with my bike on the BART train at rush hour—it was just another day for most of these people. And yet, was it ever just another day? All of us deep in the middle of some story that can suddenly turn.

Some of the people on the train looked sad, some looked content, and some appeared completely numb. Fact was, there were good and bad stories running along all around me, threads all. I remembered that last thread Jimmy'd pulled off a seat in one of these trains. Was this the same train? And if so, which seat would it be? I saw a lady doing her makeup in the seat that corresponded to the one we would have sat in that sweet year ago.

She looked like a clown.

Then I searched the bike for that thread and found it fast, remembering that Jimmy'd tied it right near where he'd painted *Chief Joseph* in cheap dime-store paint.

That thread's story was us.

That thread's story is this story.

55

Louis found us sleeping under a blanket. "Hoka hey!" he shouted. He clamped the new hose in place in no time while Eugene lit up his pipe. Back on the road, I asked Louis why he kept calling me Blue Truck.

He shrugged his shoulders.

"If I'm Blue Truck, I'd have a bad carburetor," I protested.

He arched one eyebrow. "Then you'd be Blue Truck with a Bad Carburetor."

"But doesn't it need to make some kind of sense—like shouldn't I have asthma or something?"

"Do ya?"

"No."

"Well then, we'll just keep it Blue Truck."

He looked at me.

I looked at him.

He was beginning to sound like one of the eight-year-olds at the Y. "You aren't making any sense."

"No, I'm not. And that's just the point."

The question that was my face. I looked at Eugene, who just grinned and leaned forward to the windshield and looked skyward and did the sign language motion for clouds, my favorite signed word—a roiling, boiling hand-over-hand Chinese tai chi expression of grace.

"Well, Blue Truck, it makes total sense if you get it."

I looked back at him, perplexed.

"You know, Blue Truck, when you just know something?" (and he pounded his heart with his closed fist).

I considered it and then I nodded. I knew. Like knowing I needed to bathe Jimmy. Knowing he was a horse and a salmon both. Seeing Eugene in the market, just like a turnip, pulled up out of the soil, and me knowing I needed a turnip. How I knew I needed to tell him everything and didn't need to talk to him at all.

"But not if you think about it," Louis warned me.

I smiled.

After a while, Eugene pulled out nail polish and set to painting my fingernails: one yellow; one red; one black; one white; and leaving the thumb unpainted.

"I'm talking about the spirit world here, and I probably shouldn't be. Smoke, he's wiser—he keeps his mouth shut."

"Well, we're all Catholics here, right?"

He looked at me again. "Are we?"

"It said so in that book."

"Catholic, eh? I wouldn't really call that the spirit world."

"I'm sorta joking."

"Sorta?"

"Well, I like Mary and churches, but I'm more of a Buddhist, I guess."

"Nam ramay kyo, all that?"

"No, not that kind."

"That's good—though I do know a woman in Manderson who got a lot of appliances using that chant. There's something to it."

I held up my hand and Eugene blew on it. Then he started in on his own.

"Lakota colors you got there, the four directions." Louis gestured with his head.

"Do I make a wish?" I was thinking I'd get four instead of the usual three.

"No." And he furrowed his brow. "The power is in asking for help, not wishing for it, Blue Truck. That's what crying for a vision is about."

"Crying for a vision?"

"Well, that's Indian for asking . . . like *really* asking." And he punched his heart.

"So then, someone like Crazy Horse asked?"

"He asked to be shown how he could serve his people."

I nodded.

"But you see, the point is: a vision answers a question. There's no wishing. It's about making a decision to serve, asking how, then listening, and then doing it."

"So, did Eugene cry for a vision?" And I looked at him, his head now resting in my lap as, holding aloft his hands, he continued painting his nails.

"Yeah, out there in Oregon, before I met him. Spirit told him to go back home."

I looked at Eugene then, considering. "How does it work?"

"Well, it's three days, three nights—sometimes four—out in the wilderness alone, fasting, praying for a vision. Asking, Blue Truck; not wishing, but asking. You ask, you get an answer. You wish, well . . ." And he shrugged.

I looked out into the forest. Endless stands of pines scattered into the distance, and I could see a meadow out there, and where the grass was thicker, I figured there was a stream. I had an urge to run out into it.

"So you just sit there, huh? You don't move around or anything?"

"There's a few ways to do it. You can make a circle and sit in it; you can bury yourself in a hole. But pretty much, it's just calling the four directions, and all your relations. And then just asking with your heart."

I looked at my newly painted fingernails.

"Man, I don't think I could handle that. All that time sitting still. I'm not good at that at all." And I thought back on my stillborn Buddhist life, my discarded zafu, committed to the street with everything else, sat on now by that punk girl, unless she'd chucked it too.

He shrugged. "You're no different from anyone else, Blue Truck. And sometimes if you don't go out and cry for a vision, it comes crying for you. The Great Spirit wants you to live, Blue Truck. You gotta start right there. You're boyfriend's dead, but you're not."

I felt my eyes begin to tear up then and, in my embarrassment, simply said, "I know."

"It's okay, Blue Truck—you can cry."

And so I did. Which made Eugene sit up and put his arms around me, rocking me and kissing my neck. I rested my head in his lap then, and was getting my breath back when I heard Louis say, "Oh shit!" And the truck swerved.

We'd been coming around a curve, and when I popped up to look what I saw before us was a deer startled and stopped in the road, its legs every which way, undecided about where to bolt. Louis swerved, but it bolted the same way, then back, and the next thing you knew we collided hard, and the deer deflected off the front bumper, shaking the whole truck, before it was catapulted off into the ditch.

Eugene exhaled loudly and Louis muttered, "Damn."

Louis slowed down, but before he came to a stop, he dropped it in neutral. Then he engaged the parking brake and hopped out, telling Eugene: "Keep the gas coming, I don't want that carburetor going."

Eugene scooted over into the driver's seat then as Louis reached behind him for his rifle, while I hopped out the passenger side, leaving Eugene to man the accelerator and hopefully prevent the truck from stalling.

We walked quickly up the shoulder to where the deer lay, struggling in the ditch, trying to pull itself up.

"Stand back." Louis aimed his rifle at the deer's twitching head and fired. I turned, but the shot echoed and came back at us from every which way.

Doing what needed to be done.

Dr. Jack No Wind. No ifs. No ands. No buts.

He stood there a minute, said some prayers or something in Lakota, and then looked at me, saying: "I'd keep it if we weren't in the park. But we've already run into the law once."

"What a waste, huh?"

"Nah, the vultures and flies and all them will get some of him before the rangers do. Hell, they might not even find him, in which case he'll get eaten up proper. Nothing wasteful about it."

We walked back toward the truck, and Eugene revved it for us, smiling.

"Now, that—that's wasteful."

"Did he mess up the front end, you think?"

We went around front and checked.

"Doesn't appear so. Just a dent or two. To go with the rest of 'em." He flicked his eyebrows up. Then he looked underneath and around where the deer had made contact. "These old cars are tough, and we only caught him as he was pulling away from us besides." He banged the hood, as if he were patting an old beast of burden.

"It didn't even stall this time."

Eugene revved the engine again, his big crooked grin filling the windshield.

"Don't waste my gas, Rupert, or I'll have to rename you Smoke That Went Out the Back End and Didn't Come Back!"

We both hopped in and off we went down the highway.

Louis looked at me with sadness in his eyes then. "How you doing, Blue Truck?"

It made me start, for it sounded somehow like he was saying goodbye without saying it. I just nodded.

We drove on to Cody, past signs for the Buffalo Bill Cody Museum.

"Sitting Bull was in that Wild West Show of his, wasn't he?" I commented.

"And Black Elk, and a whole bunch of people."

"Pretty strange."

251

"Buffalo Bill—he must be from Buffalo, huh? You must be getting close."

Used to his jokes by now, I grinned and said nothing, watching the landscape returning back to sagebrush nowhere at the lower elevations, and all of it turning purple in the setting sun. I thought how I had let myself just fall into Eugene and Louis, had gotten comfortable, enjoying the feeling that this could all go on forever. And I looked at Eugene then, dozing against my shoulder, his mouth slightly open. If I had a eucharist on me, I'd have given him communion. In the name of the father of my child, the son of our love, and the holy spirit baby that grew between us.

Some things you gotta figure out for yourself. A new way of seeing, and that's what a spirit baby was, growing in you, a gift from one man to the next.

Eugene got me pregnant with what is seen and unspoken. He'd filled me with a growing silence.

Eugene lurched forward as we rounded another curve, rousing me from my reverie as his head slid down my chest, right past my heart and into my lap, where he found the perfect pillow in Jimmy.

"How far you going tonight, Louis?"

"Well, I got this new hose and I just sort of feel like going until something else blows, you know?"

I nodded in agreement.

"You wanna be left off somewhere?"

I didn't, and only said, "I don't know."

He slowed down.

"I can't stop, as you know, but I can slow way down." He raised his voice then: "Smoke, you're on! Hoka hey!" Eugene lifted himself, and his eyes flickered. He looked around dazed as Louis pulled into the gravel.

I must have looked surprised. I couldn't beg. *Ask for nothing back.*

"Walk in beauty," Louis said then.

I looked at him, and thought, but didn't say: "But I'm on a bike; how can I do that?"

He looked back at me as if to say: "Ask how."

We hopped out, and Eugene, still sleepy, didn't get his footing and fell onto his knees in the gravel, splaying his arms out. I helped him up.

"You okay?" But he was already brushing himself off, smiling to reassure me he wasn't hurt.

We quickly maneuvered to near the moving truck, pulled the bike out, and it bounced on the shoulder's pavement. I wanted to kiss him goodbye, and he even hesitated for a microsecond, our eyes meeting, but the truck was moving and he had to catch up. Couldn't Louis drive up and circle, let us say goodbye?

It all happened so fast.

Sleepy Eugene, back in the cab, waving goodbye.

He'd pulled a Jimmy, Louis had. Too soon. I saw the one brake light of the truck flash, and though a faint glimmer of hope arced like a shooting star across the empty purple sky of my weary Great Basin of a heart, I wasn't surprised to see the car veer left and then head down another highway heading north. Into more sagebrush nowhere.

The sky was deepening to indigo, but I stood there in the gravel holding the bike and watching that one red light get smaller and smaller, until it disappeared for good around a hill.

Two old crows, birds of prey, flown off into the night.

I mounted my skinny nag then and rode off into the approaching darkness. Did what I do when I don't know what to do. I pulled. Took everything I had not to turn up that same road and follow them. I rode right past that turnoff, and I knew as I did that I'd never see them again; we weren't on the same road anymore.

No brick walls here for me either—God's knuckles were already a blessed, bloody mess way back in Idaho besides, soon to be shrouded in the glove of night. And I was no longer vocal enough to bark. So I just hummed and sang inside myself, finding once again a song—a lullaby really, to carry the feeling along until it fell away:

. . . *we never did too much talking anyway, don't think twice, it's alright.* . . .

I was a little in love with both of them. The man's words and the boy's silence. The man's distance and the boy's thigh so near mine. The man's jokes and the boy's smiles. The man's sarcasm and the boy's sighs. Louis's mind and Eugene's body.

And all of it held in Jimmy's cupped hands.

56

On the BART train there were a dozen people buried in the newspaper, so thick with stories you'd see people fold it up and put it down with a sigh. There were babies, who didn't know what they were in for, kids starting to notice that nothing's as it seems, and a whole bunch of adults wrapped up like packages in their business suits and dresses. I looked out the window at the flashing lights that once again reminded me of deep-sea fish with organic lightbulbs on their heads, and I thought about salmon, and dogs, and little pullets catching rain . . . whelps, calves, smolts, and shoats. Two seats to my left, a boy was drawing a horse on his sketchpad.

And then up we galloped into the rising sun, the hulking port cranes standing around like grazing dinosaurs. What's a baby crane? A chick?

57

I reached Greybull and found a campground. In the morning, I went looking for breakfast and saw the town was on a river.

"What river is that?" I asked my waiter at the diner as he delivered my pancakes.

"That's the Big Horn River."

"As in Custer?"

"No. That's the Little Big Horn you're referring to. That's north of here a spell."

"So is there like an even bigger big horn or a middlin'-size big horn?"

"They come in all sizes, son." And he walked away, as if he'd heard that joke one too many times. Or maybe he was serious?

I dug around in my bags for my map, to chart the day's course—and maybe even get a straight answer to my smartass question. I realized in doing so that I hadn't looked at a map since Idaho Falls; I had just let Louis guide me eastward.

When I found the maps, there were other papers folded up with them I didn't recognize at first. But when I opened them up I saw they were drawings Eugene had done. They were sexual drawings of us fucking and sucking, and yet they weren't nasty at all. They were full of spiritual symbols: mandalas or medicine wheels, with cherubic-looking thunderbirds shooting thunderbolts while we did the same from our cocks in the very center. There was another of our two mouths open, our tongues tangled as great snakes, with buffalo, horses, birds, and stones pouring out. In that picture, my eyes were cerulean blue and his were black as lava. Some were blue truck drawings. I could tell from the lines being shorter—except for when he drew my hair, which, since it was a curly mess, was unimpeded in the rendering by blue trucks or anything else. That made me laugh.

Better not laugh too hard, or I might cry.

Pull.

I tucked them away for later, and unfolded Jimmy's map to chart the day's course. I'd be heading south to Worland, then east over the Big Horn Mountains. I put the map away when the waiter returned with the coffee pot, and I asked for the bill. He didn't look at me, just kept looking out the window into the middle distance. In the bathroom before I left, I looked in the mirror. My eyes were bluer than I'd ever seen them.

The sink looked like the one Jimmy and I'd first made love on back on Shotwell Street. I splashed water in my face, and looked at my eyes and my cheekbones and my scruffy chin, trying to conjure up his. I kissed the mirror, but I couldn't see or feel him. There was just the promise left: *Take me back the way I came . . . road's the place for lost souls.*

58

The BART train finally slowed down to the platform, and then the doors slid open. I hesitated—the platform like a question. He's not there when I roll out. And I didn't look down toward the end where I first saw him as I followed the hurrying crowd to the exit. But after I got onto the elevator I turned around and waved to where he'd been as the doors closed like a final curtain.

59

I headed south (what color was that? And I looked at my fingernails: red). I followed the Big Horn River, through a town called Basin and past mountains that looked like heaps of ice cream.

Kissing Eugene.

He too, disappearing and yet expanding into everything just like Jimmy.

I pressed on, singing pop songs in order to pull . . . *Carefree Highway, let me slip away, slip away on you* . . . and hearing Eugene humming those Indian songs. All the way to Worland, where a big green highway sign got my attention. It read: "Buffalo 97 miles."

"Huh?"

I took a left and headed for it.

Almost made it too.

Miles and miles I rode, right through a town called Ten Sleep—named for time, a lady in a minimart who I bought a bottle of Crazy Horse from told me: "Number of nights between one Indian camp and another." But there were no Indians out on that highway—just big-rig trucks, and lots of them. I white-knuckled my handlebars, clenched my jaw, gnawed on my tongue—like a hand it was, running down the brick wall of my teeth. Too many trucks. Buffalo herds of them. Me running, running hard like a horse, hearing the deafening sound of an enormous migration, like drums, and then voices, like birds—crows cawing, finches whistling, and finally geese honking loud right behind me—and I was pulled into the song of it all—I sprouted wings, great black wings—and I flew. . . .

Oh shit," in the immortal words of Louis No Wind. But I was the deer this time, airborne and on my way into the ditch on the side of the road. Which, as I flew outward over it, I realized was more than a ditch. More like a whole creek bed, deep and sloping down, down, down. A beautiful cottonwood, like a great green flower, sat in the vase of the little canyon, and it whispered a koan: *Hoka hey.*

I let go of the bike and leaned back, strangely calm, time arrested. We separated like a rocket from its booster. Me the booster, left to fall away, while the bike continued on into the great green, silvery blossom of Venus, undulating in the breeze.

I landed hard on my butt, toward my left side, and as I did, I felt a terrible pain stab through my left leg. I slid through stone and brush, grabbing for anything I could get my hands on, trying to slow down, my leg now throbbing, sending shooting arrows of pain into my brain, as a dusty brown cloud rose around me. In the distance I heard a crash and knew that that was the bike. It had reached the base of the tree and the water next to it, as I'd heard a splash among the sounds, which were crashing and metallic, cacophonous with bouncing rubber, the thrown-sack thud of the panniers, rocks and dirt and brush disturbed.

I waited for everything to stop—for the silence—to assess the wreck. I waited until the cloud of dust floated above me through the branches of the cottonwood, where I heard the birds again. They flew in and out of its branches, which spread out over and above me. There was the wind too, and grasshoppers, bees, flies, the water babbling—and all along the creek bed, chokecherry and willow.

Eden, the sequel.

And then the pain, like a stone, an enormous heavy glowing hot stone right in the center of my left thigh. Flat on my back, I didn't want to look. Instead I rolled my head back and looked up behind me, from where I'd come. The road. Dear lost road. It was at least twenty feet above me, and it was a steep culvert, full of brush and rocks the size of human heads or bigger. One, not far above me, had blood on it.

I got up on my elbows slowly, carefully, wincing, and looked down, spitting out grass and gravel as I did so. There was my bike, bent and twisted, having hit the tree before it could reach the creek.

And then I saw something worse—Jimmy!

The purple bag had opened, still hanging from the handlebars of the bike, and falling like sand in an hourglass, in a steady thin stream, was Jimmy, down into the piled stone, over the little flowers in their crevices, the weeds and the dirt, and on through them all into the creek, bleeding a final stream of gray blood to flow away off to who knows where.

"Jimmy! Fuck, Jimmy." I attempted to roll to the right and move toward him. The pain arrested me, excruciating and possessing all of my senses in its suddenness: like a hot wave, smelling of burnt sage and dust, tasting of stone, flushing me crimson and causing my eyes to spin dizzily, the cottonwood kaleidoscoping above me. Not a sound at all, because the pain was so loud a blast that it was everything and nothing all at once—a deafening roar, like being sucked under an ocean wave.

I surfaced, breathing heavily, flat on my back, looking into the sky, the great white buffalo clouds floating merrily along east, leaving me here, horseless.

I bent my head, my chin pressed into my neck, finally mustering the courage to inspect my leg. It was bleeding all up the side of my thigh, turning the drab green of Jimmy's old shorts a deep, dark purple. And something was sticking out, poking the pants outward, tenting the fabric—and it sure wasn't a hard-on. I guessed—no, dreaded—it was bone and that I probably had a compound fracture, because the pain was making me chew on my tongue again, grit my teeth.

Oh my God.

I was in some kind of trouble.

"Forgive me, Jimmy," I whimpered. And then it all came down. How I didn't kill him when he asked, and now how I'd failed once more—to get him back home to Buffalo. A ridiculous screwup.

I was mad and cursed the truck that had clipped me. And I cursed my stupid life, and my backasswards idiot idea of ever even coming out here. And I owed my poor mother a phone call too. I wished I'd just stayed home, or not let Louis and Eugene throw me back out on the road. And then I remembered what Louis had said: "Asking, Blue Truck; not wishing, but asking . . . the Great Spirit wants you to live."

"Great Spirit, whoever you are, please help me!"

It gave me a left hook.

I don't know if it was shock—I'd never been in any situation like that before—but I passed out as the pain passed through me again. When I woke up it was already dusk.

I knew it was time to do something, that I had to get out of there.

I inspected my leg again and the purple stain was growing. I had to stop that. I found a way to sit up and get my shirt off, wincing every time I twisted one way or the other. I wrapped it around the top of my leg for a splint, hoping to stop the bleeding, and realizing as I did so that I'd now likely freeze to death as night was approaching—one sorry-ass Boy Scout.

I looked around. Bees, birds, and bats were flying in and out of the tree. I looked up at it: a big BVM. Three wishes and they're all the same: get me the fuck out of here alive.

Wisher.

I put out both arms and tried to see if I could drag myself backwards up the slope, but when I moved but an inch on my butt, the pain slammed into me like a wall that then proceeded through me and out the other side (a deep bass wave-like sound, looking sort of Rothko as I closed my eyes, close hot heat like in the sauna at the YMCA). I gasped: *Fuck*.

I craned my neck around again and looked up, and I knew I'd never be going up there. So I rested. Maybe someone will come. If ever there

262

was a time I needed to run into Louis and Eugene again, this was it. I thought of them, imagined them, tried to will them up that road.

Wisher.

I'll be here for a while most likely, I realized then. Probably through the night—and then some. Probably the rest of my life, which wasn't looking long at all. Short.

However long it was going to be, I'd need to get my sleeping bag to stay warm. I leaned up again on my elbows, breathing deeply through the pain, and scanned the wreckage for it.

"Motherfucker!" I cursed; I'd heard him honking. They always honked, those trucks. Like mooing cows. I took it as a warning, like always, stayed as far right on the shoulder of the road as I could. But he kept honking, and then I was airborne. He must have clipped me. There must have been someone coming the other way. I tried to re-imagine the shoulder, how much room there'd been. It was a curve, definitely a curve, so a truck would play it safe, swing wide outside. One man's safety is another man's danger. How Vietnam of him.

Oh, what did it matter? The only thing that mattered was that he was somewhere getting help. Fat chance. It must have been midday when he hit me, if that. And it's got to be going on seven or eight—the sun's setting. They'd have come by now.

Of course I didn't get his plates! And what would it matter? Why am I asking myself stupid questions?!

I located my sleeping bag, right where it should be. I always carried it on the rack that extended over the back wheel of the bike, and it was still attached by the bungee cords I'd used to secure it. A big blue ripe piece of fruit, just out of reach.

I thought of how nice it would be to have a dog fetch it and bring it to me, perhaps a friendly raccoon; a bird of prey could pick it up in its talons and drop it off. Couldn't it have broken free in the wreck and ricocheted off the tree into my arms?

Wishing.

It was at least ten feet away. Ten feet was forever. Ten feet right then was as far as Buffalo was from San Francisco. Ten feet was the fucking moon.

Maybe it'll be a warm night.

Wishing.

Wouldn't it be nice to have a stick, or a lasso, or a harpoon, or really long arms . . . *And we could be happy . . .*

For a long time, I just looked at it.

Asking instead of wishing," Louis had said. "That's what crying for a vision is about."

Does anybody know what crying for a vision is really all about? Lights, please.

Well, if I was Linus, what I needed right then was my blanket. And it was ten feet away. I could ask.

"Great Spirit, help me get to that tree." Praying to somebody else's God—Jesus Jimmy, Mary and Chief Joseph . . . all the Buddhas . . . Thor, . . . uh, Diana, Innanna, Krsna, Rama, Isis. I ran down the checklist from my spiritual wanderings in the great midway of alternative religions that was San Francisco. Whoever's on call, for God's sake! (Oh *him.* He's the one I left out—the one who's not real keen on letting cups pass.)

At least I'd be moving downhill. Yelping and barking, I dragged myself, clawing at the dirt, roaring through the pain, my knuckles tearing on stone and brambles. Stopping to rest, another wall passed through me, which this time felt like cement, about two feet thick. I groaned and shivered. I'd moved three feet.

Fuck. I gotta do it again. And again. And then probably one more time. I should get there by next week.

I wondered how close I'd come to Buffalo. Buffalo, Wyoming, like some mocking joke, had teased me with that highway sign, promising just ninety-seven miles. But the real Buffalo—hell, that was another two thousand miles down the road. *Who cares?* If I don't die, I'm going home. Jimmy's already headed downstream as it is. Better luck next time, eh Jimmy? I looked at the purple bag, near-empty now, a sad wrinkled sack, the testicles of it drained of all life, its contents sprinkled like powdered sugar on the stone and sagebrush, and the rest of it running down the creek—salmon in a stream, sure thing, Jimmy. And a tear rolled down my cheek.

For the next three feet I sang out to meet the pain head-on. And no 1969 pop tune would do. I sang punk: *Why don't you dance with me?! I ain't no limburger!*

Whoosh. This time the wall of pain was a solid steel door passing through me. I clamped my teeth, shuddered, and breathed deeply.

Four more feet to go. I can't do it. Whatever song would do now? *God Save the Queen!*

Whatever it was that time—granite, iron, I don't know. But it didn't pass through. It came down like a hammer; slammed me like a fly to the wall, and I was out.

Some hours later I awoke shivering, the air cool and damp and dark. I was leaning slightly toward my good side, and I looked over to see how close I was to the bike. Very, but not quite. I was able to reach out for the sleeping bag, but couldn't quite get hold of it. I went for the stuff sack's string that hung down into the spokes. I just kept stretching, then pulling my arm back and to my chest and stretching it different ways, bending it at the elbow, moving it around, trying to limber it up, breathing into it like they'd taught me in yoga. If I could make it just a tad longer . . .

"Ahhhh!" The pain got me again. I'd stretched and felt a harpoon pierce my leg. But after the harpoon had gotten through threading me like a needle, I noticed I had my hand on the stuff sack string, and I clung to it for dear life, even as I felt the pain begin to emerge again. I roared as I worked my index finger into the loop of it and yanked.

The bag flew over and hit me in the head as I passed the 2001 monolith.

"Yes, yes," I whimpered in sado-masochistical bliss, breathing heavily.

Now I had to get into it. And no Jimmy to help me. So I told myself:

"Okay, Shame, unzip it."

"Take a breath."

"Now, unzip it all the way."

"Okay, good."

"Take another breath."

"Now, drape it across yourself."

I couldn't see getting into it—it being a mummy bag, a disturbing analogy considering. I lay my head back in a rather prickly shrub. How had I slept in this state? I looked up into the branches of the cottonwood, the underside of its leaves shimmering silvery in the moonlight.

I heard a car go by. "Hey!" I shouted.

Is this what I was going to do? Yell from twenty feet down a culvert every time a car went by? They'd never hear me. And they sure couldn't see me. I remembered the road then, how it had banked around the curve, obscuring any view down into the creek. I hadn't even known there was a creek down here until I was airborne over it. The hell with my *Heys!* then. I oughta be saying "Hoka hey," and to myself.

The realization of that began to grow in me as I considered it. How's anyone ever going to find me? Even if Eugene and Louis had ended up on this road, they would have had no reason to stop. I realized then that I *was* going to have to climb that hill if I hoped to survive. Crawl it. There was no other way. And if each three feet equaled a concrete wall, I'd be taking on a small city.

Something else hit me then. The wind. And I heard it then for the first time, whistling and hollow, blowing down the canyon. Ghostly. Me and death giving each other the too-long look.

I inhaled fear; I exhaled hope.

What did that Buddhist dude say? Beyond fear and hope—something like that.

Sounds like a good place to me. *But what was it—where was it? What were they getting at? It's hopeless, so there's no need to be afraid?*

I really needed to understand that just then.

But I was getting more terrified by the minute. I'm likely going to starve to death, in pain, right here, while the world just floats right on by above me like these cloud herds of buffalo. But as I looked up for them, I saw the clouds were gone, and the night was full of stars. Far away. As far away as the road. Too, too far.

Everything is hopeless, the Buddhists droned on—all you got is *right now.*

Easy for them to say on their zafus.

I needed a pillow. If I was going to die miserably, I wanted to be comfortable doing it.

A pannier bag would do. I got up on my right elbow and looked for them. One was smashed between the bike and the tree, out of reach, while the other had been flung down toward the creek. And it was wet. Not from the creek either. Bleeding it was. Shit, that's the malt liquor. *Et tu, Crazy Horse?*

I looked at empty Jimmy then, swinging in the hopeless wind, royally purple in the moonlight. Purple as old blood, the journey done. My pillow, my comfort. Empty and gone.

The bike had hit the tree sideways and it was bent into a boomerang, so that even though the back of the bike had been within my reach, the front of it was ninety degrees away, down across some rocks and hanging over the roots and boulders above the creek. Out of reach. And all those strings hanging on it. Poems never written. All those stories. *Now they're prayers, eh Jimmy?*

Not wishes, but prayers.

I looked at my hand then, all scraped and dusty dirty. And there were the nail-polished fingernails from Eugene. *God, was that just a day or two ago?* It suddenly felt like years. Long, long ago.

So much for *right now.*

I wished I were back there.

Wishing.

What did Louis say about those colors? Sacred colors of the Lakota. The four directions. You call those when you cry for a vision. *And this . . . shit, this is it.*

You ain't no different from anyone else, Blue Truck. And sometimes if you don't go out and cry for a vision, it comes crying for you . . .

I was growing feverish and thought I'd actually heard his voice and looked around for him. Then I looked hard at my nails again.

He said to ask.

I don't want to die screaming, or whimpering.

Ask.

All I got left.

"Great Spirit, if I'm gonna die, I'd like your help."

But how does that serve anyone but me? And I didn't know who I was talking to besides.

"Great Spirit, sir . . . uh, ma'am . . . I humbly ask you how I might serve my people from this rather compromised position." And it occurred to me then that even if I died I could at least leave some semblance of how to do it right, and if nothing else the *Buffalo Bee* or whatever it was could run a story that said a young man got himself into a bad situation and yet he died with dignity by . . . *going beyond hope and fear?*

I didn't want to die.

Ask.

"Great Spirit, can you help me get out of here and show me how to be in the world? Show me how to serve?"

I held up my hand then, looked at the chipped, dirty nail polish, and called the four directions as my witness: yellow pinky for the east, and pointed my arm to Buffalo; white index for the north (I swung my arm left up the creek); red for south (and toward the tree I pointed); black for west (and over my shoulder went my hand, reaching back toward San Francisco). And me the thumb right in the center.

"Great Spirit, help me out, brother; I don't know what I'm doing." And I thought of old Rumi poems I used to jabber when I was Tammy Faye and Jimmy was losing his patience:

268

Where did I come from, and what am I supposed to be doing?
I have no idea.
I looked over at the empty purple bag. I'd never known how to love him proper. I did want something back. "Show me how to love the world, Great Spirit."

I didn't want to die whimpering, but I whimpered then as my sad little life ran by me like the water in that creek, trickling by, off to nevermore. I cried—for the failure of it all, for the pain in my leg, for the terrible circumstance I was in; I cried for Jimmy and all he'd been through, for my father and my mother, for all the hollow-eyed boys at ACT UP meetings, pleading "no more." I cried and I cried, and I cried until I cried out.

I'm tired of being lost. Can I go home?
Help Mr. Wizard.
No more wishing.

I was burning with fever by then and looked up at the constellations, twinkling, me muttering: *. . . just ask . . . the stars . . .*

I fell asleep and dreamed. And I dreamed I was in the sauna at the YMCA and every boy who I'd ever been with came in, one after the other (a very big sauna, a stadium) with towels around their waists: there was Alejandro and Tran, Peter, Eddie, Yau, Tom, Mark, Larry, José, Deshawn, Sven, Henry, the Sages, Catnip, the Fennels, Willow, Gingko, Ginseng, Lars, Lawrence of course, the numerous nameless frat boys from Wheeler Hall, and the legions of anonymous guys from wherever, ad infinitum. Next came my mother, a larger towel to cover her breasts, and in her arms, which she had folded before her, she held the framed photo of my father, who suddenly smiled and said, "Hi, Seamus." That got me. Doc Pinski came next, in all his rotundness, followed by Julie, Sam, Tanya, a whole crew of ACT UP guys and girls, my friends from the road—Ralph, Carl, and Ellen; the church lady and the dickering farmer from Idaho; the Marine from INEL; all the waiters and waitresses, hotel maids and receptionists; Mandy from the Y and all the little kids too—Miguel and Carlos, Mo and Ivan and Alice and

269

Eustacia, so sweet in their little gym towels. Even Cavanaugh lurked in, and stood in the corner.

Finally Jimmy, his nostrils flaring, horse that he was. My heart leapt. My man, my groom, my best friend, my love. My relation. I'd never cried in a dream before.

Jimmy.

And then I woke briefly, the sun shining straight into my eyes . . . midday. . . . I'd survived the night.

I was thirsty.

I fell back into the dream of all my relations. I'd forgotten to call them, but they'd come.

I was back in the sauna and I was looking for Jimmy. But it was so hot in there, and there were so many of us, and he'd been way on the other side, and I was tired and thirsty and felt like falling. I needed something to drink. If I could just kiss Jimmy, and feel the cool night air of his mouth . . . if I could just kiss him, it would slake my thirst.

"Jimmy," I muttered.

But he wasn't there, and all the white towels turned to snow and then a big white sheet on the rickety bed on Guerrero Street, and I was with Jimmy, naked, and he held his finger to his lips and pointed at the ceiling. And a movie of our whole life together played there. There he was on the platform as the movie began, and me finding him. We rode the train to San Francisco and Chief Joseph was sitting on the BART train a few seats down. He held his finger to his lips as well. I watched our life in silence—stern looks from Tanya, sweet smiles from the twins, the many embraces of James Damon Keane. The sun rose and fell quickly over San Francisco and Mount Tamalpais, the fog rolled in and out, and Jimmy grew thinner and more peaked, and I grew sadder. And then I turned my gaze from the ceiling screen to look at Jimmy naked next to me and he was a skeleton. I woke with a start and it was night and the cottonwood was a green Virgin Mary and it told me to go back to sleep, and I did.

And Jimmy wasn't there.

Then I was on a gray-white horse riding across what looked like a vast salt plain. I rode faster and faster until it was hard to move and the salt thickened, first to white mud and then to white stones and finally, it was bones—bones two or three feet deep. And it hurt as they rose around me and nicked my shins, and the horse could barely move through them, the bones pressing against us, dense and sharp and unforgiving. The horse was snorting and struggling and sinking as if in a current that was too strong. And all the while that mahjong sound of bones rattling and spilling everywhere.

And then I saw a huge shadow approaching across the endless horizon of bleached white bones, and something came down from the shadow and seized me and pulled me up, up. And I strained to look up and see, and there was Eugene, who had sprouted huge black wings from his shoulder blades, and he was smiling his kind, crooked smile, and I whispered his name as we rose.

I tried to ask him where he was taking me, but the words came slow like a record at the wrong speed. I wanted to say it didn't matter, that I'd go, no matter where it was. I was lost and I'd go.

But it was hot, so hot, and then I saw the sun—the sweet sun—and called out to it by its name: *Jimmy!*

And I was blinded by it. And then Eugene let me go.

And I fell.

Hot and blind and shedding and snapping.

And falling.

And I awoke again to the sun in my eyes, my forehead on fire.

After a while I slept again, and I was a burning thing flying through the sky, through cloud herds of buffalo, intent on the earth. I was a meteor, a mass of lava, sweating and throbbing and hot and heavy as stone. And I looked down and below me was Idaho and I was coming down, and all I could see was the sagebrush desert with a blue truck in the middle of it and Louis under the hood. I was the blackberry pie in the sky falling to create the Craters of the Moon! I tried to yell a warning to Louis but no words emerged. *Bam!*—and I hit the earth hard.

Bam!—and it felt like those doors that I'd passed yesterday, like interplanetary kidney stones.

I awoke to dusk and strained my head to see my throbbing leg, purple and burning like a mass of lava. And then I slept again and I was a bird flying above the lava—a bird on unsure wings. And the lava cooled and was Craters of the Moon again, but something more. It wasn't lava now, but a thing that once lived and was now dead—an enormous buffalo, on its side, a stream of blood, like a river—a river from underground, the very one Eugene and I had made love alongside in the cave—flowing crimson into the sagebrush nowhere that was scattered with bones. And the river flowed through them, soaking them red, inundating and running through them as they piled up, clacking in the babbling stream—and I could see the gray streak of Jimmy's ashes in the bloodwater, and I followed it.

Jimmy.

And then the blood river ran faster and the bones piled up into cataracts, and pretty soon there were larger things in the riverbed—white metal wreckage: washing machines and refrigerators, dryers, ovens, and then there were cars, all bone-white as ghosts: Jeep Cherokees and Dodge Dakotas, Winnebagos, Impalas, Mustangs, Pintos, Falcons. And there were people struggling to get out of them as they filled with blood. They were the Edward Curtis chiefs from the book: Red Cloud and Dull Knife, Sitting Bull and American Horse—and another in the shadows I couldn't quite see—shaking the door handles, banging on the windshields. Like horses that have fallen and can't get up.

All submerged in the red tide.

And the water filled with all sorts of things, and when I tried to make them out, they all turned into salmon. And we were on the crest of a great wave, some of the salmon flying out in front. Into sagebrush nowhere. And then out in the distance I saw hundreds of *2001* monoliths in a long snaking line, which as I got closer I saw were dominoes, thousands and thousands of dominoes, receding into the sagebrush forever ahead of us. And on the white circles of the dominoes were the faces of my queer brothers, ashen, emaciated, some covered in lesions, some peaceful, some raging, some demented, oblivious, asleep: Kyle and Vance, Gavin and Josh, Mark and Henry, half the boys I'd just seen in the sauna, ACT UP people and legions of others I'd never known, but who I'd seen on the streets of San Francisco. Even Thomas and Franco, my brothers for the love of Jimmy.

The salmon flung themselves ahead of the bloody tide, hitting the first domino, and when it fell and went under, the next and the next, and so on. All of those faces falling. And then there were butterflies and birds slamming into them, locusts and grasshoppers, flies and frogs. All of those faces and all of those dominoes swallowed by the red wave. The din of them falling, so fast and heavy, pounding—like wild horses, buffalo, rain, drums, clacking mahjong pieces.

I covered my ears, closed my eyes.

Then the river of blood no longer flowed, but was like a great sea and it was rising all around me, boiling and rising. And I had to tread water or I'd drown. But I couldn't keep my head up. Something was pulling me, pulling me by my left leg, pulling me under, back down. I struggled, flailed with my arms, swallowing great gulps of blood, my tears gray and ashen, muddying the bloody flood.

And then in the distance I saw a shore: green grass, RVs, geese in formation in the distance coming toward me. It was Unity Lake, and all my relations, there they were again, in their white towels, sweating in the hot sun. I swam with all my might toward them, pulled and pulled to get away from whatever held me. But I was moving so slowly, and the birds were coming so fast. The formation of geese grew into a huge black cloud of birds, cawing—a murder of crows and vultures that dove like pelicans into the red lake of blood, scooping it up in their craws that then dripped like those skull cups held by wrathful deities in Tibetan tankas.

I thought of the bardo then, and figured I must be dead. *None of it's real*, Jimmy'd read to me—*just the illusions of your own mind*. Beyond hope and fear.

And then the red water roiled and boiled, and from it rose a great white Buddha, enormous and fat, laughing, with blood running off his body from surfacing, and a big red clown's nose and a giant red smile painted on his face. A black crow perched on one of his shoulders, the wind rustling its feathers, and he was seated on a giant lotus flower where kneeled the twins in their little towels like altar boys, both with holy jars of Best Foods Mayonnaise, full and overflowing with diarrhea. And all my relations on the shore grinning crooked like Eugene does, with a sigh, and then a big hearty laugh.

And something pulling my leg.

"*Tell all the people that you see . . .*," the laughing Buddha sang out, quaking. It was Jim Morrison's voice from that song me and my mom would sing to evoke my father.

"*Tell all the people that you see . . .*" And he just kept laughing, he could barely get the words out—and then he sprouted ten thousand arms and they all swung out like "cut it," and there was a huge clap, and then black stillness.

My eyes opened to red sirens in total silence. There were cottonwood leaves all around me, like I was up in the tree. The light of day, but overcast.

Then the sound came . . . voices, radio dispatch, boots in gravel, and snapping branches.

Some man's voice: "I saw smoke, figured a car had gone off the road . . . so I stopped . . . but there wasn't any car . . ."

I winced. I was being put in one of those aluminum stretchers on ropes. There were two men, one on each side of me guiding the basket through the cracking branches and leaves, as the ropes began to pull me up. I wasn't dead, and I smiled at them.

My relations.

One smiled back: "You're gonna make it, buddy, you hang in there." A horseboy.

It was raining lightly, and I opened my mouth and I drank of it, closing my eyes, and as I did I saw Jimmy, in full health, dye-blond and scruffy, his big brown eyes and his say-nothing smile. He held one finger to his mouth, and with the other hand he reached out a wet finger to place on my tongue like a eucharist, and then he blessed me: *In nomine Patris, et Filii, et Spiritus Sancti.* And I knew then that I was forgiven, . . . and Jimmy . . . it must be day forty-nine . . . Jimmy's being born.

Somewhere near the top I heard the man's voice again:

"That lightning bolt musta split that tree right in half, and covered him over . . . only reason I went down was because I saw something sparkling. . . . I'm a scavenger . . . steep though . . . but I've found a lot of things on the side of the road—once a whole Coleman stove, umbrellas, flashlights, shoes . . ."

I opened my eyes to see him, talking to a fireman, next to his F-150. The Frogman of Wyoming . . . one last greeting from Jimmy . . .

And into the ambulance I was trundled; the doors closed, the siren sang, and they took me to Buffalo.